Nobody's Pretty Girl

Nobody's Pretty Girl

A Carly Styles Novel

A Story of Secrets, Lies, Love, and Healing

By

K.J. Knudson

This book is a work of fiction. Names, characters, places, and incidents

are the product of the author's imagination or are used fictitiously.

Any resemblance to actual events, locales, or persons

living or dead, is coincidental.

Copyright © 2024 by K.J. Knudson

Cover art by: Prisca Kolkowski Learmann

We support the right to free expression and the value of copyright.
The purpose of copyright is to encourage writers and artists to produce
the creative works that enrich our culture.

The scanning, uploading, and distribution of this book without
permissions is a theft of the author's intellectual property.
Thank you for your support of the author's rights.

First Edition: May 2024

Prologue

Stupid, stupid, stupid Bitch! He knew he should have killed her when he had the chance. Now she was running around out there in the woods. But it was cold–so cold she would surely freeze to death before the cops could find her. He'd go out in the morning and find her skinny-ass naked body frozen to the ground. Those stupid cops out there – calling her name over and over; tramping through the woods pretending they knew what they were doing. What a joke they were!

"Carly, Carly, it's Jack."

"Carly, Carly, Carly, Carly"

Maybe if they yelled "Stupid Bitch" she would answer. She was probably dead already. No problem. He had a nice grave all ready for her. He dug it before the ground froze up. He'd find her in the morning and throw her in it. It wouldn't be hard to find another dumb blonde to take her place. There was an endless supply of them out there. Pretty young girls who came flocking to Nashville looking for their big break. Yeah! Hah! Like that was going to happen. Bunch of no talent hopeful wannabes coming in with a dream, only to get laid by some fat producer and then thrown out with the garbage. One after another, a whole long line of stupid bimbos ripe for the picking.

What a joke she was! Thought she was better than him. All sweet and smiling – thanking him for being a fan. What a load of crap! Just another no talent wannabe! She couldn't even sing! Sounded more like a cat in heat! In the morning he'd put a chain around her neck and drag her back through the snow. Kick her into the grave like a dog. If she was still alive maybe he'd let her beg him to rape her one more time and then kill the stupid bitch. He was tired of her. She was worthless. She used to be pretty. No one was going to recognize her now. He left his mark on her. Some of his finest work. Too bad it was all going to be covered with dirt.

They kept calling her. Stupid worthless cops! They were never going to find her. Shit! He had her all to himself for four days. Now they were out there in the dark yelling at each other in the woods like a bunch of little boy scouts. They wouldn't find him either. They were too damn dumb. And he was nobody. No name. Just nobody. But he knew where to go. He knew these woods. Not like the stupid cops who spent all their time writing tickets and giving boring lectures to little kids who couldn't care about anything a cop would say. He heard sirens wailing in the distance. Shit! They were so far away they were never going to find her. No way the stupid bitch could get out to the highway. Maybe they ran her over. That'd be just what she deserved!

Chapter 1

"Carly, Carly – oh my God! Carly" Jack wasn't sure it was a person at first. He started flinging the snow away from her body. He took off his glove and laid his hand across the side of her neck to feel for a pulse. He felt a faint throbbing and heaved a sigh of relief. He tore his jacket off and wrapped it around her naked body. She was motionless and her eyes were closed. He picked her up out of the snow and a small, tattered blanket fell away from her body. She was almost unrecognizable. Her face was battered and bruised. He started screaming at the other deputies.

"Go block off the highway. I have her. I found her. Turn on the sirens - the lights."

"Hurry – oh Christ! Hurry! bring me your jackets." He wasn't sure he could keep her alive. She wasn't moving. She didn't answer him. Her eyes were closed. His heart was pounding in his chest as he ran with her. They couldn't wait for the paramedics. He cursed at them. Damn the budgets and all that crap! He knew they were closing in on her location. He had begged them to wait at the highway. He headed toward the lights and the sounds of the sirens.

"Open the back of the Sheriff's SUV," he screamed. "There's a portable oxygen unit in that car. Get it out and start it up. Bring me your jackets – the ones you're wearing, we need body heat. Get me anything that is warm." He felt the panic rising in his voice. Volunteer searchers ran over with blankets. Tears were streaming down his face. Carly was his wife's sister, his curly haired daughter's favorite auntie. She was his family for God's sake – who could do this to her? Why? Why?

They pulled her into the back of the Sheriff's SUV. She was so cold he couldn't tell what color her bare feet were. Maybe purple, maybe black. He started covering her with the deputy's jackets. One of the volunteer searchers wrapped big blankets around her feet. Another Deputy jumped in the back with him and Carly.

"Go!" he screamed at the driver. "Go! Call the hospital! Tell them we found her! Tell them to get ready! Oh God! Somebody call my wife and tell her we found Carly. Oh God, Carly. Breathe, please breathe, please, please, breathe."

The Deputy in the back spread his body out alongside Carly, trying to warm her with his body heat. It was just so damn cold. Her face and body were covered with frost crystals. Jack wrapped another jacket around her head. Her face was covered with blood, her hair was matted together on one side with dried blood. Jack put his head down close to her face trying to feel her breath. The other deputy hooked up the oxygen unit and fit it onto her head.

"Carly breathe, it's Jack. You're safe – just breathe, breathe, breathe for me." He was shouting and the tears kept streaming down his face. He stared in horror at the abrasions and cuts on her body. There were open sores and blisters on her arms along with marks that looked like she had been bitten by an animal.

"You're safe Carly, it's over. It's Jack, please breathe, please, please breathe." He stopped for a moment and heard her take in a breath of air.

"I'm so sorry, so sorry it took us so long to find you. Just breathe - good girl - in, out – in, out -keep breathing. Hang on Carly. We're almost to the Hospital. We're going to warm you up. You're going to be okay. Can you hear me? Can you open your eyes for me? It's Jack. No one's going to hurt you again. Hang on – you're going to be okay." He wasn't sure about that. She was motionless, lifeless, her skin was ghostly white. He wondered how long she had been out in the cold. Christ! It was probably only 20 degrees out there. He cursed the damn paramedics again who insisted on waiting for his call. He'd give anything to have a helicopter right now. He had no way of knowing how low her body temperature was. He saw what looked to be human bite marks and some burns on her chest and felt the bile rising in his throat; he thought he might be sick. She looked like she had been mauled by a wild animal. He thought about the son of a bitch who had done this to her, and he wanted to yank out every tooth in his head. He silently made an oath to track down this kidnapper if it took him the rest of his life. He tried to regain control and concentrated on keeping his voice calm and reassuring. In, out, just breathe he prayed. She made a low moan that almost sounded like the word *Jack*.

"Hang on Carly, we're almost there." He was lying. They were out in the middle of nowhere. It was miles to the nearest hospital. They were flying down the highway and the siren was screaming so loudly he could barely think.

"Christy is waiting there for you." Another lie. It might take his wife hours to get there. He wondered how long he could keep Carly breathing. The color of her skin was frightening. He thought she might die at any moment. It was horrifying! He had never lost a family member before. Not now. Not now, he prayed.

Chapter 2

Jason couldn't remember the last time he visited a nightclub. He felt a bit self-conscious, maybe a bit overdressed, and even a little bit old. The crowd was young. There were guys in cowboy hats and jeans, ladies in tight, skinny jeans and sequined shirts. He saw two pretty girls and an empty barstool next to them and decided to snag the seat and try to blend in. They smiled at him as he asked if the seat was taken. The red head answered, "My husband was sitting there but he had to go do a little surveillance for a perp, so he probably won't be back soon. If he wants his seat back, he'll just throw you out of it." she laughed.

"Sounds promising," said Jason. "Is he a big guy, can I take him?"

"Big enough," said Christy. They all laughed. "I'm Christy, and this is Carly".

"Jason Kingman, nice to meet you."

"Oooh, last names," said Carly. "Christy, we can google this man and see if he is more than just the guy with the prettiest eyes we have ever seen,"

Christy had a surprised look on her face. It wasn't like Carly to flirt with strangers. Since her kidnapping, she kept her distance from men and never spoke to anyone she didn't know. But this was an amazingly attractive man, and he was giving Carly a smile that could melt a woman's heart. He was the kind of man you would expect to see with a gorgeous, expensively dressed woman clinging to his arm. If Christy had to label him, she would say wealthy and sophisticated. He was looking at Carly as if she was the most beautiful woman he had ever seen. Of course, she was beautiful, and she was even smiling back at him. But flirting with a stranger?

"Perhaps you are forgetting that I am very married, Carly."

"I wasn't thinking about you right this minute," Carly laughed. "Sorry," she said, "we're just having a little fun with you. We usually pick on Jack, but he's abandoned us."

"I'll save you the trouble of doing the Google research. I'm just a boring attorney from Kentucky."

"You came down here tonight from Kentucky?" Carly asked.

"I'm just over the state line, so it's not far. A friend of mine was here last week and told me how fantastic the singer was, and he said I should come down to hear her. I'm hoping the band is playing tonight."

"You're in luck. They will be back on stage"- she looked at her watch - "in about 10 minutes. Are you a musician?" Carly asked.

"Oh, no. I've been teaching myself to play guitar, and now I'm going to try to learn some piano – just got a little keyboard."

"Wait 'til you hear…" Carly elbowed Christy and cut her off mid-sentence.

Jason looked up and saw a rough, scruffy looking man coming toward them. He wondered if this was the husband who was going to throw him off the barstool. But the Christy girl was beautiful, dressed to the nines, and didn't look like she would be with this guy.

The man suddenly ran right up to Carly, grabbed her arm, and yanked her off the barstool. She let out a blood curdling cry and started screaming "No, no, no!! Don't touch me, don't touch me" over and over hysterically.

Jason jumped off the bar stool and pushed him backwards. "Hey, what are you doing! You can't grab her like that!"

"Mind your own business, asshole," he yelled and tried to grab for Carly again.

Jason grabbed the attacker's arm, twisted it behind his back, grabbed the other arm, knocked his feet out from under him, and threw him to the floor where his head made a resounding Thud! when it hit the concrete. He stomped his boot into the middle of his back and said, "You might want to be more careful about who you call an asshole, little man."

He saw Christy frantically screaming into her phone, and then two uniformed sheriff's deputies came running toward him and a big, tall good-looking guy who seemed to be flashing a badge at him. Jason's first thought was – *oh shit! Am I about to get arrested??*

"I'm Deputy Jack Granger. Nice work buddy. We'll take it from here."

The deputies reached down and handcuffed the scruffy guy and hauled him to his feet. He was screaming, "He broke my arm! You're hurting me! Take the cuffs off."

"Not one chance in Hell you scum bag. We are going to cuff and hogtie you until you are back in prison where you belong. Take him to lockup and don't take the cuffs off, guys. He's a snake."

Jason looked over at Carly who was sobbing and shaking violently. Christy was trying to calm her without much success. Jason looked at the deputy and mouthed the questioning words, ex-husband, boyfriend?

"Stalker! Kidnapping, woman beating felon. We just got word he escaped from a prison work crew, and then he comes right back here to terrorize her."

"Wish I had known," replied Jason, "could have broken a few more bones."

"Yeah, we saw you take him down from across the room and we were a bit stunned when we saw how quickly you had him down on the floor. We were running over to back you up. Turns out you didn't need our help. You in law enforcement?"

"No, no. I'm an attorney but trained with the Army Rangers years ago. Sometimes comes in handy."

"I guess," laughed Jack. "That was amazing!! And just what that bastard deserved!"

Jason walked over to Carly, took off his jacket and put it over her shoulders. She was shaking and rocking back and forth and sobbing. Christy made a motion to him indicating that Carly didn't like to be touched.

He sat down and pulled his barstool closer to her and asked, "Can I put my arm around you?"

She was sobbing so hard she couldn't answer, but he thought she nodded her head. He slid his arm cautiously around her and Christy looked surprised. He noticed that she didn't try to hug or comfort her.

"Breathe, take some big breaths, very slowly, okay? He's not coming back. The deputies are taking him to lock up. He's not going to hurt you. I can stay right here with you if you want."

He thought she nodded again, but it was hard to tell because she was shaking so badly. He saw the bartender slide what looked like a cup of tea toward her.

"Doug made you some tea, Carly. Can you take a sip?" asked Christy.

Jason held the cup up for her and she took a small sip. The tea sloshed over onto the bar because she was still shaking. He set it down and pulled her over gently toward his shoulder and she rested her head against his shoulder. Christy gave him another one of her raised eyebrow surprised looks.

He rocked her gently back and forth. "He really scared you, didn't he? I'm sorry. I didn't know he was going to try to hurt you, or I would have stopped him before he grabbed you."

She had her hands crossed over her chest and was gripping each opposite arm so tightly that her knuckles were turning white.

"Let's put your arms into my jacket so you can be a little warmer. Can I rub your back and try to warm you up a little?" She shook her head violently and he saw a look of *"O God please don't do that"* on Christy's face. But Carly slipped her arms into the jacket, and he pulled her back onto his shoulder again. The band started playing again but nobody around them moved.

Jack walked over to the group nearby. "It's not a sideshow people. Go dance or drink yourself silly. She doesn't need you staring at her."

Jason was trying to put the pieces of the puzzle together in his mind. She kept rocking back and forth, so he gently started rocking slowly with her to the rhythm of the music. Jack and Christy just stood by looking helpless, but Jack was keeping a watchful eye on him. No one offered any advice about what to do to help her. He wondered if he should suggest calling the paramedics, who could give her a mild sedative. But she was their friend and might not want his opinion. *So, I'm sitting here holding a beautiful woman in my arms, he thought. When was the last time that happened?*

Her sobbing gradually subsided, and Jason held out his right hand to her. "The music is nice," he said. "Would you get up and dance with me?" She didn't reply. "My ex-wife always said I was a very good dancer, and she wasn't one to be lavish with the compliments." He thought he saw a slight smile on her face, but she didn't take his hand. A couple of pretty, young girls came over to the bar and asked him if he would dance with them.

"Thanks, but no," he said. "I think I have a dance partner right here."

As they walked away, he heard them mumble, "Yeah! Good luck with that. She probably hasn't been on the dance floor in years."

"What do you say?" he asked Carly. "Do you think you might want to get up and dance with me for a few minutes."

She shrugged her shoulders, but she didn't take his hand. He kept holding his hand out and slowly she touched two fingers of her hand very gingerly to his. He led her toward the outer edge of the dance floor.

He remembered Christy had told him about the no touching rules, so he asked, "Can I put my hand on your back?" She nodded, and he pulled her in a little closer with his arm around her.

"See," he said, "I haven't stepped on your toes yet." And he thought he saw a flicker of a smile.

The music ended but went right into another song without a pause. The guitarist was prompting people to get out onto the dance floor. "Christy, Jack, Rod, Claire – come on – we know you can dance. And I see our favorite girl out there with a tall, handsome stranger, so let's keep dancing."

Jason was wondering about the singer he was hoping to hear, but there was no sign of her. The song ended and the guitarist announced they were dedicating the next song to the bravest and strongest person they had ever known. The song started out with a beautiful melody -

'Can you open up your arms, and let me hold you?
Can you open up your heart and let me in?
I can chase away the demons that haunt you in the night,
I can slay all the dragons in your dreams.'

Then nearly the whole club started softly singing the chorus. He felt Carly put her hand up around his neck and she laid her head on his shoulder. He thought she was crying again. He suddenly began to slide the pieces into place.

"They're singing this song to you, aren't they?" She nodded a little.

"It's beautiful, and you are the singer I came to see, right?" She didn't reply, but he thought he knew the answer. He saw Christy and Jack watching her protectively and another Sheriff's deputy standing nearby.

The guitarist announced the next song. "This is one of Carly's favorite songs, so we are singing it for her. She sings it better than we do, but we are going to give it a try." Then they launched into a nice rendition of "Colder Weather", a song by the Zach Brown Band, that Jason liked. When they got to the last verse, he sang some of the words to her softly and she put both arms around his neck and drew in closer to him. He forgot about the "no touch" rules and wrapped both arms around her. She was soft and warm in his arms, and he tried to imagine how the perp he had subdued earlier could have ever hurt this woman. It was one of those moments he hoped would never end.

Chapter 3

The band announced their closing song for the evening and reminded everyone this would be the last dance. When the song ended the band started packing up their equipment and customers were heading for the exits.

"I need to go backstage and thank the band for their song. Would you come with me, Jason?"

"Sure. I can do that."

"We'll all go with you, Carly," said Jack. "I'm keeping an eye on you, just in case."

"What else could happen tonight?" Carly asked.

"Never ask that question," said Jack. "That's when all hell breaks loose."

Carly thanked the band for the songs they dedicated to her and apologized for not joining them for the last set.

"I think you need to come home with us tonight, Carly. We can stop at your house and get some things for you. Just tell Christy what you need, and we'll pick it up. Can we drop you off somewhere, Jason?"

"No, I walked down from the hotel. I can walk back easily enough."

"Yeah. No one who was here in this Club tonight is going to try to mug you on the way home."

"No, I want Jason to stay with me. I don't want him to go back to the hotel yet."

"Carly, we're going back to our house," said Christy. "You know you'll be safe there."

Carly started to cry. "No, I want Jason to come with us. I feel safe with him. I'm so afraid..." her voice trailed off as she started sobbing again.

"I can come and sit with you a while, if it's okay with your sister," Jason said. He saw the signs of panic coming back onto her face.

"Okay," said Jack. "Let's go back to the house and have coffee and we'll sort it out from there."

Jack stopped the car at a small red brick house on a corner in Nashville and he and Christy both got out. Jason could see large guard dogs lunging at the fence and growling. He heard Jack give them a command and they settled down a bit. Jack and Christy went into the house and came back with a cute little dog and a small duffle bag. Christy put the dog into the back seat with Carly and he wiggled up into her lap and tried to give her wet kisses.

"This is Charlie," Carly said as she looked up at Jason. "Not exactly a guard dog, but he's cute, and we used to do a lot of hiking together."

"Seems like you have plenty of guard dogs already. Are they always here at your house?"

"They bring them over at night. It's a little scary when they all start barking. I never know who's out there. Sometimes I have to call Jack to come over."

"That's a hard way to live. Do you have a security system for your house?"

"We tried that, but it didn't seem to work."

The wheels were turning in Jason's head. Here was this young, frightened woman living in a house alone, surrounded by snarling guard dogs. He wondered how many nights a week she suffered panic attacks.

They got to Christy's house, and she made coffee and a special tea for Carly. "I hope this tea will help you sleep tonight, Carly."

"It smells wonderful, but if it does, it will be a miracle. I think I'd like to sit and talk with Jason for a little while if that's okay with everyone."

"Maybe," said Jack, with a hint of distrust in his voice. "Tell us what you do, Jason. Do you live in Nashville?"

"No. I live in Kentucky just over the state line. I'm an attorney, but I also train thoroughbreds."

"Racehorses?" asked Jack.

"Yes. Lots of racehorses."

"So, what brought you down here tonight?" Jack asked with a note of suspicion in his voice.

"I came to hear Carly sing, but I didn't know her name yet. My law school buddy told me the club had a fabulous singer, and we had planned to meet up down here tonight. Sadly, he was called out of town because of illness in the family."

Christy looked over at Carly. "I think you should get in bed and try to sleep, Carly. You've had a very stressful night."

"They will be pressing additional charges against that goon, Carly, so we will all have to go to court Monday morning for his arraignment. Jason if you are still in Nashville on Monday, we could use your testimony as well."

"Sure, no problem. I'm certainly familiar with court proceedings. Who is this guy and how did he get to the club if he was in prison?"

"Carly doesn't like us to talk about him, but he was convicted of kidnapping and assault against her about two years ago. He escaped from a work crew today and came to the club after her again. He seems to have a mentally deranged fixation about recapturing her. This was his second escape from a work crew."

"What's going on with the prison system in Tennessee that allows this felon to escape? How can they put him on a work crew if he has already had one escape? Are they that desperate for highway crews? They have a prison full of men."

"I wish I knew the answer to those questions, Jason."

Jason looked up dumfounded. "Two Escapes? That's hardly fair to Carly. She could probably sue the state for mental anguish based on two escapes."

"Spoken like a lawyer," said Jack.

"Well, it shouldn't be allowed to continue. It's probably taking an enormous toll on her health. Perhaps you could petition the state to have him sent to a more secure facility."

"If you think you could do that, I would be the first to jump on your bandwagon. It makes me sick to see what he is doing to her, and what happened tonight went way over the line. I wanted to shoot him, but there were just too many witnesses."

"You can't shoot him, Jack. Please remember you have a family."

"Maybe I should get a gun," said Carly. "I don't have a family. I think I might like to shoot him."

"I could get you a carry permit, Carly, if you feel that threatened."

How much more threatened do you want her to feel, thought Jason. She had a serious meltdown right in front of all her fans in the club and couldn't stop shaking! She has snarling guard dogs in her yard every night. How much worse would it have to get?

"Perhaps you could look into hiring a bodyguard. Have you had attempted break-ins at your house?" asked Jason. "Is that why the guard dogs are there?"

"There's no money left for a bodyguard," said Carly. "All my savings were eaten up by medical bills for the injuries I suffered during the kidnapping. I still owe the doctors and hospitals a ton of money for my care, and yes, I have had at least four attempted robberies at my house."

Christy talked Carly into heading to bed before the conversation could get any more depressing.

After they left the room, Jason looked over at Jack. "Haven't there been any victim's advocacy groups stepping up to help her with medical bills?"

"No, not yet" said Jack. "We started a GoFundMe account online for her and there have been some donations. One anonymous donor gave her $50,000 for treatments to save her feet."

"Now that's a donation! Any idea who provided it?"

"No. Possibly one of the pop stars here in town. There was plenty of news coverage about the kidnapping on every media outlet. Some of the local musicians have made donations to her GoFundMe account."

"She said she had huge medical bills. Should I assume she suffered a lot of injuries at the hands of the kidnapper?"

"More that you would ever think possible, Jason. Injuries so egregious you would find it hard to believe one human could possibly do this to a fellow human being."

"So she was lucky to have survived then?"

"I'm not sure she felt lucky. She said she wished she had died. What she went through during her recovery was horrible. Christy sat with her for 21 days before she woke up from her coma. We tried to have someone with her whenever she was awake. She was in constant pain, and we didn't want her to give up. Her college friend Sean came out from Utah and stayed with her whenever he could. His whole family came out a few times and they gave Christy a much-needed break from her bedside vigil. It was an endless nightmare, battling with the insurance company, battling with the doctors. I was afraid Christy might have a breakdown before it was over. Sean's father is a doctor and he challenged some of the medical staff at the hospital when they started talking about amputating her feet. He told us he was not going to let that happen, and he found the equipment they needed for her treatments and had it sent to Nashville. Then they got that nice donation so there was a way to pay for it."

"Wow! That's quite an ordeal you went through. Where did you find Carly after she escaped from the kidnapper?"

"Out in an extremely remote rural area south of Nashville. They were holding her in an old, abandoned cabin."

"This kidnapper sounds awfully vicious. Do you think he intended to kill her?"

"He told her he was going to kill her. He was going to let her choose how she wanted to die."

"Oh, vicious and sadistic. Sounds like he was extremely violent. Have other young women gone missing in Nashville in the last few years?"

"Yes. There have been some. Why?"

"He sounds like a killer. Maybe a serial killer. Have you taken cadaver dogs out to the area where that old cabin is located?"

"You think we need to search for bodies? Isn't that what cadaver dogs do?"

"They do. We used them in the army. If they are well trained, they can sniff out bodies that have been in the ground for years. You don't think this was the kidnapper's first rodeo, do you?"

"Christ! I never thought about other victims. We didn't search for other victims out there. Maybe she was the only one who got away."

"Possibly. How many women have gone missing here in Nashville?"

"About 9 or 10, I think. Some were very young. Maybe 10 or 11 years old. Most were classified as possible runaways.

"Or possibly dead. I did a study about serial killers in law school, and they tend to escalate the level of violence they inflict upon their victims. It sounds like Carly's attack was very violent if she had so many injuries. It's worth looking into."

"God, the sheriff is going to have a coronary when I suggest taking cadaver dogs out there. He's always pinching those pennies. He never wants to spend money on overtime hours to take down these felons."

"Well, if he starts finding bodies, the public is going to thank him. Ten young girls seems like an obscene number. When did they start to go missing?"

"Over the last 2 or 3 years I think. Possibly a little longer."

"Whoa! That would be a lot of murders even for a serial killer. Were any of the missing girls ever found?"

"Not that I recall, Jason. I don't think I'm going to sleep well tonight just thinking about this possibility. The sheriff has been telling the parents the girls are certainly just runaways, but I never believed that line of crap. Usually, we can locate teens that are runaways and get them into some counseling to improve the home situation. I don't think 10 or 11-year-old girls have the resources, the money, or the guts to be a runaway. Runaways are usually older teens who partner up with lousy boyfriends who talk them into leaving home."

"Young girls can be easy prey for a killer. They can be overly trusting. I would check it out. Just take a few dogs out there, and the handlers can tell rather quickly if they are finding anything. It doesn't take them long to pick up the scent if there are bodies buried there."

Their discussion was interrupted by screams coming from the bedrooms. Both Jack and Jason jumped to their feet and ran toward the sound. Jack had his gun out before they even reached the door. Christy was in the room with Carly trying to soothe her.

"I think this is one of those night terrors they talk about."

Jason went up to Carly's bed and tried to talk softly to her. She was flailing her arms and screaming for help. Much to Christy's surprise Jason reached over and picked her up out of the bed and started walking toward the door.

"Wait, wait, where are you going?"

"Just in here," Jason said as he headed for the family room. He sat down in an oversized recliner and pulled her gently into his lap.

He started talking to her in a soft voice. "You're okay, Carly. This is Jason. I've got you. No one is going to hurt you. Just breathe. Breathe slowly now. Take a big deep breath, hold it, and then let it out. Good girl. Let's do that again. Big deep breath. Hold it, and then let it out. Good girl."

She stopped screaming and let her body lean up against him.

"Do you want to take her back to her room now?" asked Christy.

"No. It's just going to start again if we do that. Night terrors are horrible demons. I had them when I left the military. Let's just keep her here for a while and see what happens."

Christy looked doubtful, but she went into the bedroom and came back with a blanket to spread over Carly.

"She might wake up and panic because you are holding her. She doesn't like to be touched," advised Christy.

"I know. She told me. But I think she'll be okay as long as she feels safe. That was a horribly frightening experience she had tonight at the club. It probably just came back to her in a dream."

Carly opened her eyes and looked up at Jason for a moment.

"It's Jason. Remember? From the club tonight? You had a bad dream, so I'm going to sit here and hold you for a little while, so the dream won't come back again. Is that okay?"

She nodded without speaking and laid her head back on his shoulder.

"I'm going to tuck this blanket around you, so you won't get cold, and I'm going to put my arms around you to keep you safe, okay?"

She nodded again. Jason took the blanket and tucked it in all around her and kissed her on the forehead. "Sweet dreams, Carly. Sweet Dreams!"

Jack walked into the family room with his coffee and sat in a chair at the other side of the room from Jason. "Do you think she's going to be okay?" he asked.

"Okay for tonight, or okay long term?" Jason asked.

"Both, I guess. It seems like she is getting better and then she has these horrible nightmares."

"It's probably PTSD. I think she needs to see a good therapist. He can diagnose her symptoms and start some sessions with her. I know one therapist here in Nashville I would highly recommend. I know he has experience with PTSD and with rape victims."

"Her insurance won't cover any more therapy, Jason. That's just one of the many things they have refused to provide. She has no money left, but there is some money in the GoFundMe account. Do you think she should see a female therapist?"

"I don't know that gender really matters. It's the expertise and the personality of the therapist that matters. She needs someone she can open up to. Has she told you or Christy many details about the attacks?"

"Not really. Usually she will tell Christy everything, but this time she has not shared anything about her ordeal."

"Not surprising," said Jason. "Victims of vicious rapes can turn the blame inward and start blaming themselves for what happened. It's a very agonizing thing to have to talk about – even to a sister."

"We have to find a way to keep this bastard in jail. Every time she sees him again every bit of progress she has made is just thrown to the winds. It absolutely derails her. If you have any ideas about how we can get the system to keep him confined, please let me know."

"We could initiate a lawsuit against the state for negligence and mental anguish. That would surely get their attention. Laws give the accused the right to face his accuser, but only in a court of law. He has no right to confront her again after his sentencing. Who do you think is trying to terrorize her by breaking into her house?"

"That's a bit of a mystery. We haven't caught anyone yet, but the evidence of their intent to break in is undeniably there. Broken windows, footprints outside, jammed door locks. Neighbors have reported seeing a man at her windows at all hours of the night."

"Does she have any other relatives she could stay with until these issues are resolved?"

"No. She has friends in the band, but I don't feel comfortable letting her stay with them. These attempts have been going on for about a year. That's why we have the guard dogs at her house every night."

"I don't see how she could live under these conditions and have any sanity left. No wonder she is so frightened."

"We've done everything we know how to do, Jason. We took her to therapy until the money ran out. We took her for physical rehabilitation until the money ran out. We secured plastic surgery for her until the insurance company refused to pay for any additional procedures. She has permanent scaring and mutilations they refused to acknowledge were a result of the kidnapping. They used that as an excuse to deny benefits. We've tried to rescue her house from foreclosure proceedings without any luck. We have been stymied at every turn by the roadblocks thrown up when trying to deal with these companies."

"Have you hired a lawyer?"

"No. We just don't have the kind of money it would take to hire someone to take on all these damn companies."

"Sadly, they are probably going to ignore you until you take legal action. If you want to forward some information to me about the conflicts you have had with these different companies, I can look at the paperwork and let you know what I think. Again, Carly may have a legitimate lawsuit against any one of these providers. Medical insurance providers are notorious for denying any claim they simply do not want to pay. Why did she have to get a $50,000 donation to save her feet?"

"Again, the insurance company refused to pay for the treatments. In the end, the treatments did save her feet from amputation, but they still refused to classify the treatments as medically necessary."

"Seems like you have the proof right there that the treatments were medically necessary. Did they think it would be better for such a young woman to live the rest of her life without feet? All these decisions can be appealed, but I doubt you or Christy had the time to go through those lengthy processes. That's how the insurance companies defend their actions. They point out that every decision can be appealed. But patients who are so sick they are fighting to stay alive don't have the ability to appeal these decisions. It's a vicious fight that insurance companies seldom lose."

"I think we have found that out, Jason. The insurance company even denied payment for the initial lifesaving treatments she received when we brought her into the hospital. I never thought she was going to survive, but they did save her life through extraordinary measures. Personally, I considered her survival a miracle. Then the insurance denied payment because the procedure was not preapproved, and it was what they termed an unorthodox treatment."

"So, they wanted her to die while the hospital was awaiting their approval? Life saving measures are generally exempt from the preapproval clause."

"It all gives me a headache, Jason. We weren't equipped to deal with these problems. We don't have any experience dealing with medical insurance, but Carly doesn't have anyone else."

"I'll try to help you if you would like me to. I created a foundation for veterans so I can help them with these types of problems. I have a lot of experience dealing with medical insurance and hospitals. Sadly, we don't treat our veterans better than anyone else. Sometimes just a letter from an attorney will cause the insurance company to rethink their decision. It's always worth a try. I think they should repay you for the $50,000 you provided for the treatments to save her feet. That would be a good place to start. If they repay you, you could put the money into an account and use it for some of her other medical expenses."

"She doesn't have the money to pay you, Jason, and we have already provided as much help as we are able to give."

"You don't have to pay me; I'll use money from my Foundation to finance your protests. If we can get her an appointment with the therapist I have in mind, I can use money from the Foundation to finance that as well."

"That's very generous of you to offer, Jason. I'm not sure Carly will be willing to accept help she can't finance herself. She has always supported herself and has been very independent in her financial life. She has never asked us for a penny before this happened. She is devastated by the loss of her financial independence as well as the loss of her personal independence."

"I can understand that. She is dealing with losses in every part of her life, and she did nothing to deserve this. She can't even live peacefully in her own home. Let's give it a little time and then we can see how she feels about accepting some help from me. I'm sure you and Christy must feel like your lives have been turned upside down by this tragedy."

"Yes," said Jack. "Luckily our marriage is strong, but it has been sorely tested."

Carly started to whimper and cry a bit as she started to wake up.

"It's okay, Carly. No one is going to hurt you. Just sleep. Just sleep. I'm watching out for you. You're safe. Can you feel my arms around you?"

She nodded a little and put her head down on his shoulder again.

"It's sad to see how frightened she is," said Jason. "How terrible it must be for a woman to know this horrible man is trying to capture her again. It's not like she has any chance in hell of defending herself against him. And sadly, he knows that."

"Well, I think he learned not to mess with you, Jason. He was certainly no match for you."

"They do teach soldiers how to defend themselves in the army. It's part of that basic training."

"We have to find some way to protect her from this bastard. I tried to get the sheriff to fund a bodyguard for her, but he wouldn't authorize the expense. We need to find a way to force the state to keep that damn perp locked up."

Christy walked out into the family room. "Are you ever going to come to bed, Jack?"

"I'm okay here for now, my love."

"I think Carly will be fine. You can come to bed, Jack."

Christy walked into the kitchen and came back with a bottle of water for Jason.

"Thanks, Christy"

Carly woke and cried out a little. Jason started singing a little song to her, and she quieted down and snuggled her head down into his chest.

Christy watched in amazement. She sat down abruptly in Jack's lap. "I guess if you aren't coming to bed, I will just have to sit out here with you, and I want you to sing to me."

Jack looked up at Jason like he wanted to strangle him.

"Okay, love, I'll come to bed, but no singing, okay?"

"No, Jack, I want you to sing to me."

Jack made groaning noises of protest and followed Christy down the hall.

Jason grinned at Jack's dilemma and sang a little bit more to Carly.

Chapter 4

Jason looked down at Carly sleeping in his arms. He could remember the nightmares and the horrible dreams he himself had experienced. He used to have visions of the bombings and battles he fought in Afghanistan, and after his parents were killed, he had horrible dreams about their death, seeing them being run over by a huge semi-truck and killed. He wondered how any man could have hurt and abused this woman so violently. He had a kind of reverence for women. He knew they weren't put on earth to be abused and exploited by men. His mother had often cautioned him about being mindful of the feelings of young girls. She had reminded him that young girls could become quickly infatuated by a handsome young man and they could be easily hurt. He wasn't a player. He heard married men in the army bragging about their wonderful, faithful wives, and then saw them sleeping with the very next woman they could seduce. His own young wife had found someone new and gotten a divorce before the second year of his marriage had ended, but he hadn't been unfaithful to her. She just didn't want to live life as an Army wife. He couldn't blame her. He had only been home once in the two years they were married. It had been a hasty marriage. They thought they were in love, but they were too young and didn't have the maturity it took to make a long-distance relationship work. His mother had been right about that, too. She had urged him to wait until his military service was finished before he thought about marriage. But he had wanted someone to come home to, someone who would be waiting for him, missing him, someone who would pray for his survival. So, his young wife had simply divorced him and moved on with her life. She married a local businessman and had the child she always wanted. He didn't begrudge her that happiness, but he was devastated by the cruel way she handled their breakup, and he had been lonely since he had come home. Sure, there were women out there who would like to keep him company, but he just couldn't seem to connect with anyone who held his interest. Carly felt soft and warm in his arms, and she snuggled into him and moaned softly as she slept. He loved the way she felt in his arms and wished he could hold her forever. Jack had told him a little about the ordeal she had endured at the hands of the kidnappers, and it was clear that she was still suffering from the trauma and had never received the kind of help she needed to recover from such a horrible ordeal.

She cried out in her sleep and Jason pulled his arms around her even more protectively. "I've got you Carly. You're okay. No one's going to hurt you. Just sleep. Shhh! Everything is okay." He hummed a little melody to her and rocked her gently until she relaxed into him again.

"Good girl. Just sleep," he whispered. Every time she moaned it tugged on his heartstrings. He wondered if it would ever be possible to build a relationship with a woman who had been so abused. He didn't know, but he knew he wanted her. The first time she smiled up at him with her pretty green eyes he had been smitten. But that was before the attack of the escaped kidnapper. After the attack she was hysterical and inconsolable. He had subdued the kidnapper before he could hurt her, but the fear that he saw in her eyes made him wish he could have done more to the man than just stop him. He couldn't remember ever seeing anyone that frightened, even among the soldiers in his unit. She wasn't just frightened; she was terrified to the point of becoming incapacitated. No one should ever have to experience that level of fear, he thought. As she slept, he thought about ways he might be able to help her. He wanted to take away all the memories that were making her suffer, but he wasn't sure anyone could do that. He still had some of his own memories he fought with. The frequency of his nightmares had begun to diminish, and he hoped he could find some help for Carly to soften her horrible memories as well. Since they had only just met that night, he wondered if she would even accept any help from him. He had the resources and knowledge to get her some excellent therapy, but he wasn't sure if she would be receptive. He remembered his own introduction to therapy. His grandma and Roy, the ranch manager, had found the therapist and forced him to go to his appointments. He told them he didn't need help, but he couldn't deny he had spent one horrible night searching the house for a gun so he could end it all. That had done it for Grandma. She was a strong woman, and she was hell bent on getting him help. She removed his dad's old guns from the house and had Roy lock them up in the stables. Then she asked Roy to move into the house with them to help her survive the nights when he had flashbacks. Jason was grateful to them now. They hadn't just let him wallow in his grief, and he had finally decided to go to law school and try to help other veterans. He still missed his parents every day, but he was learning to control the grief and the anger.

Jason watched Carly as she slept. Gradually he dozed off. He heard Christy coming into the room to make another check on Carly, but he kept his eyes closed. He mulled over the conversation with Jack in his mind. It didn't seem right that they had received so little support from the community or from any victim's advocacy groups. He smiled to himself as he thought about his grandma and Aunt Nettie who just loved to get on the computer and do searches. He had purchased computers for them to keep them away from his own computer. Here was something they could research. Maybe they could find some groups who would provide funds to this struggling family. He saw the pain in Christy's eyes every time she looked at her sister, and he realized this ordeal had taken its toll on the whole family. Jack had said Carly didn't have any other family members, and he wondered what might have happened to them, but that was a question for another day. For now, he had to figure out how to get them to trust him enough to get some help for Carly.

Early in the morning he felt Carly squirming in his arms. She looked up at him in panic, at first, but as soon as he spoke to her, she relaxed and laid her head back on his shoulder.

"What happened?" she asked. "How did I get here?"

"You had a bad dream, and I remembered you said you didn't want to frighten Lindsey, so I brought you out here."

"Was I screaming?"

"A little bit, but you stopped as soon as I picked you up."

"Did I wake up Lindsey?"

"No. Lindsey was fine. Christy and Jack were worried about you, but you settled down and went back to sleep as soon as I told you that you were safe."

"Wow! I don't remember anything. Have I been asleep all this time?"

"Yes. Do you feel a little better now?"

"I don't think I have ever slept this long. Most nights I can't sleep at all."

"With all those snarling dogs outside your windows, it's a wonder you could ever sleep."

"It's hard, but they do protect me."

"I'm wondering why someone would keep trying to break into your house. Do you have anything of great value inside?"

"Oh, no. Just some old furniture and my old piano. I certainly don't keep any money in the house because I don't have any money now."

"When did the break-in attempts start?"

"It started before the trial for the kidnapper. Jack thought they might be trying to silence me before I could testify at the trial, so they moved me to a safe house for a while. After the trial was over, I moved back to my house, but then the attempts started again."

Jason listened without any comment. Thieves generally target houses with valuables, and it didn't seem like she had anything of great value. He thought they were targeting her, but the kidnapper was in jail, most of the time. He didn't want to alarm her any further, so he kept those thoughts to himself.

"Have you been here all night with me?" Carly asked.

"Yes. We've been sleeping together," he teased.

She had a startled look on her face.

"I'm teasing you," he said with a smile.

She smiled up at him with her pretty green eyes and said, "Well you are the most handsome man I have ever spent the night with."

"Well, well, well. Someone is feeling better today," said Christy from the doorway. "How about we all have some coffee, and you could give Jason a chance to get up and stretch his legs."

"Don't know about that. I'm very comfortable here," said Carly.

Just then they heard a wail coming from Lindsey's room.

"Could you please go get her Carly? I'm making breakfast. Be sure to introduce her to Jason."

Carly started to get up slowly. She looked up shyly at Jason. "Thank you. Thank you for making me feel safe last night. It's usually so hard for me to sleep."

"Anytime," said Jason with a smile.

Carly went down the hall to pick up Lindsey and carried her into the kitchen to her mama.

"Mommy, Aunt Carly still has her pajamas on."

"So do you, Lindsey."

"But I just woke up. Aunt Carly gets up early. Daddy says she gets up before the chickens."

Christy laughed. "Well Aunt Carly got someone to sing her a lullaby last night and she just woke up too." Christy looked over Lindsey's head and smiled at Carly.

"Lullaby?" asked Carly.

"Oh, yes, Carly. He sang to you."

"I wish I could remember. Was I awake?"

"Yes. It would have put me to sleep for sure. I tried to get Jack to sing to me, but he was such a poor sport."

Jason walked into the kitchen and the conversation stopped abruptly.

"Sorry. Am I interrupting something?"

Carly blushed.

"Mommy said you can sing lullabies," Lindsey blurted out.

"Oh, dear, I forgot how quickly she picks up on everything these days," explained Christy.

"Quite all right. Do you want me to sing you a lullaby tonight, Lindsey?"

"Can he Mommy? Can he?"

"We'll see, Lindsey. This is Jason. He is Aunt Carly's new friend."

"Can I call him Uncle Jason?"

"He isn't really your uncle, so let's just call him Jason, okay?"

"Okay, mommy."

"How about you take Aunt Carly down to your room and let her help you get dressed."

"Can I help with anything?" Jason offered.

"No but help yourself to some coffee. Were you able to get any sleep last night?"

"I did doze off for quite a while. Carly was very quiet once she was sound asleep. She said she usually doesn't sleep more than an hour or so."

"That might even be an exaggeration. Some nights I don't think she sleeps at all. It's sad what this has done to her life. Last night you mentioned something to Jack about PTSD. Isn't that what affects soldiers when they have been in a war?"

"Yes. It's what they used to refer to as shell shock. But it can occur in anyone who has suffered a horrible trauma. How long was Carly held by the kidnapper before she escaped?"

"Four days."

"Ouch! That's a long time to spend wondering if you are going to live or die."

Carly walked back into the kitchen with Lindsey in tow and the conversation ended.

"It's Sunday, Carly. Do you have any plans?"

"Well, I guess I should take Charlie and go home," she offered.

"Jack doesn't want you to go back to your house yet. Let's wait until this kidnapper is safely back in prison."

"Okay. I could take Lindsey and Charlie to the park."

"No, Carly. I don't think you should go out alone."

"I could go with you," offered Jason. "Then I could take you to lunch."

"Oh good," said Lindsey. "Can we go to Burger King?"

"I think Jason was inviting Aunt Carly to lunch, my little moppet," said Christy.

"Lindsey can come too," added Jason.

"Oh good. I think I'm going to like Uncle Jason."

Carly and Christy smiled at each other when Lindsey persisted in adding the uncle title. *"This is one cute little girl, thought Jason. Almost as cute as her Aunt Carly."*

After breakfast, Jason said, "How about if I go back to the hotel for a shower and change of clothes, and then I'll come back and pick you up in my car."

"Sounds fine," said Carly, "but the park is just a block away."

"But you might be forgetting about Burger King, Aunt Carly. The King just might not be within walking distance."

"So true," said Carly. "We'll get ready and watch for you."

After Jason left, Christy looked over at Carly. "Do you feel comfortable going out to the park with him?"

"Yeah. I think he is big enough to take on any potential kidnappers today. I wish I could keep him as a bodyguard. He makes me feel safe."

"I'm glad, Carly. You deserve some peace in your life, even if it is just for a while."

"I'm dreading tomorrow. I hate having to look at the kidnapper's horrible face again. Do you think they could do the hearing without me?"

"I don't think so Carly. You are the one who was assaulted, so we will all have to testify as witnesses to that assault. Jack told me this morning that the perp wanted to know if he could press charges against Jason for breaking his arm."

"I wish he had broken his neck," said Carly. "That's what he deserves."

"Maybe next time," Christy quipped.

"Oh, God, please don't let there be a next time," said Carly.

"Are you sure you feel comfortable going out in a car with him? You don't know him very well."

"We can walk down to the park with Charlie and Lindsey first, and if I don't feel comfortable, I'll just come back here, okay? He seems nice, don't you think?"

"Yes, he does, but you know Jack is always suspicious of anyone who wants to cozy up to you. He didn't believe he was really a lawyer, but he looked him up on the internet as soon as he went into work this morning and he is a member of the bar in Kentucky."

"So, we know he isn't a liar then."

"Well just be cautious and don't rush into anything. He is a devastatingly attractive man."

"I hope you didn't say that to Jack."

"No, I don't want to bruise his ego. Just try to keep it casual. I can see by the way Jason looks at you, that he might be wanting more than just casual friendship."

"I'm not ready for anything more than casual, so please don't worry about me."

Jason came up to the door and Carly let him in, giving him the once over after listening to Christy's comments. He had on some nice jeans, a button-down shirt that almost matched the color of his eyes, and a leather jacket that she immediately wanted to touch to see if it could possibly be as soft and supple as it looked.

"Let's walk to the park so I can take Charlie, and then we can bring him back here before we go visit the King for lunch."

"Works for me," said Jason. "Is Lindsey ready to go?"

Hearing her name, Lindsey came running down the hall with Charlie on a leash. "We are ready, Aunt Carly."

It was nearly dinner time before the trio returned. Christy had started to get worried, and she wished Carly had a cell phone so she could check up on them. Carly came in the door wearing a big smile, and Jason was holding Lindsey in his arms.

"I didn't realize you were going to be gone so long. Is Lindsey all right?"

"Yes, she just got a little tired and fell asleep in the car on the way back."

"Did you have fun, Lindsey?" Christy asked.

"Mommy we went to Burger King, and I ate all my lunch, so Aunt Carly said I could have ice cream. Then we went to the Fun Place, and Jason and I played all the games there. Jason gave me lots of quarters, and I won a bracelet." She held her arm out to show off her new bracelet.

"Sounds like Lindsey might be ready for an early bedtime. I'm almost ready with dinner and Jack is going to be coming back late, so we can eat if you guys are ready. Jason, I hope you can stay for dinner."

"I would like that. Thank you. We had a great afternoon with your daughter."

Christy noticed the smile he gave Carly as he gently set Lindsey down on her feet.

They all played some games with Lindsey after dinner until Christy announced that it was Lindsey's bedtime.

"I guess I should head back to my hotel," Jason announced.

"No, please don't go. I feel safe with you here, and Jack isn't home yet. Can you stay here again tonight? Please?"

Christy wasn't sure what Jack was going to think about this when he got home, but she decided not to cross that bridge yet. After she got Lindsey off to bed, she walked back into the family room and found Carly and Jason sitting on the couch talking. Carly had her head leaning up against Jason's shoulder, and Christy tried not to show her surprise. She heard her cell phone ringing in the kitchen and went to take the call. When she was finished, she walked back into the family room.

"Jack is going to be very late tonight. There has been a shooting up north of town and they have a suspect cornered. He asked if you might stay here tonight with us, Jason. His brother is up there on duty also, and he doesn't want us to stay alone."

"Sure. I can stay. That's not a problem."

"Okay. I'll bring you some blankets and pillows and you can sleep on the couch."

"I hope I don't have one of those nightmares again tonight. Please wake me up if I start screaming."

"We can try," said Jason. "It's not always easy to wake someone when they have night terrors."

Christy came back with blankets and pillows. "I brought you one of Jack's t-shirts. The shirt you have on looks a little too nice to be slept in."

"Thanks. That will be great."

Christy and Carly went off to bed and Jason laid down on the couch and wished it was just a little bit longer. He thought about Jack and how hard it must be having to be away from his family for such long days. But he was glad Jack hadn't come home and asked him to leave. He had enjoyed such a great day with Carly. When they were at the park, she had even let him hold her hand for a short time. He woke up suddenly when he felt a small tap on his shoulder.

"Jason, can I talk to you?"

"Whoa, Carly. I didn't hear you coming. Are you alright?"

"Yes. I was trying to be quiet so no one would hear me. I just needed to talk to you."

She was shivering a little from the cold.

"Come here and get under these blankets and tell me what's wrong."

He pulled the blankets up and she laid down on the couch next to him.

"I just get scared sometimes when I'm alone. Then I start shaking and I can't stop."

He thought she was going to cry.

"You don't have to be alone. You can stay here with me. Put your back right up against me and I can keep you warm."

She moved over a little closer to him and she could feel the warmth of his body. It felt comforting. She liked the feel of his body up against hers.

"Can I put my arm around you, Carly?"

She nodded and he reached out and pulled her even a little closer to him.

"Okay, I'll keep you safe, and you see if you can go back to sleep and not have any of those terrible dreams."

He stroked her face lightly and kissed her on the cheek. She made a little murmuring sound and he felt her pushing closer against his chest. He watched her quietly as she drifted off to sleep.

A few hours later, he heard Jack come in the door. "Don't get up, it's just me, Jack," he said.

Jason was hoping he wouldn't turn on the lights and notice Carly sleeping there with him, but he went straight to the bedroom in the dark.

Carly woke up early the next morning and looked over at Jason. He smiled at her and hugged her closer.

"No dreams last night?" he asked.

"No. I don't even remember trying to fall asleep."

"Well, you went right to sleep after we said Good Night. It was probably less than 5 minutes."

"I guess I should go back to my own bed before Christy gets up." She started to move toward the edge of the couch.

"Wait, wait I hear footsteps."

"Aunt Carly, I've been looking for you. I went to your room, and you weren't there. I thought maybe you went back home."

"No sweetie, I just came out here to talk to Jason to keep him company."

"Was he lonely?"

"I think he was a little lonely, sugar."

"I like Jason, Aunt Carly. He has twinkly eyes."

Carly and Jason both started to laugh.

"Twinkly eyes. That's a new one," Jason laughed.

Carly saw Christy creeping up behind Lindsey getting ready to scoop her up and spirit her away.

She gave Carly a look that said, '*What is going on here?*'

"Lindsey, I think I hear Daddy calling you. Let's go see what he wants."

She scooped up Lindsey and left the room quickly.

"I'm guessing this is what you didn't want your sister to see?"

"Pretty much."

"We could pretend you had a terrible dream and had to come and sleep with me."

"We could…" Carly turned over toward Jason and touched the side of his face gently. "You must be the best sleeping pill ever. I've slept all night for 2 nights in a row. I never thought that would happen again."

"You need it to happen every night. You need your sleep to get better. You could come home with me after the hearing today and I promise I can keep you safe."

"Where is home, Jason?"

"Up in Kentucky on a ranch. We have security devices throughout the house, and we have security patrols on the property day and night."

"What are they protecting?"

"The horses, the buildings, the family, our employees. We need to be very careful not to let strangers onto the property. There have been ranchers who have lost their entire stable of horses to nighttime fires."

"That sounds awful!"

"Yes, it is a tragedy, but we have taken a lot of measures to make sure it never happens to us."

"Kentucky seems like it is a long way from here…." She let her thoughts trail off and felt Jason gently pulling her closer to him. She felt all her muscles tighten and then gradually began to let them soften as she sank into the warmth of his body. And what a body it was! Even through the T-shirt she could feel all the muscles winding through his chest. She looked down at his arms and they were nothing but ribbons of muscle up and down the entire length of each arm. He had one leg draped over her body, and she wanted to reach down and touch it to see if it felt as muscular as his arms. She felt her breath starting to get heavier and she almost felt like she was gasping for air. *Not now, not now, she told herself. This isn't the time!* She tried to hold her breath and stop breathing.

Jason leaned over and whispered in her ear, "It's okay, Carly. I feel it too. It's okay to have feelings. Just breathe. It's okay. We're not going to do anything about them. Just try to enjoy the feeling and the warmth."

He rocked her gently in his arms. Carly couldn't remember ever feeling like this before. She couldn't remember anyone holding her so gently, tucking blankets in around her to keep her warm, and now whispering softly in her ear. She wondered what kissing him would feel like. It was nice yesterday when he held her hand.

She heard footsteps coming down the hall and tried to just lie there quietly.

"Look, Daddy. Aunt Carly came out to talk to Jason because he was lonely."

Jack was carrying Lindsey. He looked over at Carly and said, "I see that. I think someone has some 'splaining' to do today."

"What's 'splaining', Daddy?"

"That's what Daddy is going to do. He's going to 'splain' how to make pancakes."

They hurried into the kitchen and closed the door behind them.

Carly looked at Jason and started to giggle. They were both laughing when they heard Christy walk through the room and into the kitchen. Carly looked over at Jason and thought maybe he was going to kiss her. She reached her hand up toward his face and kissed him gently on the mouth. He wrapped his arms around her back and pulled her up across his body and covered her mouth with his. He heard the kitchen door open and then quickly close again. She didn't pull away and he deepened the kiss, not wanting it to end. They laid there quietly afterwards just listening to each other breathe.

"I guess I shouldn't have done that," she said.

"No? I was hoping we could do it again." He reached down and gently lifted her chin up towards his face and covered her mouth with his kiss. Her head was reeling. She felt him pull away when they heard the kitchen door open.

"Hey, you two! Are you remembering we have a court hearing today? Jack and Lindsey are making pancakes, and the coffee is ready. Are you okay today, Carly?"

"Yes, I'm fine. I got a lot of sleep last night."

"That's great. Do you want me to start running a bath for you?"

"No, I can do that. I'm just dreading this hearing today."

"I know you are. But we are all going to be with you, and you will be safe, right, Jason?"

"Absolutely. If he starts to act out, maybe I can break his other arm. That might slow him down."

Christy laughed. "I think Carly was hoping someone could break his neck. Okay, Carly, if you need something to wear just look in my closet and pick something out."

She went back into the kitchen and Jason reached over to kiss Carly again. "I'm not going to let him hurt you today, and there will be bailiffs in court to restrain him. Try not to look at him. Keep your eyes on the lawyers or the judge. He wants you to look at him so he can see your fear. If he starts yelling or acting out, they will probably take him out of the courtroom." "Oh, God, Jason, I don't want to do this! I don't want to go." She started crying and Jason tried to rub her back to soothe her.

"I promise it will be okay. I'm going to ask the judge for a moment in his chambers and see if they can't find a way to keep this perp locked down a little tighter."

"I hope you can. I don't want to keep doing this."

"No. You shouldn't have to. This should have been over for you a long time ago. You shouldn't have ever had to lay eyes on him again."

"Do you think the judge will let you talk to him?"

"Probably. Since I am a member of the bar, they will usually give you that courtesy."

"Breakfast is almost ready," Christy called from the kitchen.

Carly ran off to get her bath and Jason folded up the blankets he had used and went to find his shirt so he could look more presentable. He went into the kitchen for coffee.

"Did Carly have nightmares again last night?" Christy asked.

"I don't think so. She came out to talk to me and fell asleep. I don't think she even woke up again after that."

"Good story," said Jack with a smile.

"She's upset about having to confront the kidnapper again. She doesn't want to go to court today, but I told her we would protect her."

"We will, even if I have to shoot the bastard."

"Who are you going to shoot, Daddy?"

"Oops! Nobody. Daddy isn't going to shoot anyone. I was quoting a line from a movie!" he lied.

Christ gave him a look! "This has to end, Jack. The system can't continue to put her through this agony. It's destroying her!"

"Jason and I talked about some ideas he had for stopping this horrible drama. We can see what the judge recommends and talk about it afterwards. Jason is offering to help her as an attorney without payment, but I told him Carly might not be willing to let him help her."

Christy looked up at Jason with a sly smile. "Well, I think she might be softening to that idea."

"What exactly does that mean? What did she tell you?"

"Oh, she didn't have to tell me anything, Jack. I'm her sister. Sometimes actions speak louder than words, right Jason?"

Jason didn't answer. He looked embarrassed. Christy was waiting for him to blush, but guys don't usually do that. They just turn away, which is exactly what he did.

"Okay, I guess I have been left out of the loop. Maybe you can fill me in on the way to the courthouse. We need to drop Lindsey off at my brother's house. Do you know the way to the courthouse Jason?"

"Not really but I have GPS in my car."

"Carly knows where it is. She can ride with you."

They ate breakfast without much further conversation, and they all got ready to go.

Carly started crying as soon as she got into the car. Jason wanted to wrap her up in his arms and hold her. When they got to the courthouse, he parked the car and reached over to her and held her in his arms. He forgot to even ask if she wanted him to hold her.

"It's going to be okay, Carly. We are all there for you. Don't look at the perp and don't respond if he yells out anything."

Carly started to cry again as soon as she had to take the witness stand. The judge spoke softly and gently to her, and she was able to answer a few questions.

Before anyone knew what was happening the kidnapper rolled himself over the top of the defense table and started to run toward her. The bailiffs ran out to grab him, but Jack and Jason were already in front of him before he could reach Carly.

"You lying bitch! I should have killed you when I had the chance. You just wait. I'm going to find you and I'm going to kill you. You're as good as dead! As good as dead! Just wait!"

Carly collapsed down onto the floor of the witness stand. Jason went over to pick her up.

She was crying hysterically. The judge started yelling orders at the bailiffs and the defense attorney and ordered handcuffs and chains for the kidnapper. He was pounding his gavel to bring order back to the court. He called for the paramedics to come in for Carly, and they took her off to a room next to the courtroom and Christy went with her. The judge called for a 20-minute recess to give Carly time to recover.

Jason asked for permission to approach the bench. The judge looked at him quizzically and Jason explained that he was a member of the bar in Kentucky and a friend of the family, and he would like to speak to the judge in chambers. The judge granted his request and Jason and Jack followed him back to his chambers.

Jason explained this was the second prison escape for the defendant, and he asked the judge if the state could find a way to keep this prisoner locked up.

"You can see what this is doing to the victim, Judge. He goes to her place of employment to attack her, and she is living in fear. She needs this to be over."

The Judge called in his law clerk to put in a message to the warden of the prison.

He sighed, "I remember his trial. He is a vicious felon as I recall. I see no need to use him on a work crew or use him anywhere outside the prison walls. He threatened the victim again today. I agree that this must end. We will hold a sentencing hearing as soon as it can be scheduled. In the meantime, I will ask the warden to keep him in a maximum-security cell."

"Mr. Kingman, if you are a member of the bar in Tennessee, I would urge you to petition the court to have this prisoner sent to a maximum-security prison."

"I'm not a member of the bar in Tennessee, but I believe I can petition for reciprocity and get admitted to the bar in Tennessee. If not, I know a lawyer here in town who will do that."

"I would urge you to do that, sir. As soon as possible."

Jason and Jack looked at each other as they left the chambers.

"What do you think he was trying to tell us when he said, 'as soon as possible'?" Jack asked.

"I think that he doesn't trust either the warden or the prison system here. Maybe he doesn't trust either one of them. But there was a message there, and it was pointed! I'm going to get my friend Donnie to draw up a petition as soon as he can possibly get it done. I hate to say this, but I think Carly's life is in danger. Is it possible there was more than one kidnapper, and the second one might still be out there?"

"Carly never mentioned two of them, but she won't talk to us about the kidnapping. I'll ask Christy. If anyone would know it would be Christy."

Jason's head was spinning. There was something very wrong with the way this case had been handled. The attempted break-ins at her house didn't make sense. The prisoner just threatened her in court, and it was clear he meant to have her killed. Putting this vicious felon on a work crew didn't make sense. Letting him escape twice was totally unacceptable for any prison system. He wondered if Jack shared his feelings, but he didn't want to bring it up, yet.

They went back into the courtroom and the Judge pointedly asked the defense attorney if he was finished with his questioning of the victim. The defense attorney finally said yes as the judge was giving him a steely stare. Other witnesses were questioned, and the hearing ended as the judge ordered the defendant sent back to the state prison immediately to await additional sentencing.

Jason took Carly back to the car, and she started crying again. He held her in his arms and stroked her back gently until her sobs slowly subsided.

"He's going to kill me, Jason. You heard him. Everyone heard him. What am I going to do?"

"Let's go back to your sister's house and I'll tell you about an idea I have for you, okay?"

She nodded silently, and he started planning how he could convince her to go home with him for a few weeks. There was something wrong here, but he just couldn't put his finger on the source of evil.

Chapter 5

After the court hearing, Jason took Carly back to Christy's house while Jack and Christy went to pick up Lindsey from the babysitter. He told Carly about the ranch where he lived in Kentucky and asked her if she would like to go home with him and stay at the ranch until the kidnapper had been transported back to prison. He showed her pictures of the ranch on the internet so she could get an idea how it looked. He told her about the security patrols that guarded the property and assured her that she could feel safe there. She hesitated at first, but then decided it might be a good idea to be further away from the kidnapper.

When Christy got back, Jason could hear her trying to talk Carly out of her decision to leave while Carly was packing up an overnight bag. Jason could tell that Christy and Jack did not want her to leave with him, but in the end, Carly decided to go to the ranch and left with Jason.

Once they were on the road, Jason kept making sideways glances toward Carly, wondering if she was still okay with her decision. She was looking nervous, so Jason wondered if he should ask her if she had changed her mind.

"Carly, I'm going to pull off up here and gas up before we get back up to the ranch. They have a little store here if you want anything – like coffee, water?"

"No, no, I'm okay, Jason. I don't need anything."

"Okay. I'm just going to get gas then."

Jason got back in the car after he finished fueling up and looked at Carly. "Carly are you okay? Do you feel uncomfortable? Do you want me to take you back to Nashville?"

She didn't answer right away, and Jason thought maybe he knew the unspoken answer.

"I can take you back to Nashville if you want me to. It's okay. Whatever you want to do is okay."

"No. No, Jason. I don't want to go back. I don't know… Are we close to where you live?"

"Yes. We're fairly close now. There's an overlook just ahead, and I'll pull off there and show you where we're going. You can see where the ranch is and think about it for a few minutes. Then if you want me to take you back, I'll do that. I feel like I talked you into coming up here, but I don't want you to feel uneasy about it. That wasn't my intention. I only wanted you to feel safer. I saw how frightened you were when you saw the kidnapper at the hearing. Nobody should ever have to feel that frightened."

"I was hoping to never see him again in my entire life, and I never dreamed he would escape. I guess he made it clear that he intends to keep coming for me. He said I was as good as dead."

"But he's back in prison and you're here with me, and I promise I won't let him hurt you. When Jack and I went back into the Judge's chambers today, that was the question we asked the judge. What is wrong with the prison system in Tennessee that they can't keep this dangerous felon in prison where he belongs? Okay, let's drive up to the overlook and I'll show you where the ranch is, and you can decide what you want to do. If you want me to take you back to Nashville I will."

"I did want to stay with you, Jason. I felt safe last night when I slept on the couch with you. It made me feel better. I wasn't as frightened when you put your arms around me. I went to sleep."

"Good. Let's drive up and take a look, and then I want you to do what's best for you. But I would love to have you come up to the ranch and spend a few days with me." He secretly hoped that she just might want him to put his arms around her and hold her again tonight.

As they drove up the road, Carly saw the sign on the side of the highway that said, *"Welcome to Kentucky"*, and she felt the knot tighten in the pit of her stomach. *What am I doing here? She asked herself. What am I doing? Christy didn't want me to come up here. Jack didn't want me to come. I don't really know Jason very well. Now I'm a long way from home. Was this a foolish idea? Kentucky! I don't know if this was the right thing to do.* She thought back to the last few nights she had spent at Christy's house. She had to admit that there was something about Jason that seemed to calm her. Even though she didn't like anyone to touch her, when he had wrapped his arms around her, she felt protected and safe. He had whispered reassuring words to her. He even sang to her a little. She felt like a little child being tucked into bed when he wrapped a blanket around her and kissed her on the forehead. She couldn't remember anything like this from her own lonely childhood, but she imagined that somewhere there were children being tucked in bed by their parents like this every night.

Jason drove into a small parking area. They got out of the car and walked around to the front of the vehicle. "Okay. I'll show you where we are going. Look over to the left, and you can see lots of long white fences. That's the ranch, and the fences go all the way around the ranch. You can see part of the house from here. There's a big gate where we enter the property and then the house is off to the left. If you drive past the house, there are more buildings for people who live here and stables and barns for the animals."

"I thought you said you lived here with your grandmother."

"I do. I live here with my grandmother and Aunt Nettie. We live in the house but there are other people who live here too - like Roy - the manager - and Robbie and Bruce, our trainers. The people who work here year-round live on the property and have houses."

"So, all these people have houses right on the ranch? It's not just one house? Do any of them live in your house?"

'No, no. They don't live in my house. Only Grandma and Nettie live in the house with me. Other people who live here and have families have their own house."

"It looks awfully big. I thought it was just a small farm."

"Yes. It's big! We have a lot of horses now, and we need to provide stables for them, and then we have a track so they can be trained."

"What are the horses for? Do you sell them?"

"They're racehorses. Thoroughbred racehorses."

"Do they go to a racetrack?"

"Exactly. You've heard of races like the Belmont, the Preakness, the Kentucky Derby, right?"

"I've heard of the Kentucky Derby, but I've never been to see it."

"Well, we have to take you to the Kentucky Derby. I started going when I was young. If we had horses running in the Derby, the whole family would go to Louisville for the week."

"You had horses that ran in the Derby? Your horses?"

"They belonged to the Ranch. They were my dad's horses, as he was still alive then. We had a big box in the stands and my dad would invite friends and family to come to watch our horses in the races. I loved it as a kid. Back then I wanted to be a jockey."

"When is the Derby? Is it just one race?"

"The Derby is on the first Saturday in May. There are lots of races that day, but the Derby is the big event. People come from all over to attend. Ladies wear big fancy hats, and people bet like crazy."

"Do you bet on the horses?"

"No. I'm not much of a gambler. I think my dad and my mom used to do some betting, but it's not really my thing. So that's what the ranch looks like."

Jason reached over and gently took her hand. "Carly, can I put my arms around you and just hold you for a few minutes?"

She didn't reply, but she nodded. Jason put his arms around her and when he felt her leaning toward him, he stepped closer and pulled her into his arms.

"I'm so sorry. You've had a bad couple of days. Or maybe it's really been a bad couple of years. I promise I can keep you safe on the ranch. Can you let me protect you?"

Carly was quiet in his arms, and she let him hold her. He felt her sigh heavily and she put her head on his shoulder. He remembered what it was like last night when she was lying in his arms. He wanted to feel her soft and warm against his body again. He fantasized about what it might be like to have her in bed next to him. He stroked her cheek gently. He asked himself what was happening to him. He couldn't remember even thinking about being with a woman since he came home from the army. Now here he was suddenly having all kinds of fantasies about this woman. He looked at her again and said, "Carly, if you want me to take you back to Nashville, it's okay. I'm not going to be angry. You can tell me what you want to do."

"No, I don't want to go back. I want to stay with you, Jason. I need to feel safe for a few days. I need some time to recover and try to calm myself."

"Okay. Let's go to the ranch, and if you don't feel comfortable there, I'll take you back to Nashville in the morning. Is that okay?"

"Yeah," she whispered. "It sounds okay."

"Grandma and Nettie are fixing dinner for us, and they are looking forward to meeting you. I told them a little about you. I let them know you don't like to be hugged and don't want to shake hands, so there won't be any hugging or shaking – and no kissing. Unless you want to kiss me like you did this morning. I would be okay with that!"

Carly looked up at him and smiled shyly. "I think you kissed *me*, Jason."

"Not the way I remember it, but I know I kissed you back. I would let you kiss me again right now if you wanted to…I'll kiss you back." He leaned his head down toward her and she reached up and kissed him gently on the lips. The kiss deepened and then he just cradled her gently in his arms. He couldn't quite understand what it was he was feeling when he held her. She made his heart beat faster. He felt a little breathless.

When Jason and Carly got up to the ranch, he introduced her to Grandma and Aunt Nettie. They had a nice dinner of Lasagna accompanied by good wine. They talked about the ranch for a while, and then Jason told Grandma and Nettie that Carly was a singer and he met her when he was down in Nashville at the Rosebud Club. He briefly mentioned there had been an incident at the club when a prisoner who had escaped came into the club on Saturday and tried to assault her. He said he thought she would be safer at the ranch until they could transport the felon back to prison where he belonged.

"Oh, gosh," said Grandma, "that must have been horribly frightening!"

"Yeah, I was frightened. I hoped I would never see him again. He was given a nice long prison sentence."

"Why would he come after you at the club?"

Carly hesitated for a moment and looked at Jason. He realized she didn't want to answer.

"Grandma, this was a man who kidnapped Carly a few years ago, but she escaped from him. He walked away from a prison work crew and came into the club and tried to grab her."

"Oh, my word. It seems like if he escaped from prison, he wouldn't come back to find you again. Wouldn't he want to run and get as far away from prison as he could?"

"If he were a smart felon that's what he would do, but obviously this guy is not smart."

"I'm so sorry to hear that, Carly. I'm glad you are okay."

"I was very frightened, but Jason was sitting next to me, and after the guy grabbed me, Jason pushed him away. I'm not sure how he did it, but Jason had him down on the floor in just a few seconds."

Grandma chuckled. "Well, that's Jason. He's pretty strong. That felon picked the wrong person to tangle with that night. Is that what you did, Jason? You put him down on the floor?"

"Yeah. It was easy. He wasn't a big guy. But he really went after Carly and flung her right off the barstool. I didn't know who he was or why he came after her, but you just can't put your hands on someone like he did. You can't go around flinging pretty ladies off a barstool."

"No," said Grandma. "I guess he got your message, huh?"

"I hope so," said Jason.

They talked a bit more about the Rosebud club and Grandma said, "I hope we get to hear you sing, Carly. We would really like that."

"It would be nice for me, too," said Jason. "I went down to Nashville to hear her sing, but after that felon tried to grab her, she wasn't in much of a singing mood, were you, Carly?"

"No. I couldn't stop shaking."

"But it's better now, right? You feel better?"

"Yes, but I'll always be afraid of him."

"Well, stick with our Jason, Carly. He would never let that jerk hurt you," said Nettie.

"We're going to start getting dessert out," said Grandma. "I hope you are all still a little hungry."

"I'm going to go down to check on the rooms down the hall for just a minute. You can stay here, Carly. Just sit tight and pick out your dessert. Pick one for me, too." He had called the housekeeper and asked her to check on the rooms and make sure they weren't too dusty. He didn't think anyone had used those two rooms in quite a long time. The rooms were an addition his father had built onto the house while Jason was in the military, and he thought it would be ideal for him and Carly. There were 2 bedrooms on either side of a bathroom, and there was even a little kitchen where he could make coffee in the morning. He wanted to give her a room, but he didn't want to be too far away from her just in case she had night terrors again. He hadn't told Grandma about the night terrors yet. He was hoping she might not be able to hear Carly if she was screaming. He knew he should tell Grandma, but maybe tomorrow would be soon enough. It looked like the housekeeper had put new sheets on the beds, and there were candles and flowers in the room for Carly. He went back to the kitchen where everyone was having pie.

"Oh, Carly, how did you pick my favorite pie?"

She looked up at him sheepishly and didn't answer.

"Grandma told you, didn't she? She knows that cherry pie is always my favorite. We even have some cherry trees here on the property that we pick for the pies. We planted them when I was little because I loved cherry pie so much."

Carly smiled. "I confess. She did tell me you loved cherry pie."

When they finished, Jason asked Carly, "Any chance that you might feel like singing?"

"No, not tonight. Maybe tomorrow."

"That's okay. We have a nice piano here if you would like to play it."

Grandma looked up at him quickly, thinking, *'yes, we have a nice piano here that just got delivered this morning.'* But she didn't say anything.

"Do you want to see it?"

"Sure. Where is it?"

"Over in the Great Room," Jason said. He hadn't seen it himself because he ordered it over the phone from one of the suppliers in town. He walked into the room and thought *'Oh, my God that thing is big!'*

Carly walked into the room and said, "Oh, Lord, I thought you were talking about a little piano like a spinet or a studio piano, I wasn't thinking about a piano like this. This is almost as big as a concert grand."

"Would you play something for us? I'd like to hear how it sounds when someone talented plays it. I'm not a very good piano player. I'm just learning."

Carly started playing and it had a beautiful sound. "Wow! You are so lucky. I've never had a piano like this. Even the college didn't have anything this nice! This is beautiful!"

"Do you know much about it or what kind of piano it is?"

"Sure. It's a Bosendorfer. It's made in Germany. When I was little and lived on the farm, I wished for a piano like this. We had an old farmhouse piano. I taught myself to play little songs that I heard. But it wasn't anything like this. This piano is gorgeous. Jason, this could be the piano of my dreams."

Maybe it will be the piano of your dreams, thought Jason. It could be yours. But he didn't say it.

"That's good. I'm glad you like it."

Carly started playing again. Nettie and Grandma came in to listen.

"That piano has a beautiful sound," said Grandma.

"Yeah," said Jason, as he looked at Grandma and whispered, "for something I picked out over the phone."

"Jason, that's what you did? You bought it over the phone?"

"Yeah. I thought it would be nice for her to have a piano. Maybe she'll stay a little longer."

"I thought she was just going to stay overnight."

"I don't know. Maybe she'll want to stay longer."

Grandma gave him the eye. "Jason, what's going on here?"

"I felt bad for her. That guy came after her in the club, and she had a complete meltdown. It was awful to watch. She was so horribly frightened. I've spent the last two days with her. She didn't want me to leave her and go back to the hotel."

"Well, you are a big guy, Jason. She must have felt nice and safe with you around. Especially after you took down the perp in the club."

"I guess she did. I stayed with her at her sister's house, and I went to the court hearing."

"That's nice. I'm sure it made her feel better."

"I hope so. It's terrible to be that frightened. I learned a little bit about the kidnapping from Jack, her brother-in-law, who is a deputy in Nashville. He was at the club Saturday night, but he just wasn't close enough to Carly to stop the perp. The deputies were at the entrances because they had been warned the guy had escaped, but somehow, he got past them and got right over to Carly. But I was there, so it was okay."

"Yeah, I can't imagine you would ever let some jerk hurt a woman."

"There was no chance of that. I wanted to punch him right in the face, but I didn't. I just dropped him down to the floor and put my foot on top of him until the deputies got over there."

"Did he fight back?" asked Grandma.

"No. He didn't really have a chance to fight back. Besides, I think I broke his arm or broke his wrist. Nothing he didn't deserve."

"Sounds a little violent," said Grandma.

"Well, he was very violent. You wouldn't believe how he came at her. I thought he was just walking over to say something to her. I thought maybe he knew Carly or her sister Christy. But he grabbed her viciously and threw her right off the barstool. Then I pushed him away and asked him what he thought he was doing. He said, 'Mind your own business, asshole.' So, I dropped him right down to the floor."

"That wasn't a smart answer for him, was it?"

"No, but if he was a smart guy, he wouldn't have come back there to grab her."

They listened for a few minutes more and then Jason said, "Carly, would you please sing just one song for us? How about the song the band sang for you – 'Colder Weather' – I love that song."

"Okay, I guess I could sing that one." She started singing and Jason was amazed by her voice. He knew now why Donnie had told him to go to Nashville last Saturday.

"That was great, Carly. It's one of my favorite songs. I play it on my guitar sometimes."

"You do, Jason?" asked Grandma. "How come you have never played your guitar for us?"

"I'm not very good yet. I need to practice more."

"We would still like to hear you play, Jason," said Nettie.

"Okay, another night. Do you want to play some more, Carly?"

"No. But I'll come back and play in the morning. I love this piano. Can I take it home with me?"

Jason laughed. "I don't know. Would it fit in your house?"

Carly paused for a moment and said, "Sadly, no. It's probably bigger than my living room"

"Well, that might not work then."

"I was just kidding, Jason. I wouldn't take your piano."

They walked down to the other end of the house and Jason explained a bit of the layout to her.

"While I was in the Army my dad built this addition on the house. It's a nice little suite of rooms, so I thought you and I could stay down here. We have two bedrooms separated by the bathroom, so you can sleep here, and I'll sleep in the bedroom on the other side. If you get frightened or have a bad dream, just call me and I'll come in to see what's wrong. I'll be very close."

"Okay," Carly said hesitantly.

Jason looked at her questioningly for a few moments. "Do you feel comfortable with this? Is it okay?"

"Um, Kind of…" She didn't continue and he looked at her and tried to figure out what she was thinking.

"You can use this bathroom, Carly, and I can give you some privacy. I can use my bathroom down the hall."

She looked at him again and just said, "Okay."

"Is anything bothering you, Carly? Are you okay?"

"Yes, It's okay. It's fine. I just hope I don't wake up during the night and start screaming."

"It's okay if you do. It might happen, but it's not a crisis, no one will hear you. Grandma and Nettie won't hear you. It will just be me."

"Okay. I'll just change and get into bed."

"I'll leave you here for a few minutes so I can run down to my room and get some things I need."

When he came back, Carly was already in bed. He walked over and sat on the edge of the bed near her.

"Everything okay now?"

"Yeah. It's very comfortable."

He had an almost overwhelming urge to kiss her goodnight, but he didn't want to startle her. He wanted to touch her one more time before they said goodnight and wished she might reach out to touch his hand or his arm. She didn't, so he said goodnight and walked over to his room and got into bed. He wished she was next to him like she was last night. He worried that she might not be able to fall asleep by herself in a strange place. He wondered if she was still frightened. He wondered if maybe she was thinking about him. Maybe she wanted to curl up next to him again. Maybe that's what she wanted but was too shy to ask him. But then again, maybe she had no feelings toward him at all. Maybe she just didn't want to be afraid and that was all she needed from him. He tried to go to sleep but the thoughts kept coming.

Chapter 6

Jason dozed off for a few minutes and woke up to a strange sound he couldn't quite identify. He thought Carly might be crying. He waited a few minutes debating about whether to give her some space or go in and talk to her. He turned to get up and saw Carly standing on the other side of his bed.

"Carly, you startled me. Are you okay?"

"Sort of, I guess. Can I talk to you for a few minutes?"

"Of course, you can," he answered, and pulled back the covers on the other side of the bed for her. Her eyes were wet with tears, and he wanted to reach up and brush the tears away, but he was afraid any sudden movement might frighten her.

"Are you frightened, Carly?"

"I always feel frightened. I've been frightened ever since the kidnapping. I feel like I'm just waiting around until he comes back for me so he can take me away and kill me." Carly laid her head on the pillow and started to sob.

Jason reached over and touched her arm lightly. "No, Carly. I'm not going to let that happen. You're safe here. Remember I showed you all the security devices we have here? I'm not going to let anyone come here and hurt you. I'm so sorry you've had to live with so much pain."

"He's watching me and waiting for the right time. Then he's going to kill me like he said he would. He told me all the different ways he could kill me. He asked me how I wanted to die."

"What a bastard he is. He should be back in prison by now. Let's check with Jack tomorrow and make sure he's back where he belongs. Do you want to stay here in my room with me tonight? You don't have to sleep in the other room by yourself if you don't want to. I gave you your own room because I didn't want you to think I was expecting anything from you."

"I wasn't sure...." she hesitated, "I wasn't sure if you would want me to come in here and sleep with you, but I think I'd like that if you don't mind..." her voice trailed off and she looked at him questioningly.

"I don't think I will mind," he smiled. "I think I will like it. Who doesn't want to wake up in the morning and find a pretty girl lying next to him in bed?"

She sobbed a little and nodded her head. "I never thought I would say this, but I don't feel so afraid when you hold me. My whole life is falling apart. I just can't get myself back on track again. I don't know what to do."

He reached out for her and pulled her over toward him very gently. "Let's start with this, Carly. I'll put my arms around you, and you can tell me if it makes you feel better." Her body felt tense and rigid, and she was breathing through her mouth with small panting breaths.

"Shh! Shh!" he whispered, holding her gently. "Just breathe slowly, deep breaths in...out... real slow. Just try to relax. Can you feel my arms around you?"

She nodded and her breathing slowed down a little. It didn't sound like she was panting for breath anymore. She let her body lean toward him a bit more. He moved a little closer until their bodies were almost touching. She was wearing a pink silky shirt with long sleeves and some cute little pajama shorts. Her beautiful curly blonde hair was falling gently around her face. She looked up at him quickly with her gorgeous green eyes and then gently laid her head against his shoulder and sighed. He had a sudden fantasy where he was softly touching every inch of her beautiful body. He wanted her like he had never wanted anyone before in his entire life. He took a deep breath and sighed noisily to bring himself back to reality.

"Jason? Are you okay?" she asked.

"I'm good. How about you? Feeling better?" She nodded.

"What he did to you was horrible," Jason whispered. He pulled her gently a little closer to him and her body felt so warm pressed against his bare chest. He suddenly wanted to kiss her, but he was afraid it might make her pull away from him.

"When you have nightmares do you relive some of the things that happened with the kidnapper?"

"I see all of it again, Jason. I only want to forget it, but the dreams bring it all back to me." She started sobbing again. "He was very brutal to me. I never knew anyone could be so cruel. I'm ashamed of some of the things that I did. Some of the things he made me say. I told him I loved him. I said I wanted to stay with him, and I wouldn't run away."

"You did what you had to do to survive, Carly. You were playing his game. Then you beat him at his own game. That's nothing to be ashamed of. You're still here because you were so strong. I'm glad you're still here. I'm glad you're here with me." He stroked the side of her face gently and kissed her cheek.

"At his trial, the kidnapper told everyone I asked him to rape me. He said that I liked it. He said that every time he raped me, I asked for more. He said I asked him to blindfold me so I could pretend there was another lover who wanted me. At the end he said he was going to pretend to kill me and then bring me back to life and we were going to go away together and get married. He said he slapped me and hit me because we were pretending he was a villain who was attacking me. He said the bite marks were from a mean dog that he killed in order to save me."

"Wow! This bastard was quite the storyteller. But the jury didn't believe him, did they?"

"I think some of them did. I had to testify at the trial. The defense attorney made me admit that I said I loved him." Carly started sobbing uncontrollably.

"Nobody believed that Carly. They knew you only said it to stay alive."

"When I told the jury he made me say things and held a gun to my head and threatened to kill me, the kidnapper jumped out of his chair and tried to run up to me. He was screaming at me and calling me a liar. He kept screaming, Liar! Liar! Liar! Until they got him back in his chair and chained him down. I couldn't stop crying after that and the judge had to call a recess. The paramedics came in and gave me a sedative. Christy took me back to her house and said I needed to stay with her until the trial was over."

Carly had her head on his chest, and he could feel her warm tears running down his side.

"I'm sorry. I'm so sorry. I didn't mean to cry like this. I promised myself I would be strong and I wouldn't cry tonight."

"It's okay, Carly. It's okay to cry. Maybe it's good to let it all out. You can tell me anything you want. It's okay." He gently stroked her back and he could feel the sobs wracking her body. She was rocking her body back and forth against his arms.

"I'm getting you all wet."

"It's okay. I'm waterproof." He heard a small hiccup in her sobs and thought that he might have made her smile. He held her close to his body and gently rocked her back and forth as she cried.

"You should probably take me back home. You could just take me back to my house and leave me there."

"Why? So, you could go home and cry all alone? I'm guessing you have already spent a lot of nights crying all alone. Am I right?"

She nodded her head weakly.

"So why would that be better? Isn't it nice to have someone here with you? To have someone hold you. You shouldn't have to cry all alone, Carly. You shouldn't have to be all alone. Have you been able to talk to your sister about what happened to you?"

"Not much. Some things I don't want to tell her." She started sobbing and shaking more violently. "I've been so alone. I can't go anywhere because I'm afraid. I'm afraid to go out. I'm afraid to stay in my house. I'm so afraid. It might have been better if I had just died. I don't feel like I have a life anymore."

"No. You were strong enough to save yourself. You're going to be strong enough to get through this. I think I might know some ways to help you. Would you let me help you?"

"Why would you want to help me?"

"Because I think I might be able to. Isn't that a good reason?"

"But you don't even know me, Jason. My life is such a mess you won't believe it."

"My life was a mess once, so maybe I might be just the right person to understand what you're going through. I wasn't injured and physically abused like you were, but I had some real problems I had to work through."

"What happens to people like me, Jason? What happens to people who owe so much money to hospitals and doctors that they will never be able to pay all the bills? Will I get sued over and over again until there is nothing left, not even my house or my old piano?"

"No, Carly. You have to ask for help. Jack told me about a GoFundMe account they set up for you. That's one way to get help. Then there are agencies and foundations that help victims of violent crimes. I can help you find some of these if you will let me help you."

"It's hard. It's hard to ask people for money. I've never been that kind of person. I didn't have a real family, so I always had to make my own way. I don't like to ask people for help. Even when I was little, I never asked for anything."

"Well, you must have been a very unusual kid. You don't have any family except for your sister, Christy? No parents or grandparents?"

Carly was quiet for a while and Jason thought that her tears were beginning to subside. He kept rubbing her back gently, and it seemed like some of the tension in her body was softening. Finally, she answered, "Christy isn't my real sister. She's not a biological sister, but we grew up together. I lived with her family until I went to college. They were our neighbors. After my mother died, I lived with them. We called ourselves sisters. Nobody knew we weren't real sisters."

"What about your father? You didn't stay with your dad after your mother died?"

"No. After he killed my mother, he shot himself. So, Christy and her family took me in, and I stayed with them. When I was little they didn't tell me that my mother was dead, so I thought she just went off and left me behind. I waited for her to come back for me."

Jason felt himself at a loss for words after her disclosure. Finally, he asked, "How old were you when this happened?"

"I was in first grade, so I was probably six." Jason felt the blood rushing from his head and thought he felt his heart turn.

"You were six years old when your mother disappeared?"

"Yeah, I was pretty little. Christy found me the next day. I was hiding in the chicken coop. She knew that was one of my hiding places. Sometimes I had to go there and hide when my father got angry. I heard people calling me, but I was afraid to come out until my momma told me it was okay. When I was in the chicken coop I heard a loud pop – like maybe from a gun, and then I heard another one a little later. I guess that was when my father shot himself. After they found me, Christy took me back to her house and I started living with Christy and her parents. We went to school together and we started calling ourselves sisters. We were just like sisters. We still call ourselves sisters. Her mom and dad were good to me. I used to call them mom and pop. I wondered if it was okay for me to stay with them, but nobody ever said I couldn't, so I just kept going to school and stayed with Christy. We shared everything – our clothes, our shoes, - everything but boyfriends. Christy had all the boyfriends. We didn't share those. When I lived there, I tried to be good. Christy liked to go out to parties, and she wanted to try drinking and smoking. I didn't ever do that. I didn't want to get into any trouble, and I hoped they wouldn't notice me, and they wouldn't send me away. I tried to help in the house and her mom would say I was her 'good girl'. There was an old farmhouse piano there and I liked to play it, so I would play very softly so it wouldn't bother anyone. Sometimes when I wanted to cry, I could go play the piano and make up little tunes so I wouldn't cry. I wanted to be a big girl; I didn't want them to see me cry. I didn't want them to send me away. I liked it there. They were good to me. Her dad called her "Red", and he called me "Blondie". We went to high school together and we were so close, we told each other everything. We told everybody we were sisters. I don't think anybody knew what happened to my parents. When we finished high school, her dad gave us some money he had from selling off part of his land, and we both went to Junior College in Nashville for a few years. Then I got into singing, and that was my life after that. I wanted to sing and perform, and I learned to read music at college, and I got to take some piano lessons. That's when I met Sean, and he taught me a lot about music. He was the best friend I ever had. No one ever talked about where my mother was – they didn't adopt me or talk about adopting me. Later when I started performing in some little clubs, I found a song by the band Reckless Kelly called "Nobody's Girl" so I started singing it. My mother used to call me her pretty girl. After she was gone I was Nobody's Pretty Girl ever again. That was me – Nobody's Girl. One night when I sang it Christy came up to me afterwards and she was angry. She said, "Why do you sing that song? I hate it when you sing that song. It's like you're singing about yourself. You're saying you're Nobody's Girl and you're my girl. You're not Nobody's Girl. You're my girl – I love you."

"So, I stopped singing it. I still sing it at home sometimes, but I don't sing it at the club anymore. It seemed to really upset her."

Jason looked over at her and he could see the tears rolling down her cheeks, and he took his hand and gently brushed the tears away. "You're not Nobody's Girl. Everybody loves you. You can't be Nobody's Girl."

"That's what I was. I wasn't anybody's girl. I didn't belong anywhere; I didn't belong to anyone. I didn't know what an orphan was then, but I was the orphan that nobody wanted." Carly rolled away from Jason and grabbed her pillow and started sobbing again.

"Oh, God, Carly. You were such a little girl when this happened."

"I shouldn't have told you that. Christy and I made a pact when we were just little girls and swore we would never tell anyone we weren't real sisters. Her parents made us promise we would never talk about my parents. I never told anyone that before. Please don't tell Christy I told you that."

"Your secret is safe with me. I won't tell her. You can talk to me about it if you want to. I'm not going to tell anyone."

"I always tried not to think about what happened. I was afraid my father might hurt me after I saw him shoot my mother, so I ran and hid in the chicken coop."

"Oh, God, Carly. I lost my parents when I was on my way home from active duty. I was leaving the Army. They were both killed in a terrible highway accident while I was flying home. But I was an adult, not a little child like you were, and I fell apart. I hear you talk about this, and you say, 'things just went on, I went to live with the neighbors, and that was it' and I'm thinking, oh my God, you must have been the strongest little girl on the planet. How could a little girl lose her mother like that? You saw your dad shoot your mother? How could you do it? Remember the night I met you and your band sang that song for you? At first, I didn't realize they were singing to you, and they said the song was for the strongest, bravest, person they ever knew. I asked you if they were singing to you, and you said "Yes". They didn't even know about this part of your life. I feel kind of ashamed. I was a grown man and I let my life fall apart and here you were, this little girl, and you say you just went on – you went to school, you tried to be good, you tried not to let people notice you. You hoped they wouldn't think about sending you away. So, all this time, as a little girl, you thought about getting sent away. I'm so sorry! My parents – I always knew they really loved me – and then I think about you. I don't even know what to say, Carly. I don't know what to say to you. I want to just wrap you up in my arms, and I want to take care of you. And I know you don't want – don't want me to touch you. And I don't blame you. You've been through hell. But that's what I want to do right now. I just want to hold you. I want to take care of you. I don't want you to ever feel this kind of heartache again. Can you let me hold you again? Just for a little while?"

Carly moved over closer to him and laid her head on his chest. He could feel her body relaxing into him. As he gently caressed her back, some of her tense muscles seemed to soften. Slowly she pulled her hand up and wrapped it around the top of his shoulder. He could feel her fingers rubbing very softly against his skin.

"It's been a long time since I've been able to be this close to anyone," she said. "I didn't think I would ever want to let anyone hold me like this. But Saturday night when you were holding me on your lap at Christy's house, I felt so peaceful with your arms around me. I felt like I was finally safe. That no one was going to hurt me. I felt like you were there for me - just for me."

"I was there just for you. I kept hoping Jack wouldn't ask me to leave. I wanted to hold you in my arms all night. I felt how relaxed your body got when you drifted off to sleep, and when you woke up once I just rocked you back and forth a little until you dozed off again."

Carly had little soft fuzzy socks on her feet, and she was rubbing her foot against one of his feet and then gently rubbing her foot up and down his calf.

"I like the way your feet feel with those soft fuzzy socks," he whispered.

"Sorry. I didn't realize I was doing that." She pulled her foot away.

"I liked it," he whispered. "It's kind of like having a soft little kitten rubbing against your leg."

"I have to keep my feet warm, or I start to feel panicky. I worked so hard to save them that I try to always keep them warm."

"Tell me about what happened to your feet."

"They were frozen during my escape from the kidnapper. I lost a part of each foot, but at least I have enough left to walk on. It took me a while to figure out how to balance myself after the amputations. I still have exercises I do to practice keeping my balance. It was a long time before I could walk on them. I guess I'll never be a long-distance hiker or climb Mt. Everest, but I'm grateful every day that I still have my feet."

"I'm glad you have them. Life would be hard without feet. I guess that's something we don't think about until something like this happens. Carly, I want you to know you are safe with me. I wouldn't ever hurt you. I'm just not that kind of a guy. I don't want to do anything that makes you uncomfortable. If you ever feel uncomfortable or want me to move away from you, you just need to tell me."

"Okay," she nodded.

Jason looked up at the patio doors and he could see the beginning of daybreak edging up to the house. He stroked the side of her cheek gently with the back of his hand. "Let's see if you can go to sleep for a little while. It's almost morning."

"I'm sorry. I think I cried all night. You should have taken me home."

"No one is going to take you home, Carly. I think you should stay up here for a while."

"I think I would like to stay longer if you wouldn't mind."

He gave her a slow smile. "I would like that. Would you like to go for a ride with me tomorrow on my horse, Charlie? We can ride double on him. He's a big horse and he won't mind."

"Could I fall off?"

"No. I'm not going to let you fall off the horse! There's a nice trail we can take up to the North end of the ranch, and maybe we can get Grandma to pack some lunch for us. I want to talk to you about some ideas I have. I think there are a number of ways I can help you, if you will let me. I told you I'm a lawyer, didn't I?"

"Yes. You called yourself a boring lawyer."

"Well, this boring lawyer might be able to help you with some of your medical bills that are worrying you. Have you talked to a therapist about the nightmares you have?"

"I did some therapy at the rehab center, but my insurance coverage ran out and I couldn't afford to pay for any more sessions. Mostly the therapist just gave me some pills and told me to get lots of rest. I couldn't walk, so I wondered how much more rest I could need."

Jason smiled at her answer. "That seems like a good question. If I can find a good therapist for you, would you consider doing some sessions with him? I know someone who would be a wonderful person for you to talk to."

"I can't do that, Jason. I don't have any money left. The medical and doctor bills have taken everything I used to have. I thought I had enough money saved for any emergency, but I guess no one ever anticipates having something like this happen to them. I lost all my income for over a year. I'm still not working as much as I used to. I just can't afford to do anything. I need to try to save my house, but I don't even think I can do that. I've always been able to take care of myself, and now I can't."

Jason saw tears beginning to fill her eyes again. "It's okay, Carly, don't cry. I just want to help you. I think a good therapist can help you deal with all the horrible memories this kidnapper has left with you. I have a Foundation I started to help Veterans who have been traumatized by war or suffered the loss of limbs. I've learned a lot about therapy, and I know some excellent therapists. I can use money from the Foundation to help you, just like I use it to help Veterans."

"But I'm not a Veteran, Jason."

"Maybe not, but you certainly are the survivor of a terrible trauma, so I think that qualifies you for help. Let's talk about this tomorrow. Right now, let's see if you can sleep for a little while. I need to get up in a few hours to go check on a few of the mares who are getting ready to foal. I try to get them out for a bit of exercise every day. We keep tabs on them so we have a general idea when they will give birth. If you wake up and I'm not here, I will be down in the barn. But Grandma and Nettie will be here with you, so don't worry. All the doors will be locked."

Jason watched as Carly slowly drifted off to sleep. He felt so much sadness when he looked at her that his own eyes filled with tears. *Nobody's Girl, he thought. That's how she thinks of herself. How sad it must be to feel like you don't have anyone to care about you. No parents, no grandparents, no family; only a sister who wasn't really a sister, after all. She went to live with the neighbors. How did that happen? She said they were good to her, but he had the sense there was something missing in the equation. Maybe something that she was never told.*

He couldn't remember much of the song, but he thought it sang about '*breaking in a broken home*' and in the chorus it said, *'you're nobody's darling, you're nobody's girl'*.

He thought about his own parents and how much he missed them. *'I had them for nearly 30 years, he thought, what would my life have been like if I lost them when I was only six?'* He couldn't even imagine that, but he knew he would have had two sets of loving grandparents, plus Roy and Lucy, and everyone else on the ranch who would have cared for him. How does a little girl end up with no one? No one.

He drifted off to sleep and woke up a few hours later. Carly was curled up next to him and he hated to move away and wake her up. He pulled away slowly and put his pillow up against her back. He left her a note on the nightstand.

"Good morning! I went out to tend to the mares. Grandma is going to save some breakfast for you and some coffee. I'll come back for you in a little while and we can go for a ride on Charlie. We're going to have a great day!"

Jason went down to the kitchen to see if there was any breakfast ready. Grandma gave him a little smile as he walked in. "Did you have a good night, Jason?"

"It was okay. Carly is still sleeping. I left her a note. We were awake for a long time last night, so she may sleep for a while. Can you save some breakfast for her?"

"Of course. Are you okay, Jason?"

"Yeah, just feeling a little sad for her. She has had quite a struggle. I think I can help her with some problems, and she needs some good therapy, but I'm not sure if she will let me help her."

"Give her a little time, Jason. You've only known her a few days, haven't you? She probably doesn't feel like she knows you well enough to accept help from you."

"I guess." Grandma put a plate of food in front of him. "Thanks, Grandma. Do you think you or Nettie could pack a lunch for us? I'm going to take Carly on a ride to the North section and show her the ranch when I finish with the mares."

"We can do that," said Grandma. She looked over at Jason. "She's a beautiful, talented girl, Jason." She saw a slow smile creep across his face. '*Aha*' she thought. '*He has a little twinkle in his beautiful eyes.*'

Chapter 7

Grandma Gwen was checking some of the messages on her phone when she thought she heard Carly walking down the hall.

"Good morning," said Carly.

"Hey, Carly, Jason asked me to save some breakfast for you and some nice hot coffee. I have some eggs I set aside for you. Do you like scrambled eggs, is that okay?"

"Oh, sure, that's great. That was nice of you. I hope I'm not disturbing you."

"Not at all," Grandma replied. "I was just checking some messages on my phone, but there's nothing important today."

Grandma went over and poured Carly some coffee and handed it to her.

"Thanks. I didn't realize I was going to go back to sleep and sleep this long. Usually, at home, I can't sleep at all! For some reason I fell asleep again this morning. I heard Jason get up and get in the shower, and then I guess I went right back to sleep."

"That's okay," said Grandma. "It's nice and quiet here. Sometimes that makes it easier to sleep."

Grandma brought Carly some eggs and sausage and asked her, "Would you like some toast or bagels with that Carly?"

"No, thank you. This will be just fine. When I woke up again, Jason was gone, so I guess he had some work to do this morning."

"Yes. He's checking on one of the mares. We have a mare who is about to foal, so he checks on her every morning to make sure she's all right, and then he tries to get her out for a little exercise. She's due to have her foal very soon. If you wake up in the middle of the night and Jason is gone, that's where he's going to be - down in the barn."

"Do you all go down to the barn when the mare is giving birth?"

"I don't always go, but Jason and Roy are always there, and sometimes Robbie. It just depends on how it's going. Sometimes the births are easy, and sometimes you need to be there just in case things aren't going smoothly. Jason said he was going to take you for a ride this morning."

"That's what he mentioned, but if he's busy he doesn't have to do that. I can play the piano."

"I think he was counting on it. I fixed a lunch for you, and I'll tell you one thing about Jason. He gets cranky when he's hungry. Hopefully you won't see his cranky side."

"Well, I certainly haven't seen that yet. He saw my worst side after the kidnapper tried to grab me. I think I had one of the worst meltdowns I have ever had. A meltdown that would have sent most men running for their lives. But somehow it didn't seem to faze Jason. He sat right with me and kept talking to me until I was able to start to pull myself back together. Then he talked me into getting up to dance with him for a few minutes. The band dedicated a song to me and then I got weepy again. Afterwards he went back to Christy's house with us, and when I went to sleep, I had one of those terrible screaming nightmares. Christy said she was trying to calm me down, but Jason came in and just picked me up off the bed and took me out into the family room. He sat in a big chair and pulled me into his lap, and he sat there and held me all night. I woke up a few times, but every time I woke up, he just started talking to me again. When I woke up in the morning we were still sitting there, and I don't know if he even got any sleep. So, I guess he has seen the worst side of me, sadly."

"I'm sure Jason was glad to do that for you. He knows a bit about night terrors and bad dreams. He had issues with those when he came back from the Service, but don't let him know I told you that. It's something he has put behind him now. Thankfully."

"I hope I can put them behind me soon. I have so many other problems to deal with. I never realized an ordeal like this could send every part of your life into a downward spiral."

"I'm sure most people wouldn't realize that. Do you have any family that can help you?"

"No. My parents both died when I was very young."

"Oh, I'm so sorry. What did you do after that happened? Did you live with some relatives?"

"No. I didn't have any family. I went to live with the neighbors."

Oh, thought Grandma, the neighbors, huh. Wow.

"That must have been very hard. How old were you when they died?"

"I was only six."

"Oh my God. She lost her parents when she was only six years old and went to live with some neighbors."

"I'm so sorry. That must have been very hard for you when you were so young."

"It was hard. I really missed my momma, and I was so young that I didn't understand what happened, and I kept thinking she would come back for me. But of course, she never did."

Grandma looked at her and tried to make sense of what she had just said. She said her parents were dead and yet she was waiting for her mother to come back for her. She didn't want to ask Carly that question.

"It sounds like you could use some help. Maybe Jason could help you. You know he's a lawyer, right?"

"Yes. He told me that when we met at the club. He said he was a boring lawyer."

Grandma laughed. "He told you he was boring, huh? I don't think anyone would ever call Jason boring!"

"It doesn't seem that way. He didn't say he lived on a huge ranch with all these beautiful horses. Who does the ranch belong to?"

Grandmas looked up at her slowly and said, "Well, the ranch belongs to Jason."

"Oh!" exclaimed Carly. "The whole ranch?"

"I own a part of it, but mostly the ranch is Jason's, and, of course, when I'm gone it will be all Jason's. There's just the two of us left. Just Jason and I."

"He mentioned his parents had died in a car accident."

"Yes. Sadly, they did. We all still miss them."

"I know what you mean," said Carly.

"If you let Jason know what kind of problems you are facing, he can probably help you."

"He said he was going to talk to me about that on our ride today. I think Jack already told him my house was going into foreclosure. I'd like to save it, but I'm so far behind that I don't think there is any way I could ever catch up. The hospital bills and the doctor's bills took all the money I had saved. Everything I had is gone, and all I have left is my house. Probably not for long."

"You need to let Jason look at that. He's pretty good at problems like those. He has a whole group of Army veterans he helps. It's an organization he started so he could help them with problems in civilian life. If they need medical attention or counseling, he helps to arrange that. Some veterans have a hard time readjusting to civilian life, especially if they have lost a limb or sustained serious injuries. It's hard for them to become productive, and if they have a family to support, it can be even harder. He has a lot of experience working with banks and insurance companies, doctors, and counselors. If I were you, I would let him look at any paperwork you have. He is very persistent and doesn't usually take 'NO' for an answer. Just between you and me, I think he likes doing this because he can push them around a bit and try to make them look at his point of view. Then he generally comes out on the winning edge."

"Really?" asked Carly. She laughed a little. "He doesn't seem pushy like that."

"That may be a different side of him than what you have seen, but I think he can be very persistent when he wants to get something from insurance companies or banks. I wouldn't hesitate to let him try to help you. It couldn't hurt."

"I just hate to take up his time with my problems. I have so many now. My life used to be so much more peaceful. I never had all this stress about money."

"All the more reason to let him help you. Maybe he can get rid of at least one of your problems."

"Yeah," Carly said softly. "Maybe I'll...Maybe it would be a good idea..."

"I'm so sorry the kidnapping left you with all these problems. It must be hard to put your life back together again when you have so many things hanging over your head."

"Yeah, it really is. I guess I shouldn't talk about this. It's too depressing."

"I can understand how that would be depressing all right!"

Grandma watched as Carly swiped at a tear that had started to roll down her cheek.

After Jason and Carly had gone off to bed last night, she had researched Carly's kidnapping on the internet. There were hundreds of news stories depicting the events, and some of them went so far as to discuss the rapes and the brutality of the crime. It seemed like there was a no holds barred policy about her ordeal. She wondered why these reporters felt it was necessary to spread Carly's pain across the pages of their newspapers.

"I fixed some lunch for you and Jason, so when you are finished with breakfast, I'm going to take you out to the barn on our golf cart. Jason is down at the family barn getting Charlie ready."

"I could probably walk down there if you just show me where the barn is."

"No, I have to take some paperwork to Roy and that's where he is."

"I hope I'm not taking Jason away from anything else he needs to do."

"We're not busy now. He just needed to check on the mare to make sure she wasn't getting ready to foal today. Unfortunately, most of the foals seem to be born in the middle of the night."

"Oh!" said Carly, "then how do you know when it is happening?"

"There are some signs before it happens so we can usually figure out when the foal is coming. It's usually about 1or 2 am in the morning."

"I should have brought my camera with me. These foals could make some dynamite pictures. I didn't realize what it would be like up here. I think I was picturing something a lot smaller."

"It is big. The ranch has been in the family for a long time, and each generation added more land. I think we're maxed out now. I don't think there is any more land available."

"I grew up on a little farm with the neighbors, but we didn't have any horses. Just a few pigs and chickens. I've never ridden a horse before."

"Well, if you want to learn how to ride, Jason would be an excellent teacher. He has been riding almost all his life. He said he's going to take you for a ride on Charlie today. You're going up to the far Northwest corner of the ranch. There's a gorgeous view up there, and it's a great place to have a picnic. It's the highest point on the ranch."

"That sounds nice. I'm a little bit nervous about riding a horse. I hope I don't fall off."

"I'm sure Jason won't let you fall off the horse. I'm sure he is going to hang onto you. I wouldn't worry about that, Carly. Jason is very strong. He has lots of upper body strength from dealing with all these big horses."

"I noticed that last night. Not very many men have arms the size of Jason's."

"I think that's what happens when men go into the Army. He was in the Rangers Airborne Division, and I think it's a very strenuous program. He didn't look like that when he left home. He was a little scrawny, but he looked different when he returned. "

"I guess that would do it."

"I think the Rangers program is a tough way to go when you are in the military, but Jason did well. He earned a lot of medals, saved a lot of lives."

"Really?" asked Carly. "That's impressive."

"Yes. But he won't tell you that."

"Why not?"

"He doesn't like to talk about it. In fact, he doesn't like me to talk about it, but I tell people. We are very proud of him. He tried to get rid of all the medals he was awarded, but I wouldn't let him throw them away. I have them in my room. I can show them to you when he isn't around. I thought if he ever had a son, it would be nice for his son to see the medals."

"That would be nice. I would like to see them." Carly paused for a moment. "I asked Jason last night if I could stay here a little longer. He said I could. I hope that's okay with you. I don't want to be a bother or outstay my welcome."

"You are more than welcome to stay as long as you like. This is a big place. We have plenty of room and lots of security. You should feel safe up here, and we could get to hear you play our lovely piano some more."

Carly hesitated for a moment, "I..I..I think I will feel safer here. At the hearing on Monday the kidnapper broke loose and tried to come at me again. He told me he was going to kill me. He said I was as good as dead. I can't seem to get his words out of my head now."

"Oh, my Lord! That has to be a horrible feeling. He did break out of jail last week, right?"

"Yes. And that was the second time."

Grandma's head spun around, and she looked at Carly. "The second time? The second time he escaped from prison?"

"Yeah. They use him on work crews for the highways and then he escapes."

"Why would they put someone like that on a work crew? That's insane! Maybe we should all write to the Governor in Tennessee. You really do need to stay up here with us. There's something wrong with those people in Tennessee."

"That's what Jason said. I don't know what would have happened if Jason hadn't been sitting next to me last Saturday."

"Did you know Jason? Did you guys know each other before that happened at the club?"

"No. He just happened to come in and sit down next to me."

"Well, that turned out to be a good thing. Jason didn't let him hurt you, did he?"

"No. Jason stepped in between us and pushed him away. When the guy tried to grab at me again, Jason grabbed his arm and twisted it around behind his back and the next thing we knew the guy went flying down to the floor."

"See, that Army Ranger training can really come in handy!"

"I guess that was it, huh?"

"That jerk picked the wrong time to go after you while Jason was sitting there."

"Yeah. I'm trying not to think about what could have happened."

"No. Let's not think about that. Are you ready to go for a ride with Jason?"

"Yes. I'm a little apprehensive but ready to go."

"I'm sure you will have a good time. Here's the lunch. I'm going to give it to you so that we won't forget to give it to Jason. Let me grab the paperwork I need to take to Roy, and we'll go out to the cart and take all this down to the barn."

As they rode down to the barn, Grandma showed Carly some of the buildings along the way. When they got down to the barn, she saw Jason had Charlie tied up to the fence, saddled up, and ready to go. She noticed Jason had a blanket rolled up and tied behind the saddle. *Okay, Jason, she thought. Well maybe that's for the picnic –or maybe something else?*

Jason walked over to the golf cart and Carly handed him the lunch.

"Your grandma fixed you some lunch, Jason."

"That's great. Thanks, Grandma!"

"I told Carly you get a little grumpy when you're hungry."

"Grandma, you didn't have to tell her that."

"I just thought I should warn her,"

Jason smiled at her. "Grandma, I'm not grumpy."

"Jason, when you're hungry, you're grumpy. You have been ever since you were a little kid."

"Okay, maybe. Maybe."

He put his hand out for Carly and helped her out of the cart. They walked over toward Charlie still holding hands.

Gosh, this is so cute, she thought.

Grandma took out her phone and started snapping pictures. Jason put the lunch into the saddle bags and went up to Charlie's head, holding Carly's hand again. He was tapping Charlie on the nose and talking to him.

Grandma laughed. He's probably telling Charlie to behave and be a good boy. No funny stuff today.

Jason showed Carly how she could get up into the saddle. She seemed a bit reluctant, but he got her foot in the stirrup, and he put his hands at her waist and just boosted her up a little and boom! She was on the horse, right in the saddle. Jason took her foot out of the stirrup and lowered it down for himself, put his foot into it and swung up behind her.

"This is cute, thought Grandma, and she started taking pictures again.

Jason heard the clicking sound from her phone. "Grandma, are you taking pictures?"

"I might be…"

Jason laughed. "Okay, Carly, look at Grandma, so she can take your picture."

Carly looked over at Grandma and Jason kissed her on the cheek and held his lips there for a few seconds. Grandma started snapping pictures again.

"Okay, Grandma, do you have your picture now?"

"Yes, Jason. I like that one."

"I thought you might," he laughed. "We're going off on a ride now. No more pictures."

Gwen heard him click his tongue to Charlie and they started walking away. *Well, thought Gwen, they are cute together. She sighed. Seems like a nice girl. Maybe she might be right for our Jason. I hope so, she thought. It would be nice to see Jason happy again, and he did look happy today! I guess we'll see what happens. She thought it was cute that Carly asked her if she would mind if she stayed at the ranch a little longer or if she thought Jason would mind. Gwen laughed to herself. Oh no, I don't think Jason is going to mind a bit. Especially if you're keeping him company in that bed down there. Good for Jason, she thought. Why wouldn't he enjoy having a pretty woman like this in his bed. Seems about time! He's been sulking around here for over a year. Maybe this will change things for him. She smiled to herself. I guess we will see.*

Gwen walked into the barn and took some papers to Roy.

"Hey, Gwen, I saw Jason in the barn this morning. He certainly looked much happier than usual. Anything new?"

"Oh, yes! Wait until you see the pretty young woman he brought home with him last night."

"No! Really? A woman?"

"Yes. A very pretty young woman."

"He didn't tell me that, but he sure was cheerful this morning. He was goofing around, playing with the dogs and horses. I didn't see even a hint of his usual unhappy face."

"Well, she is very nice and very pretty. She's a singer at the Rosebud Club down in Nashville."

"How the hell did Jason meet her?"

"He was down at that club on Saturday night. He went down there to hear her sing. Evidently his friend Donnie told him about her, so he went down to hear her, but instead she was assaulted by a man who had kidnapped her a year or so ago. The man had escaped from a prison road crew and went back to the club to assault her again."

"Oh my God. She was kidnapped?"

"Yeah. I think it was about 2 years ago. You probably heard it on the news. Everybody in Nashville was out looking for her. They organized huge search parties and were combing the woods for her."

"Oh, that's who it is?"

"Yeah. Her name is Carly… Carly..uh.."

"Carly Styles," interrupted Roy. "Yes. I remember. It was on all the newscasts. They had tons of people looking for her in Nashville."

"That's what I remember too."

"Didn't they find her about 3 or 4 days later? If I remember correctly, she had been savagely raped and brutally beaten and was nearly dead when they found her."

"Yes. I looked up the story on the internet last night after they went to bed. There were more horrible details in the newspapers than anyone could possibly think were appropriate to print. I hope she never saw some of the things those reporters wrote about her kidnapping."

"That's who he brought up here?"

"Yes. He met her at the club on Saturday when the kidnapper came after her. Jason happened to be sitting next to her and she said Jason stopped him and threw him down on the floor."

"Well, that does sound like Jason. Oh, crap! I saw that on the news. That was Jason? Shit! I didn't even recognize him. It wasn't a very good video. It was all blurry, like something taped from a bad cell phone."

"Yes. That was Jason."

"So that's how he met her?"

"Evidently. He said he spent the last three days with her. After he took the kidnapper down, she didn't want him to leave her."

Roy laughed. "Can't say I blame her. Jason is a big powerful guy. She probably felt safe with him. If you didn't feel safe with Jason, who could make you feel safe? Right? Smart move on her part."

"They stayed down in Nashville at her sister's house for two nights and then Jason asked her to come up here."

"So, they showed up here last night? Did you know they were coming?"

"Yes. Jason called me and we fixed dinner for them."

"Do you think there is something going on between them, or was he just trying to get her away from Nashville?"

"I think maybe both."

"You think Jason is interested in her? He hasn't shown much interest in dating or going out anywhere at night in the last few years. I thought maybe the debacle with little Lisa had caused him to give up on women. She turned out to be a real cruel bitch."

"I've worried about that, too, but I see signs that he might have some feelings for this girl."

"Okay, Gwen, what leads you to that conclusion? You are always the romantic one."

"When I brought Carly up to the barn, Jason came over and gave her his hand to help her out, but as they walked over to Charlie, I noticed that he kept holding her hand."

"Okay, well ... that's a maybe."

"When they rode off, he definitely had his arms firmly placed around Carly to hold her in the saddle with him."

"That's a good thing. We don't want anyone falling off horses here."

"When I was snapping some photos, he kissed her on the cheek and held his lips there while I was taking the picture."

"Hmm..interesting. Maybe you're right, Gwen. Maybe Jason has found somebody. I hope so. He needs a little more joy in his life. The divorce with Lisa and the death of his folks seems to have taken quite a toll on him."

"No, he hasn't really gotten over either one of those things, but I haven't heard him mention Lisa for a long time, so maybe she is only a distant memory by now."

"I hope her memory is very distant. She turned out to be a real piece of work. Did he get out of that marriage without having to make any concessions to her? I never really heard about the details."

"Oh, yes. Lexie took care of that. She made Lisa sign away any rights she might have claimed to Jason's share of the ranch. Once she found out what Lisa had done, she refused to be the one to tell Jason until Lisa signed a waiver. Lisa was anxious to get the divorce so she could marry the father of her baby."

"Well, that was nasty business; making Lexie go to Germany to tell Jason what Lisa had done after he was so badly injured. Lisa should have gone herself and not made Lexie do her dirty work."

"I think it would have hit him hard either way. I'm sure he thought Lisa loved him. I think he loved her, but they just couldn't sustain a long-distance relationship. Certainly, she wasn't mature enough to do that."

"Well, I hope this can turn out to be a good thing for him. This Carly has evidently been through a horrible ordeal, so she may be somewhat fragile."

"One thing you do need to know about her, Roy, is that she doesn't like to shake hands or be hugged. I noticed last night that Jason was very careful around her. But this morning he didn't seem as careful."

"I can understand that. If she was raped and brutalized by that kidnapper the way they described it on the news, she probably doesn't want anyone to get too close to her."

"She seemed okay today with Jason. She let him take her hand and he helped her up on the horse. Hopefully everything is going okay now."

"That's too bad something like that could happen to a nice young woman. Where do we get these crazies? I hope they lock that guy up and keep him locked up this time. It doesn't seem fair that he should get another chance to terrorize her."

"Evidently he has escaped twice already."

"Twice?? They couldn't figure out after the first escape this psycho wanted to get away?"

"She said he came after her at the club both times."

"So, he's a real stupid psycho, huh? Comes back to get her and gets captured again. You would think he would run like hell once he was free."

"At the hearing on Monday, he broke free and tried to attack her. She said he told her that he was going to kill her. That she was as good as dead!"

"Ugh!" said Roy. "That must be frightening. Just imagine someone saying that to you."

"I think she is extremely frightened. Probably why she said she would like to stay up here a while longer."

"Either that or it's Jason."

"Let's hope it might be Jason."

"I need to find a way to meet her when they come back. I'll try to accidentally run into them."

"You could come over for dinner tonight. Nettie is cooking and doing Italian."

"Ohhh…. I'll be there."

"Okay, Roy. You'll come over for Nettie's cooking, huh?"

"And to see you."

Gwen smiled at him. "Okay. Nice save there, Roy. We'll see you tonight then. You can come meet Carly, but don't shake hands or try to hug her."

"Got it. No shaking, no hugging. I'll remember."

"If you see Robbie, you could ask him to come over as well, but be sure to give him the no touch rules. Oh, wait, Roy. I forgot to tell you that if you notice a very large new grand piano in our Great Room, you should pretend it has always been there."

"A Grand piano? Where did that come from?"

"Jason is pretending it has always been there, but it was delivered yesterday morning. It's quite large! Hard to miss it!"

"And why do you suddenly have a Grand Piano?"

"Carly plays the piano…. Got the picture?"

"Oh, Lord. He bought a piano for her? He must be hoping she's going to stay here. Is he in love with this girl? Who buys a piano for a new girlfriend?"

"I guess Jason does." Gwen got back in the golf cart and started back toward the house. She stopped for a minute and looked at the pictures she took of Jason and Carly. She found the one where Jason put a kiss on the side of Carly's face. It was really cute!! *I don't know why I didn't show Roy this picture, she thought.*

Gwen turned around and started back toward the barn. Roy saw her pull up outside and walked toward the golf cart.

"Okay, what did you forget?"

"Nothing but come over here. I want to show you a picture."

Roy walked over to the side of the cart, and she showed him the pictures on her phone.

"Here's Carly. I don't know why I didn't show you this picture."

"Oh, she is a pretty girl. Way to go, Jason!"

"Now look at this picture where he is kissing her on the cheek."

"Well, there is something there! Look at his face. I haven't seen Jason smile like that since he was a kid. Good for him. I was hoping he wouldn't die a lonely old man."

"I've worried about that – about him being lonely, being here all the time with no friends, no girlfriends. It just didn't seem right for such a young man."

"Well, when Jason does find a girl, he doesn't fool around. This one is a true knockout!"

"Jason has those beautiful eyes and he's a handsome man. It doesn't seem as if he should have any trouble finding pretty girls."

"That may be, but we haven't seen any around here lately, have we?"

"No. As a matter of fact, I was shocked when he brought her here last night. Did you know he has never, ever, brought a woman back to the house with him?"

"Never? He's never brought a woman home with him?"

"Never."

"Now I know I have to check her out when they come back."

"I wouldn't look for them any time soon. Jason had a blanket roll behind the saddle, and they took lunch with them."

"So this may be more than just a little ride, huh?"

They both laughed.

"I don't expect them back before supper time."

"Maybe not even then," said Roy with a little chuckle.

"Carly asked me this morning who the ranch belonged to, so I told her it belonged mostly to Jason. She said Jason told her he was a boring lawyer when she met him. Could you believe that Roy? He told this girl he was boring."

"What's he going to do? Tell her - 'I own a big ranch in Kentucky, and they call me Kentucky's most eligible millionaire bachelor with the pretty eyes?' Is that what you want him to say?"

"Well no, but boring lawyer doesn't fit him."

"Maybe he wasn't too interested in her."

"He seems plenty interested now. Interested enough that we have a huge new piano."

"Some young girls are very impressed by money, Gwen. I think Jason is shrewd enough to keep some parts of his life to himself. I don't think he would want women coming on to him just because he has money. If he did, he probably could have had a whole slew of women in his bed by now. There are plenty of women out there trying to get his attention."

"He obviously didn't tell Carly this was his ranch. She has no parents, no family, no one to help her through all the trauma she has endured. This morning Jason said he wanted to help her, but he isn't sure she will accept his help. I told him to give her a little time. Her brother-in-law, Jack, told Jason that Carly has a house going into foreclosure and a ton of medical bills."

"That's something Jason could help her with. He's solved those kinds of problems for lots of his veteran clients. With a little romantic interest involved, his outcomes might be spectacular."

"I think that's a good assumption, Roy. See you tonight!"

Chapter 8

Jason and Carly started riding up the trail, and as they rode along, Jason talked a bit about the history of the ranch and how it had grown through the years. Carly turned her head and looked up at Jason, and he was smiling down at her with his pretty eyes. *I can't believe I'm doing this! I can't believe I'm riding on a horse with this handsome man.* She remembered Christy had warned her to be careful when Christy had described Jason as devastatingly handsome. Truthfully, she couldn't remember ever seeing a man as good looking as Jason. It was almost enough to take your breath away. He had coal black hair that made his blue violet eyes seem even more brilliant. His features seemed like they had been chiseled to perfection on his face. Today he was wearing a black Stetson that made him look taller and even more dignified. She wondered if he ever wore the hat when he was in court. He wasn't wearing it at the club, so maybe he only wore it on the ranch. She wished Christy was here to see him wearing the hat. Christy might be even more worried about her if she ever saw him in this hat! Jason had his arms firmly wrapped around her, and she let herself lean back against his chest. As she did that, she felt him bend down and then kiss her on the cheek. Her face suddenly felt hot, and she knew it wasn't because of the sun. She looked up at him again and he smiled at her, and she smiled back.

"I'm starting to enjoy this, Jason. It's fun."

"Good. And you haven't fallen off yet, have you?"

"No. I don't think I'm going to fall off. I think you have a good hold on me."

"I do. I'm not going to let you fall off."

"Where are we going?"

"We're going to take this trail up to the far Northwest corner of the ranch. It rises up a hill and the view is magnificent. We can have lunch up there. There's another gate up there that is smaller than our main gate. We use it to take equipment in and out, but I didn't bring the key today, so we won't go out beyond the gate."

"Why would you take equipment out that gate?"

"We own more land beyond the fences and sometimes we need to go in and mow if the vegetation gets out of hand."

"So, you own land beyond these fences?"

"Just a little bit. We can go for a ride out there one day when I remember to bring the key. When we get up to the end of the trail, we can have some lunch if you're hungry, and I want to talk to you about some ideas I have for you. We could even do a riding lesson for you on Charlie if you want to try that."

"Riding by myself? I don't know about that. Maybe not yet. I'm a little nervous about this."

"That's okay. Just remember Charlie is a good horse. He won't do anything he's not supposed to do. He won't take off running with you on his back! Remember when I went up by his nose this morning and told him he had to be a good boy?"

"What does that mean?"

"It means that he and I are not going to do any of the crazy stuff we do."

"What is the crazy stuff?"

"I'll take him in the rink, and I'll show you the routine that Charlie and I do when we get back to the barn."

"Is it something dangerous?"

"No, not really. It's meant to be entertaining."

As they rode up the trail, Jason told her all about the ranch and kissed her on the side of her cheek a few times. "What do you think, Carly? Do you like it here?"

"It is beautiful! I can see why you love it! This must have been a wonderful place to grow up!"

Jason thought he heard a note of wistfulness in her voice. "If you stay for a while, we can get you riding on your own horse. We have some very gentle mares that will be perfect for you. We can do some more trail rides and go up into the woods beyond the gate. There are lots of beautiful wildflowers in the woods in the Spring and Summer. Up there they don't get trampled or eaten by the horses."

"I've never been in this area before. I didn't realize how beautiful it is."

"You've never been to Kentucky?"

"No. I never had a car when I was younger. My friend Sean gave me his car when he moved to Utah, but that was the first time I ever had a car of my own."

"Maybe you could come to the Kentucky Derby with me this year."

"Where is it exactly?"

"Louisville."

"Do you go to the Kentucky Derby every year?"

"Almost every year, except when I was in the Army. We might have a horse ready for the Derby this year. We're not sure yet, but we're working on it. We have a few that might qualify."

"Wow. That sounds impressive. Have you ever done that before?"

"Yeah. The ranch has. I haven't personally because I was gone for a few years. My dad and my grandfather have had horses in the Derby. The ranch has had a couple of winners."

"You had horses that won the Kentucky Derby?"

"Yeah. Some years back. Not in the last couple of years."

"Wow. That must be a big honor."

"Yes. A big honor and a big purse."

"A big what?"

"A big purse. Do you know what a purse is?"

"I have a purse I carry around. Like that?"

"No. The purse is the winnings for the race."

"So there's money involved for the winner."

"Yes. Big money. About a million dollars for the winner. The jockey gets 10% of the purse."

"What? Are you serious?"

"Yes. It's a big race. Your horse has to earn points in other races to qualify and there is also an entrance fee of about $50,000."

"No wonder you want to enter a horse in the Kentucky Derby."

"It's a big deal to have a winner from your ranch. It does a lot for your standings."

"I guess you know all about this because you grew up here."

"Yes. I've been to lots of racetracks."

As they were riding up the trail there were horses running all around them. One of them came right up on the trail next to Charlie.

Carly looked up at Jason. "Now what do you do?"

"Nothing. He just wants to come up to see Charlie. We'll stop here and let them say hello to each other and then the other one will probably run off."

"Really? That's what they do?" She looked at the horses and noticed that their noses met, and the new horse nickered a little at Charlie.

"They're just saying hello to each other. Now they're done and he'll probably run off."

The other horse just stood there next to Charlie and finally Jason said, "Okay, Charlie, let's go."

They rode up the trail a little further and Jason said, "Well, this is it. We'll stop up here."

"You were right. It's a beautiful view."

"It's one of my favorite places. I used to come up here a lot when I was a kid."

"You rode all the way up here by yourself when you were a kid?"

"Oh, yeah. I rode everywhere on the ranch, but I learned to ride when I was very young. I don't think my parents worried about me. I was a good rider."

"You came all the way up here alone?"

"Usually. Okay, we're going to get down. I'll go first and then I'll help you get off. I have a blanket here we can spread out. We'll put our lunch where Charlie can't eat it."

Carly laughed. "Would he do that?"

"He might. He's a bit of a food hound."

Jason took the blanket and the lunch off the saddle and gave Charlie a pat on the rump and said, "Okay, boy. Go eat some grass or something."

Carly looked over at Jason suddenly. "You don't tie him up?"

"Oh, no. Charlie won't go anywhere."

"He won't run off with the other horses and leave us?"

"Nah. He won't run off. If he gets too far away, I can just call him back."

"And he comes back when you call him? Like when you call a dog, and it comes back to you?"

"Sure. He'll come back."

"I was thinking we would have a long walk home."

"Charlie won't leave us here. He always comes back when I call him."

Carly watched as the horses walked off to the bottom of the hill. "He's pretty far away."

"Don't worry. He's not going to leave us." Jason sat down on the blanket, took her hand, and pulled her down next to him.

"Did you go back to sleep this morning?"

"I did. I couldn't believe I fell asleep again."

"That's good. You've been through a lot these last few days, and you were tired. I brought you coffee, and then when I got out of the shower, I noticed you were sound asleep. I just pulled the blanket up over you and closed the door to keep out any noise. Grandma saved some breakfast for you, right?"

"Yes. It was nice of her to do that."

"Yes, she's great. I'm sure she's happy you're here."

"Why is that?"

"Grandma likes company, and I've never brought anyone up to the ranch before, so she probably thinks you are very special."

Jason leaned over and started kissing her. She kissed him back and he asked, "Is this okay, Carly? Can I put my arms around you?"

She nodded and he kissed her again. He pulled her over against him and just laid there quietly with her. Neither one of them said anything for a long time.

Finally, he said, "You asked me if you could stay here for a while."

"Yeah, I did. Is it okay?"

"I think it would be nice to have you stay. I think we could have a lot of fun together."

"But I wouldn't want to take you away from your work and interrupt your life."

"My life isn't very busy right now. I don't have much legal work on my plate. I have one case that is pending. It's an appeal, and I'm waiting for a decision. But we do have something coming up here at the ranch that will be fun."

"What's that?"

"One of our mares is about to foal."

"Your grandma told me that. She said you went out to check on the mare this morning."

"I did. She should have her foal soon. That's our next big event, and after that we have 3 more mares getting ready to foal."

"Your grandma said they always do that at night."

"Isn't that the truth! So, if you wake up some night and I'm not there next to you, you will know I am down at the barn."

"Could I go with you?"

"You can if you want to. You don't have to."

"I like to stay with you, Jason. I don't think I want to be alone in the house."

"You can come with me. Sometimes it's a long process though. It's not over in an hour."

"Your grandma told me how cute they are when they try to get up on their feet."

"That's the best part."

"I think I'd like to see it. I'll bring my camera."

Jason leaned over her and kissed her again. "I like having you here. I really liked having you here last night. It was nice."

"Nice? I cried half the night, Jason. I'm so sorry. You should have taken me home."

"It was what you needed to do. Sometimes it's good to get things out in the open and talk about them. You can't keep everything inside you. I found a great therapist for you, and you can start tomorrow if you want."

"Wow! That was fast."

"If that's okay, I'll call him to confirm. I hope you'll decide to stay here for a while."

"I'm just sorry I cried so much. Sometimes I just can't stop."

"Who wouldn't cry after what you've been through. Remember I told you last night that I'll help you, and I'm serious about that. I'm going to look at your mortgage first, so you won't miss a deadline. Once we get that taken care of, we can look at other things, like your hospital and doctor's bills. I already called Jack this morning to have him send over all your mortgage paperwork."

"You're serious about this. I didn't think you would have started already."

"I told you I would help you. I'm not a procrastinator. I like to dig into problems and get them handled. We don't want to wait until they proceed with the foreclosure, then it's too late."

"It might be too late already."

"No, I don't think so. There's always a time allowance for an appeal to be filed. We just need to get it in before that date. I have experience with mortgages. I'm sure I can help you."

"I hate to ask you to do this for me, Jason."

"You didn't really ask me to help you. I offered to do it. And I've already decided I'm going to do this, so we don't need to talk about it anymore. We'll talk about it when I get your paperwork and I see what I can do for you, Okay?"

"That's really nice of you, Jason."

"Well, I'm a nice guy, so you probably want this nice guy to kiss you again, right?"

He leaned over and kissed her. Without asking first, he wrapped his arms around her and held her. He wondered how long she would let him hold her like that. She didn't try to move away, so they just laid there. He could feel her warm breath against his neck. Her hair smelled like lavender. He took a little piece of her hair and held it between his fingers and kissed it. She was lying very quietly in his arms. He rubbed his hand up and down her back very gently and she made a little soft sound. He did it again and she sighed. He kept rubbing her back and he felt her move in a little closer to him. He pulled his arms around her a bit tighter, and they didn't talk. They lay there listening to the sounds of the wind in the trees and the occasional whinnying of the horses.

Finally, Jason said, "Carly, do you feel safe when I hold you like this? I don't want you to be afraid. I would never do anything to hurt you. We need to find ways to make your life calm and peaceful."

"I do feel peaceful right now. I like hearing the sounds around us. Before the kidnapping I used to spend a lot of time outdoors, photographing landscapes and wildflowers; taking walks in nature, watching sunrises and sunsets."

"You don't do that anymore?"

"I can't. I'm too afraid. I'm afraid to be out alone in the woods. You heard what the kidnapper said at the hearing. He's coming back to kill me. I'm as good as dead."

"No, Carly. He's not going to come back to kill you. I can keep you safe. You saw what happened to him when he tried to hurt you. I can do a lot more damage to him if he ever shows up again. We could do some of those things together, you and I. There are some beautiful places here where we could hike and take pictures."

"I'd like that, Jason. I know I'd feel safe if you were with me. I can't hike as far as I used to because my feet aren't the same, and it's harder for me to carry my camera equipment."

"Well, we could always use our horses instead of our own feet, and I can carry your equipment for you. You can train me to be your photographer's assistant."

"That's nice of you, Jason. I would love to do that. There's a very special feeling I get when I'm out in nature. I'll have to show you some of my photos on my website. I left my camera at my house, but maybe we could go by and pick it up one of these days."

"Of course. If we go to Nashville tomorrow, we can get it. Is it at your house or at Christy's?"

"It's at my house. I haven't used it recently. I had such a hard time just trying to walk again and keep my balance that I didn't try to do any photographs."

"Maybe you could teach me about photography. I think I would enjoy it. I've always wanted to get some great photos of the horses. You could tell me what kind of camera to buy."

"You can use one of mine to see if you enjoy it. I have two digital cameras. I have an older one, and then Sean gave me a new one when they moved to Utah."

"Was this guy Sean a boyfriend? He gave you a car and then a camera?"

"No. He was like a brother, and Maia, his sister, was a best friend. They were always giving me things. I spent a lot of time with their family. I even went on some trips with them. Christy's mom and dad had moved out to a retirement home, and Christy was always with Jack, so I was sort of at loose ends. I stayed at Sean's house a lot. They tried to give me my own room, but Maia and I wanted to share her room. I really missed them when they moved away."

"Do you still keep in touch with them?"

"Yes. We email all the time. I stopped carrying a phone, but they gave me an iPad when I was in the hospital, so we can still message and keep in touch."

"Hmm, more gifts. He is sounding like a boyfriend, Carly."

"No. He was just a friend. He and Maia were the best friends I ever had. I played duets with Maia, and Sean and I entered duet competitions. People used to ask us if we were brother and sister, so Sean made up a story and said we were twins separated at birth."

"That's funny. Did you look alike?"

"People thought we did, so Sean made up the story just to be funny. I even went camping with his family. When they left, they gave me an extra tent and then I did some camping on my own with my little dog Charlie."

"Did you like camping?"

"Oh, yes. I thought it was wonderful. There are some beautiful spots where you can pitch a tent."

"Would you still like to do that?"

"I would, but I don't feel safe now. There's not much protection when you're sleeping in a tent."

"I think we have a camper van somewhere on the ranch. Remind me to ask Roy or Grandma if we still have it. I don't remember seeing it recently. My dad rarely sold anything, so it's probably around somewhere. Would you feel safe in a camper, Carly?"

"I'd feel safe with you, Jason. I couldn't do it alone."

"I wasn't thinking about sending you out alone. I think you need to be more confident about your kidnapper's confinement before you start going places alone. I got a horrible vibe from him. I think he is a very vicious psychopath."

"He certainly scares me."

"I like how we are finding so many things we would like to do together. I would also love to have you teach me more about writing songs or playing the piano. I'm going to teach you to be an expert horse woman."

Carly laughed. "Do you think I'll ever rise to the level of expert, Jason? I might be starting this a bit late in life."

"Not to worry. You have an excellent teacher!"

Carly poked him in the arm. "Just who is that excellent teacher, Jason? Could you be talking about yourself?"

Jason winked and gave her a smile that nearly took her breath away. "I might be."

Carly ran her fingers over his arm. "I can't believe the muscles you have in your arms."

"You have to have strength to deal with all these big horses. Speaking of horses, I wonder how far Charlie has strayed. I don't see him anywhere."

"I told you he was going to go off with that other horse."

"No. He wouldn't do that." Jason turned around and looked behind him and there was Charlie. He was sniffing out the lunch that was up in the tree.

"What do you think you are? A bear, Charlie? Are you going to climb the tree to get our lunch?"

Jason got up and went over to rescue their lunch. "We better eat this before Charlie gets it."

"Would he really do that?"

"He might try, but it's well wrapped. I don't think he could get this bag open, but we're not going to wait and see."

Jason opened the bag and saw that grandma had made some sandwiches for them. There was even a small bottle of wine in the bag and two small glasses. "Wow! Grandma was thinking of everything."

"We're having wine with lunch?"

"I guess so. There's water here too if you don't want wine."

"No, wine is fine. I like it. It was nice of your grandma to fix this for us."

"Yeah. She didn't want you to see my grumpy side," Jason laughed. "It sounds like the two of you had a nice talk this morning. I just hope she didn't tell you how spoiled I was as a child, or every silly thing I ever did growing up."

"No, Jason. She didn't say anything like that. She is very proud of you. She wants you to be happy. It sounds like she misses your parents as much as you do."

"Yeah, we all miss them. They were such a big part of the ranch. My dad had his hand in everything that was going on here. I don't seem to be able to do that yet. My mom was the coordinator and organizer. She had a good head for all the details. My grandma has taken over that role, and she oversees all the employees on the ranch. I'm not quite sure what my role will be in years to come, but I hope I will be able to be as successful as my dad was."

"I'm sure you will, Jason, but it seems like you are taking on a lot of work for yourself."

"I do my best work when I'm busy."

When they finished, Jason gathered up the remains of their lunch and tied the bag back up in the tree away from Charlie. He was thinking about giving Carly a short riding lesson on Charlie, but when he turned around, he could see tears streaming down her face.

"What's wrong, Carly. Did I say something to upset you?"

"No. I'm just feeling sad and a little guilty."

"Now why would you feel guilty?"

"I'm out here having a wonderful time with you, Jason. And we had a wonderful day on Sunday with Lindsey, but I owe money to all those people who saved my life and helped me recover. They never got paid for what they did, and maybe I'll never be able to repay them."

"I see," said Jason. "You shouldn't be allowed to have fun until all your debts are paid. Do you think those doctors only saved your life because they were going to get paid for it? Do you think you shouldn't ever have fun again? We talked about some things we could do together and things you would like to start doing again. Doing these things is part of taking back your life, Carly. You are entitled to have a life again. To live, to love, experience joy and feel safe. You are allowed to have a wonderful day. You need to have more wonderful days. You need to sleep at night. These are all the things that are going to help you get better."

"I guess so. I'm having a wonderful time with you. I'm sorry I keep crying. It's like the flood gates have opened and I just can't stop crying."

Jason sat down and put his arms around her and gently pulled her over toward him. "It's okay to have a great day. You're human. You have human emotions. It's okay to have fun and enjoy yourself. Do you feel safe today? Is it okay if I hold you for a little while?"

"Yes. I feel safe. What do you feel when you hold me, Jason? Do you just feel sorry for me?"

"When I hold you in my arms, I feel like I'm holding a fragile, wounded little bird. I know I need to be especially careful not to hurt him again. But I want to see this fragile bird get back up on his feet again and start to feel strong. Then I want to see him spread his wings and fly, soaring high up in the sky, testing all the wind currents, and feeling free and joyful. That's what I want for you, Carly. I want you to feel free and joyful. You don't deserve to be weighed down by all this debt and all these problems. You shouldn't have to live in fear for your life every day. When I saw that bastard at the court hearing I knew you needed to be protected. He is a very vicious animal. He should never be allowed to go free again. You shouldn't ever have to see him again. You have so much talent. You need the time and the space to grow your career, to be everything you ever dreamed you could be. You can't let this felon stop you from reaching for your dreams. I can help you, Carly. I can take over your financial problems and make them go away. I know that sounds impossible to you, but

I have the experience to make it happen. Bad things happen to good people, but thankfully there are other good people out there who are willing to help. There's no shame in asking for help, Carly. You didn't create these problems; you didn't deserve to be brutalized like this. There are good people out there thinking '*thank God this didn't happen to me*" and those are the people who are going to step forward to help you, either by volunteering their time or their money. It's okay to let them help you. You didn't create this problem; you can't solve it on your own. You can't be creative when you feel like you are drowning in debt. All you can do is tread water until it overtakes you and pulls you under. I'm not going to let that happen to you. It's not fair. I hope you can trust me enough to let me help you. Can you do that?"

Carly kept sobbing. "Maybe," she answered.

"I know Christy and Jack have been working on this for you, but maybe they need a little help, too. I can see the pain in your sister's eyes when she looks at you. They've tried everything they know how to do to help you. If you let me take over, it might afford them a measure of relief. I will need your permission to act on your behalf, and it's not going to be all sweetness and light. There are times when I will be accusing your insurance company of illegal practices and violations of your patient rights. I think your mortgage company will cave into any demands we make because local financial service businesses do not like bad publicity. They don't like having their name dragged through the mud. One thing you need to understand, Carly, is that these companies have the money. They have the means to make good on their obligations. When you sign a contract with an insurance company, they are bound by law to uphold their end of the contract. When you tell me that you had to get a donation to obtain the treatments you needed to save your feet, it makes my blood boil. That is something that should have been approved without hesitation. Think how glad they were when an anonymous donor stepped up to take over that obligation. Jack told me you have scars that could have been repaired with plastic surgery, but those procedures were denied. They don't have the right to do that to you. They can't pick and choose which injuries they want to cover. They have to cover each and every injury that is related to the kidnapping. Your feet were frozen because you escaped from that bastard. If you hadn't escaped, you would probably be dead. Were they willing to pay to have your feet amputated and then provide prosthetics for the rest of your life? That's a ridiculous decision. I'm sure we can get them to repay that donation and then you can use it for any procedures that weren't covered or use it for some of your copays. I haven't seen all your medical bills yet but based on what Jack told me about your insurance company, I think there will probably be a number of denials we can dispute. So what do you think, Carly? Do you want to jump on this train with me?"

"Maybe. Will it get nasty? What will I have to do?"

"It might get nasty, but that will be my job, not yours. All you have to do is give me permission to act on your behalf, and we can draw up a contract. If I need to get nasty, I will. It's not like I haven't done that before. You have nothing to lose here. I'll start with the $50,000 that was donated and see if we can get that back for you, okay?"

"Then do I need to give it back to the donor?"

"You can't because you don't know who the donor was. It was anonymous. We'll set up an account for you and keep it there until we determine which expenses are legitimate. Then you can use it to pay those."

"Can we put it in the GoFundMe account?"

"No. There's no reason to do that. They take a percentage of every donation, and this donation didn't come to you through that venue, so there's no reason to let them take part of it."

"I didn't know that. How do you know all these things, Jason?"

"Three years in law school and a lot of research on my own about how to help people in trouble."

"Well, I'm certainly one of those people in trouble." Carly started sobbing again and Jason pulled her into his arms. "You're trying to help me, and all I can do is cry. I'm sorry."

"It's okay Carly. Maybe it's time to let it all out. Talk to the therapist tomorrow and if you feel comfortable with him, talk about some of the things you've been holding inside. You can't keep everything inside forever. You've had some awful things happen to you. I hope you can talk about them with Dr. Mac. I want you to get better."

Jason put his hand gently under her chin a raised her head up to look at him. "Remember what I said about the wounded bird. I said I wanted it to spread its wings and fly, but I hope you don't fly too far away. I hope you will want to come back to me."

Jason held her in his arms for a while. Slowly she stopped crying and just laid quietly beside him.

"Don't look now, but there is someone behind you," Carly said.

"Would that someone happen to have four legs?"

"Yes, he does."

Suddenly Charlie reached down and butted Jason with his head. Carly started laughing.

"Oh, you think that's funny? Wait until he does it to you."

"What is he trying to tell you?"

"He must think it's time to go home. It is close to feeding time in the barns."

"Maybe he's hungry."

"Or maybe he is just being rude, huh Charlie?"

"Has he done that before?"

"Oh, yes. I fell asleep up here one day and when it got dark, Charlie came over and gave me that treatment."

"In a way, it's sort of cute. But I guess it startled you."

"Yeah, he was a little rough this time. He must be hungry. Okay, let's get you up in the saddle and we can head out."

As they were heading down the trail, Jason took a turn off and rode through some of the other pastures with horses. He thought she would ask him to slow down, but she didn't. When they got back to the barn, Jason said, "I guess there is a bit of daredevil in you, Carly. Did you like going that fast?"

"Oh, yeah. That was great!"

"Okay, I can teach you how to do that on Molly tomorrow. Just hang out here for a minute while I take Charlie back to his stall."

"Can I come in with you?"

"Sure you can!"

As soon as they walked into the barn they ran into Roy. "Hey, Roy, this is Carly. She came up here with me last night and we just went for a nice ride on Charlie."

"Yeah, I saw you down there riding through the pastures. Were you trying to scare her, Jason?"

"No. She liked it. I offered to slow down, but she didn't want to."

"Did you like it?" asked Roy. "He was going kind of fast."

"No, I thought it was fun, but I was hanging on."

"And Jason was hanging on to you, right?"

"Oh, yeah!"

"Well, you were probably safe then. Nice to meet you, Carly. Did you guys have fun?"

Carly smiled up at him. "Oh, it was a wonderful day."

He looked over at Jason. "Did you have fun, Jason?"

Jason glanced over at Roy and gave him the look. "Yeah, Roy. We had fun."

"Good. Good deal." Roy slapped him on the back and walked away.

"What was that all about?" asked Carly.

"He's just kidding me a little."

"Why is that?"

"Probably because I brought you up here to the ranch and I've never brought a woman here before."

"Never? You've never asked anyone to come here to go for a ride with you?"

"Nope."

"Jason, why not?"

"I don't know. I just didn't."

"You never met anyone you even wanted to invite to go for a ride with you?"

"No. Not really."

"Wow. I feel honored."

"Well, you are more fun than other women I have met."

"Oh, really. I'm fun, huh? After all that crying I did today and last night it's hard to believe you can tell me that I'm fun."

"You were fun today. We had a great day, didn't we?"

"Yes. It was great. I enjoyed the ride and seeing your ranch."

"Okay. It's official. You're fun. Let's go back to the house. You can play the piano for me again."

Chapter 9

Jason and Carly walked in the front door, and they were greeted by a wonderful aroma wafting through the house.
"Nettie must be fixing something wonderful for dinner," Jason commented.
"It does smell great," said Carly.
Jason took off his hat and hung it up on a hook by the door.
"I really liked seeing you in that hat," said Carly. "It makes you look like a very handsome rancher. Maybe you should wear it all the time."
"Well, I have to keep the rancher persona in check, as I often need to project my lawyer persona."
"All you would have to do is wear that hat in court and the jury would be putty in your hands."
"I'm sure glad you decided to stay up here a little longer, Carly. It turns out that you are amazingly good for my ego."
"Does your ego need any bolstering, Jason? Seems like you have a fair amount of confidence."
"What are you trying to tell me, Carly? Do I come across as a bit full of myself?"
"No. No. That's not what I meant at all," Carly hastened to add. "I just see you as someone who is very educated and knowledgeable. I might be a bit jealous. I've always wished that I had more education. I never had the chance to go to any top-notch schools like you did."
"You seem pretty smart to me, Carly. I think anyone who can outsmart a vicious kidnapper has a lot more brain power than the rest of us. Not to mention more courage than 99% of the population. You have a musical gift most people will never possess."
"I suppose. I wanted to earn a college degree, but I didn't have the money to take more classes."
"You can always go back and do that, Carly. We'll get some of these problems of yours taken care of and then you could think about being a student again. Right now, I think I'm starting to smell like Charlie, so I'm going to go down to my room and take a shower before dinner. Do you want a shower?"
"No, I can't do showers."

Jason smiled at her slyly. "Well, I guess that ends my quest to get you to take a shower with me some day."

"I have a bit of a headache, so maybe I could lie down in your room while you are in the shower."

"You can do that. Should we find you some Tylenol? Grandma has bottles of that stuff up on the kitchen shelf."

"Tylenol would be great."

Jason found the bottle, shook out some capsules for her and handed her a bottle of water. "Maybe we did a little too much bouncing around on Charlie today. Keep the water and drink some more of it. You might be dehydrated. It was a little warm out there."

They walked down to his bedroom and Carly laid down on the bed while Jason got ready to get into the shower. He sat down on the bed next to her for a moment. "Are you sure you're all right? You look a little pale right now."

"I'll be okay. I had a skull fracture and sometimes it just starts hurting again. I guess these things take a long time to heal."

"A skull fracture? How in the hell did that happen? Were you in a car accident?"

"No, Jason. The kidnapper did it."

"What? He fractured your skull? How did he do that?"

"He slammed my head against the wall in the shower."

"I guess that explains your aversion to showers. I'm so sorry Carly. I had no idea. I'm sorry about the crack I made about getting you to take a shower with me. You know I was just teasing, don't you?"

"It's okay. You had no way of knowing. It's just one of many gruesome things I didn't tell you."

"Every time you tell me about some horrible thing he did to you, I start wishing I had broken his neck on Saturday."

"I've wished that as well."

"Okay. Try to rest for a little while. We can keep the room dark, and maybe the Tylenol will help. I'm off to wash away the lovely scent of horses." He kissed her on the cheek and went off to the shower.

Carly lay very still, trying to think about the wonderful day she had with Jason. She couldn't wait to tell Christy about riding a horse, but her head was throbbing now, and it brought back horrible memories of the day the kidnapper called himself the "Evil Twin" and had dragged her into the shower and assaulted her. She would always remember it as her first close call with death. There were still moments when she couldn't believe she had survived and moments when she wished she hadn't. She started to feel sleepy, and the sound of the shower was almost as comforting as listening to a gentle rain. She pulled a corner of the spread over herself and drifted off to sleep.

Jason got out of the shower and walked into the bedroom to see how Carly was feeling. He started to say something to her and then noticed she was fast asleep. He knelt down at the edge of the bed next to her and gently touched her hand to see if she was warm enough. Her hands were ice cold. He took a fuzzy fleece throw off an armchair and gently covered her with it. He felt her forehead and it seemed warm to his touch but not feverish. He scolded himself for keeping her out so long and getting her so tired. He remembered everything she had been through in the last 4 days and thought she was probably both mentally and physically exhausted. He remembered Christy had told him Carly had only been sleeping a few hours a night. God, he thought, she must be suffering from sleep deprivation. He put on some shorts and a tee shirt and went around to the other side of the bed and laid down beside her.

"Jason? Do I need to get up now?" she whispered.

"No Carly, go back to sleep. I'll just stay here with you to make sure you are safe."

"Mmmm, that sounds nice." she said sleepily.

Jason wrapped his whole body around her and gently stroked her hair. "You're safe, Carly. I've got you. You're safe."

He watched her as she drifted back to sleep. All the muscles in her face softened and the hand she had wrapped around his arm gradually lost its grip and slid onto the bed. *What must it be like, he thought, to know that someone wanted to kill you? To know that the monster had already made a first attempt for the kill. How many times a day is she hearing the words 'you're as good as dead' echoing through her brain.*

Gwen walked down to the kitchen looking for Nettie. "Hey, Nettie, I thought I heard Jason and Carly come back to the house. Did you see them?"

"They're here. I heard Carly say she had a headache and Jason was getting some Tylenol for her. I was in the pantry, so I just stayed out of their way while they were in the kitchen. I think they walked down to Jason's old room. I heard him say he needed a shower."

"Whatever you're cooking smells wonderful, Nettie. When are you going to tell us what it is?"

"Not until dinner time. Robbie said it was one of his favorite dishes, so I thought we could all try something new."

Gwen walked down the hall looking for Jason. His bedroom door was slightly open, so she knocked softly, but there was no response. She peeked around through the open crack in the door and saw both Jason and Carly were asleep on his bed. She smiled when she saw they were lying on top of the covers and Jason had his whole body wrapped around Carly. *She must feel safe now, thought Gwen.* She closed the door quietly and walked away.

She heard Roy coming in the front door and heard the unmistakable beep of the security alarms being reset. "God, it smells wonderful in here." said Roy. "What are you ladies cooking?"

"Nettie's cooking and she won't tell me what she's fixing. She said it was something Robbie wanted her to try. You're here early, Roy. Slow day at the ranch?"

"Not really. I wanted to come and talk with you. I met Carly when Jason brought Charlie back to the barn. She's a beautiful girl, Gwen, and I've never seen Jason look happier. Maybe we can all start to come to the end of our grieving period. Are Jason and Carly back here at the house?"

"Yes. They're over in Jason's old bedroom taking a nap. Nettie overheard Carly say she had a headache. Jason's door was open, so I peeked in and saw them lying on the bed asleep. Jason had his whole body wrapped all around her."

"Good," said Roy. "After I met them, I started thinking about us, Gwen. How about we go down to your room and take a nap, or something."

"Is anything wrong, Roy?"

"No, not wrong, just something I think we need to make right."

Roy led her down the hall and closed the bedroom door behind them.

"You're starting to worry me now, Roy. Is this something about Carly?"

"No, not really. They just made me realize how we've all been living for the last few years. We're all still in mourning, Gwen. We've been grieving since George and Lexie died. It's time for all of us to get on with life. Especially Jason! He's an amazing young man and he's been in limbo since they died. Today is the first time I've seen him smile in years. That's way too long, Gwen. I hope this young woman might be just what he needs to crawl out of his depression, but if not, then we need to do something about it. Then we need to do something about us, Gwen. We need to admit what there is between us and stop denying the feelings we have for each other. I love you. I think you know that. We can make a life together here on the ranch. We both love living here, we both love Jason. We both want to see the ranch return to its glory days and hopefully have another Kentucky Derby Winner! I think if George were here, he would say, 'Go for it, Mom!' don't you think so?"

"I guess he would. When Jason is happy again, I'll know George and Lexie can rest in peace. I just don't know what else to do for him. I guess we can see where it goes with Carly, and I know you're right, Roy, it is time to start living again."

"Okay, Gwen. Let's start tonight. Let's welcome Carly and make it a celebration, not a sad family dinner. Let's have some wine and some laughter. It's time to have fun again."

Roy reached over and put his arms around her and kissed her. "Can we do that? Can we have some fun again?"

"Yes. You're right. It's time."

"And what do you think about us, Gwen? What do you think about what I told you?"

"I love you," she answered. "I guess I should go help Nettie now."

"I just heard Robbie come in. He can help her. I'm going to send him down to the wine cellar to get some wine to go with whatever it is we are eating tonight."

Roy tapped out the message on his phone and then took her in his arms and kissed her, and they laid there quietly together. He was glad he had said his piece. Since George and Lexie had died, whenever there were problems on the ranch, he always asked himself 'What would George do?' He knew this was what George would have wanted. He would want Jason and Gwen to be happy. George wouldn't have wanted his son or his mother to mourn him forever. He remembered how excited George had been when Jason was born. He had carried that baby with him all over the ranch. He taught Jason to ride a pony when he was only 2 years old. George loved the horses, but he had loved Jason and Lexie more than life itself. *I'm doing the right thing he told himself. George would want us to move on. It's time, and it seems like it's up to me.*

Carly woke suddenly with a start. "Where am I?" she whispered.

"You're right here with me, Carly. We're in my old bedroom. You took a nap while I went in to grab a shower, remember? Did your headache go away?"

"I guess it did. I feel okay. I can't believe I keep falling asleep here. Should we get up?"

"We can get up whenever you're ready. Nettie hasn't called us for dinner yet. You could go in and play the piano for a while if you want to."

"That sounds nice. Let me just go wash up a little. I might be a bit dusty from our ride." She looked over at Jason. "You look all spiffy and clean now."

"I didn't want anyone to mistake me for Charlie. It's not good to smell like a horse at the dinner table."

Carly leaned over toward him. "Mmmm, you smell good to me!" Jason reached for her, but she rolled over and put her feet on the floor and headed toward the bathroom.

When she was ready, they headed for the Great Room and Carly started softly playing the piano.

Jason wandered over into the kitchen to ask about dinner, but Robbie and Nettie didn't want him to come in. "Is this a secret dinner? What's going on here?"

"We're all going to try something new tonight. This is one of Robbie's favorites. We have some wine open if you want to start with a glass."

"I see you have a new piano, Jason, and I was told we are supposed to pretend it has always been here. Roy said you brought a beautiful woman home with you. I think we hear her playing the piano," said Robbie. "I'm anxious to meet her. Sounds like she is very talented. Where did you meet her, Jason? Have you known her very long?"

"I met her down in Nashville at the Rosebud Club last Saturday."

"I told you that, Robbie," said Nettie.

"I know, but did you meet her somewhere before Saturday? Is that why you were down there?"

"No. I just happened to sit down next to her at the club when she was on a break."

"And because you are this amazingly handsome guy, and maybe you told her you own a ranch full of racehorses and a helicopter, she decided to leave Nashville and come home with you?"

Jason laughed. "There's a little bit more to the story than that, Robbie, but if you want to stick with the part about my being amazingly handsome, I can live with that."

"Okay, Mr. Kentucky's Most Eligible Millionaire Bachelor."

"Shh! Please don't start calling me that around Carly. I don't think she has ever heard about these titles that plague me."

"She doesn't know how famous you are up here in your Old Kentucky Home?"

"Please, Robbie, don't start with this tonight. She doesn't need to know about all that nonsense."

"So, did you tell her you have a helicopter and a plane?"

"No, Robbie. Not tonight. Don't do this tonight."

"I guess you aren't going to introduce me as your pilot, huh?"

"No. Tonight you are just one of our trainers."

"Shucks, Nettie, I've been demoted."

"Well, I hear you requested this dinner we are having tonight, Robbie, so if it sets my mouth on fire, you might get demoted again."

They all started laughing. "I wouldn't serve you something spicy, Jason. You know that," said Nettie. "I hope it's something Carly will like. We don't often have celebrity visitors for dinner."

"So, do you like this woman, Jason? We are not accustomed to seeing you with a woman these days, or any days for that matter."

"Robbie! What is wrong with you tonight? Leave Jason alone. He's trying to help this poor woman who was the victim of a brutal kidnapping. She was terribly frightened when her kidnapper came after her at the Club, and Jason protected her."

"I see. So, this was more like his Knight in Shining Armor abilities than his amazingly handsome face that won her over."

"Robbie! Have you had too much wine already? Put a cork in the bottle, Jason, and take it away from him."

"I'm thinking about sending him home without dinner if he keeps this up."

"I'll be good. I promise. You must like this woman, Jason. You're getting a bit riled by just a little good-natured banter."

Robbie walked out into the Great Room for a few minutes and then came back.

"Oh, my, Jason. She's beautiful and talented! Wow! I wasn't expecting someone who would look like that. Are there long lines of young men all around the club waiting there just to see her? How long is she staying here?"

"I don't know, Robbie. She can stay as long as she wants. I'm trying to keep her safe and away from her horrible kidnapper. He made quite a scene at his court hearing on Monday. He's a very vicious felon, and he threatened to kill her. Please try not to scare her away."

"I'm quite good with a gun, Jason. If he ever comes up here, I could shoot him for you. You could just name the body part and I assure you I can hit it."

"Good to know, Robbie. If this situation escalates, we might need your gun."

"Do you seriously think he might show up here?"

"I hope not. But he has escaped from prison twice, so we all need to be very watchful for any strangers on the property."

"Roy mentioned that, but I didn't realize this bastard wanted to kill her. So, he's a true whacko, right?"

"He definitely fits that definition."

"This may sound cold, but I wouldn't feel bad about shooting a bastard like that. She must be horribly frightened."

"That's why she's here, Robbie, and we should not talk about this at dinner."

"I guess I need to start making a list of all the things I'm not allowed to say tonight."

Nettie gave him a whack with her wooden spoon. "Yes, Robbie, maybe you should! No talk about flying Jason's helicopter, no teasing about Jason's eligible bachelor titles, no gun talk, and no kidnapping questions. You could ask about the songs she writes or about playing the piano. Nothing too personal, please. Try to remember she has suffered through a horribly emotional trauma."

"No questions about family or parents either," said Jason.

"What happened to her family?" asked Robbie.

"They are all dead, Robbie, so it's not a good subject."

"Jeez, what hasn't happened to this poor girl?"

"She hasn't won the lottery, but that is truly what she needs right now."

"I'm assuming she has money problems. Is that something you can cure, Jason?"

"I'm certainly going to try. In the meantime, I'm going to keep her alive and try to make her happier."

"Do you think the bastard really wants to kill her, Jason?"

"Without a doubt. He screamed it out in court on Monday in front of the judge and a room full of witnesses. If she hadn't escaped, I'm sure she would already be dead. He is a vicious felon."

"But why? Why do you think he wants to kill her?"

"He's a psychopath, Robbie. I don't think they need a reason. The wiring in their brains has been fried somewhere along the line. She is the reason he's in prison. That might be a motive, but he had planned to kill her before she escaped. She just outsmarted him and got away."

"Do you think he targeted her because she is a well-known singer? There are documented cases of kidnappings and murders of famous celebrities."

"Yeah, I've read some of those cases. I guess there are plenty of nut jobs in this world."

"Well, I think we can keep her safe up here. Like I said, I have some serious weaponry skills and I would have no qualms about dusting them off for a guy like that. I know Roy has guns and does some target shooting. Rumor has it that your grandmother carries a gun in her purse."

"I hope she doesn't do that any longer. I have asked her to leave the gun at home. Does she still do that Nettie?"

"Gosh, Jason, I just don't have any idea," said Nettie.

"I think you do know, Nettie, I think you just don't want to tell me. To me that means yes. Yes, she is still carrying it in her purse. Am I right?"

Nettie was silent and busied herself with the business of cooking.

"I think Nettie is taking the fifth," said Robbie.

"I noticed," said Jason.

Jason walked into the Great Room and stood there silently just listening to Carly play the piano. He walked over and sat down next to her on the piano bench. She turned and smiled at him with her beautiful green eyes. *I could get lost in those eyes, he thought.*

"Lovely, lovely, lovely," came a voice from the other end of the room. Jason looked up to see Grandma in the doorway. "Could you please teach Jason to play the piano like that?"

"I can try," answered Carly.

"Grandma, what you're hearing takes years and years of practice and dedication. I think we should just keep Carly here to play for us."

"That would be nice," said Gwen. *That was your plan all along, wasn't it Jason, she thought. That's why we have this huge, beautiful piano now.*

"You can keep playing, Carly. We're all enjoying your music. Can you play something for us that you have written yourself?" asked Jason.

"I can play a solo piece that is very beautiful, but I didn't write it. My friend Sean wrote it when we were in class together in college."

By the time she finished playing everyone was standing in the doorway of the Great Room listening.

"I can delay dinner if we can get you to play some more," said Nettie.

"Oh, no, don't do that. It smells so wonderful. I'm sure everyone is anxious to eat."

They all walked over to the dining room, and Carly was awe struck by the settings on the table. There was a tall floral centerpiece with flowers that seemed exotic, and tall tapered candles that matched the colors of the flowers. Crystal wine glasses graced the table along with pretty China place settings and soft pastel napkins rolled into silver napkin holders.

"Wow! This is so beautiful. Even at the Benson's house we didn't ever have anything this fancy. Do you do this for all your family dinners?"

"We tried to make it a little special in honor of your joining us as a celebrity guest."

"Gosh, I never think of myself as a celebrity."

"We want to welcome you to our little ranch family. We have all lost loved ones in the past and we consider ourselves to be family now. We know we can rely on each other just like we used to rely on our own families, and we want you to know that you can rely on all of us and think of us as a part of your family."

"That's so nice I think I'm going to cry."

Jason wrapped his arm around her. "We don't want to make you cry. This is our welcome to the ranch dinner, Carly. Now we have to get Nettie to tell us what she has been cooking."

"Okay," said Nettie. "You can start by passing around the rice and then I will serve up the Sweet and Sour Chicken. It's Robbie's favorite and we hope it is something you like, Carly."

"Oh, it's my favorite! Whenever we did takeout at Sean's house, I always ordered Sweet and Sour Chicken. The restaurant we ordered from made it with fresh pineapple and I never tried anything else because I liked it so much."

"Well, this was also made with fresh pineapple, so I hope you will like it."

"Gosh, if you are going to keep serving me all this wonderful food, I may have to become your roommate, Jason. Or if you keep wearing that hat, I might have to marry you."

Everyone started laughing and Carly looked over at Jason who had a bit of a stunned expression on his face.

"I was kidding, Jason, just kidding. Please don't look so stunned!"

Stunned? thought Grandma, he looks more like the cat who ate the canary.

"I had my Stetson on today when we went riding," said Jason by way of explanation.

"Now if you will all excuse me for a moment, I think I need to go get my hat."

As soon as everyone figured out his meaning the table erupted in laughter again.

"No hats at the table, Jason," said Grandma. "You are going to have to charm her with your personality."

"I was kidding," said Carly again. "Really, Jason, I didn't mean that. I've never even thought about getting married. I don't think I'm the marrying type."

"Well, I'm sure you will get lots of offers Carly," said Grandma. "But you have plenty of time to make those kinds of decisions."

Grandma saw Jason giving her a frown. *I guess he didn't like the part about lots of offers, thought Grandma.*

Jason looked over at Nettie. "I thought your Italian dishes were all amazing, Nettie, but I really love this one tonight. It seems like you just can't make a wrong move in the kitchen. Coincidentally you just happened to make Carly's favorite for her welcome dinner."

"Here, here," said Roy, raising his glass of wine. "Here's a toast to Nettie's wonderful cooking and a toast to Carly. We hope you will stay here at the ranch with us for a while, Carly, and we will do everything we can to make sure you feel safe."

"Thank you so much! I do feel safer here than I did in Nashville. I know it's hard for people to understand how frightening it is to deal with the knowledge that there is someone out there who wants to kill you. At home, I hardly ever slept for more than an hour or two at a time, but this afternoon I laid down on Jason's bed while he was in the shower and actually fell asleep, and I went back to sleep this morning after Jason got up. There must be something soothing about your ranch. I may be able to cure my insomnia here."

"I think you can feel safe here, Carly," added Robbie. "We have a great security staff, and this house has a state-of-the-art alarm system. Jason can program the security patrol numbers into your phone, and all you have to do is call them if you ever feel something is amiss. If Jason isn't close by, you can call any one of us if you need help."

"That's so nice of you. I hope I won't have to do that. When I get horribly frightened, I have panic attacks, so it's not something I want you to see. Jason saw it at the club Saturday night, but it didn't scare him away. I'm hoping this new therapist can teach me how to control the attacks."

"I'm sure he can help you with that, Carly, but if we can take away the threats to you, that will lessen the occurrence of any panic attacks. Without those big dogs barking outside your windows, you should be able to get more sleep."

"Do you have big dogs, Carly?" asked Robbie.

"No. The sheriff's department has been bringing guard dogs over to my yard at night because there have been attempts to break into my house."

"Good God!" said Grandma. "I'd be afraid of those kinds of dogs."

"There are certain commands you can give them to let them know you aren't a dangerous person. Oddly enough, all the commands are in a foreign language, so sometimes I really have to think to remember them."

"I hope you can stay up here with us for a while, Carly. I think you will have a more peaceful life here on the ranch. It's very rare that anyone tries to enter our property uninvited. I think it's been years since anyone tried to get in."

"That's true," said Roy. "We rarely have problems with intruders."

"We all loved this dinner, Nettie. What other surprises do you have up your sleeve for us?"

"Nothing right now. I thought we should ask Carly about her favorite meals. Any favorites come to mind, Carly?"

"Dr. Dan used to grill Salmon steaks sometimes, and they were wonderful. Sean's mom was a fantastic cook, and she made some amazing dishes with chicken.

"Did you live with them for a while?" asked Jason.

"I did spend a lot of time at their house. I guess you could say I was living there, but it was nothing official. I didn't get my house until after they had moved away."

"Seems like we are ready for dessert and coffee," said Roy, "so I think that means we are ready to tell Carly some Jason stories. Do you want to go first, Gwen?"

"No, no, no. No Jason stories tonight. Carly doesn't want to hear those," Jason protested.

"Yes, I do," said Carly. "This sounds like fun."

"I can't think of anything at the moment," said Gwen. "He was always such a good little boy."

"Well, I have one," said Roy. "When Jason was about 7 or 8 years old, I took a call from his school while his dad was in a meeting with other ranchers. The secretary said Jason had been injured in a little accident at school and he wanted to go home. I asked her if it was anything serious, and she said he was okay, but he wanted to go home. I drove over to the school and went into the main office and Jason was sitting there very stoically. He wasn't crying, but he had bruises all over his face, and his eye was almost swollen shut and was starting to turn purple. I turned around and looked at the secretary and I asked her what the hell had happened to him and why they didn't have an ice pack on his face. She said he didn't want an ice pack, so I told her he was the child, and she was the adult and she needed to go get an ice pack. She told me that a little girl hit him. I asked her what the hell she hit him with that put bruises all over his face. Finally, she admitted the girl hit him with a baseball bat. I told her I needed to know who the girl was so George could speak to her parents. She wouldn't tell me, so I went into the principal's office and asked her what the hell was going on at this school. I told her that Jason's father was going to be very upset to see he had been bashed in the face, and I needed to know the name of the child who hit him. The principal said they had already spoken to the girl's mother, and the mother had taken her home. She didn't want to give me a name, so I asked Jason if he knew the name of the girl. He did, so I told him how sorry I was about what happened. The secretary came back with an ice pack, and I picked up Jason, handed him the ice pack and said, 'Hold this on your eye, buddy,' and started out the door. I looked back at the secretary and told her, 'A child shouldn't decide if he needs first aid, you decide and tell him what is best. It's just that simple.' I walked out and got him in the truck and told him again how sorry I was and asked him if it hurt a lot. Then he started to cry. I told him everything was going to be okay, and we would go home and find something he could take for the pain. We went back to the house and George was there waiting for us and all he could say was 'what the hell happened?' I told George that a little girl had hit him with a baseball bat. Evidently this little girl had been hitting and pinching and kicking him on a continuous basis. He told his dad, but George told him he couldn't hit her back, because boys didn't hit little girls. He told Jason to stay away from her. I'm sure George never dreamed anything like that would happen. George told Jason they were going to go talk to the girl's father. He turned to me and said, 'Maybe you should come along Roy just in case I lose my temper. You can stop me.' So, we all got in my truck and headed over to the girl's house. When we got there her father came to the door and George told him he needed to talk to him and his little girl. The man bent down to Jason and said, 'Oh, boy, you really have a shiner there. I bet that hurts, doesn't it?' George told him his daughter had done that to Jason. 'Your daughter bashed him in the face with a baseball bat.' The man seemed stunned at first and then he started yelling at his daughter to come down to the door. When she got down to the door, her father asked her, 'Did you hit this little boy with a baseball bat?' and she said, 'Yeah! And you know what he did? He took my bat, and he chased me all the way across the field until we got to the fence and then he took my bat and slammed it against the fence over and over again until my bat broke in half. He broke my bat!"

George looked at her and said, 'You're lucky he didn't break it over your head, sweetheart!'

Her dad started apologizing and he looked at the girl and asked her, 'Why would you do something like that? We don't hit little boys with a baseball bat."

She was a brazen little girl and she said, 'well I don't like him.' Her dad told her that didn't matter and there was no excuse for hitting someone. He told her to tell Jason she was sorry, and she said, 'I'm not going to say I'm sorry. I'm not sorry.' She was very belligerent, and the dad was looking at her like he barely knew who she was. So finally, the dad said, 'We will be talking about this tonight and there will be a punishment for doing this. We were supposed to pick up a new puppy this weekend, but I think we need to let that puppy go to another family. If you are going to hurt a little boy like this, I don't feel good about bringing a puppy into our home.' The little girl started screaming about her puppy and finally the mother came to the door and pulled her back. So, the dad looked at Jason and told him, 'I'm so sorry this happened, and she is not ever going to hit you again. I hope you can accept our apology and we can still all be friends; can you do that? Do you think you can be friends now?' Jason looked up at him and said, 'Hell, no!' George burst out laughing and I thought he was never going to stop. Finally, he looked at the little girl and said, 'You ever touch him again and I'm going to call the Sheriff and you will be going to reform school.' We left and took Jason for ice cream. On the way home George said, 'I think that dad needs to start saving up for bail money. Forget about college. That is not a normal little girl.' So poor Jason had a horrible black eye. George took him to the doctor the next day to have his eye checked, but he had that black eye for at least a couple of months."

"I remember that black eye," said Grandma. "Do you remember it, Jason?"

"Yes, but it doesn't bring back fond memories for me like it does for the rest of you."

"Did that little girl ever bother you again?" asked Grandma.

"I don't think I ever saw her again. When my mom came home, she was upset about my eye, and she kept me out of school for a while. When I finally went back to school the girl wasn't there."

Roy laughed. "Yeah, Lexie probably went into that school and raised holy hell with the principal. She probably got that child expelled. Lexie was a big fund raiser for your school. I'm sure the principal didn't want Lexie to take you out of her school."

"I can picture Lexie doing just that!" said Gwen. "She knew how to stand up for herself and her family. I admired her for that, and wished I had been more like Lexie when I was younger."

"So now you carry a gun around in your purse," said Roy. "Does that say, 'don't you dare mess with me now?'

"Don't be telling Carly things like that, Roy."

"I thought we agreed you wouldn't keep carrying that gun with you, Grandma," said Jason.

"I don't remember anything like that, Jason."

"Good luck with that, Jason," said Roy.

"We'll talk about this tomorrow, Grandma."

"We'll see," said Gwen.

"I think dessert is over, Carly. Do you want to play the piano again?" Jason asked.

"No, but I would be glad to help with the dishes tonight."

"No, no," said Gwen. "You are our guest of honor tonight. Nettie and I can take care of the dishes, and Roy and Robbie are always happy to help."

"Okay, but I'll help some other night. Maybe Jason and I can do the dishes together one night. I think I need to answer some emails. Christy keeps texting me wanting to know if I'm okay, and I wanted to talk to you a little bit about starting therapy tomorrow, Jason."

"Okay, we can do that. Do you want to use my computer?"

"No, I can do it on my iPad."

"Why don't you just call her? Do you have a phone, Carly?"

"No. I gave it up after the kidnapping. I didn't want anyone to be able to track me."

"You can use my phone tonight, and I'll find a phone for you. I think it is more apt to keep you safe than endanger you. I want to program all the security numbers into it for you. For now, we will usually be together, so it's not a big issue."

Jason handed her his phone as they walked toward the bedroom. "Here you go. Let your sister know you are okay. Tell her we haven't abducted you and sent you off alone on a wild horse."

Carly laughed. "That might be what she's thinking. She and Jack have been rather protective since I was nabbed."

"No doubt! I'm sure that having someone take you again would be beyond their worst nightmare. Please tell her about the security we have up here so she won't worry about you quite as much. We can stop by and see her tomorrow when we go down to Nashville for your therapy."

Carly was already connecting with Christy and telling her about riding on a horse with Jason.

Jason smiled as he heard snatches of her conversation. Her voice was animated and happy. He hoped Christy could hear the excitement in Carly's voice. He wanted to make her happy. He thought he could do that if he could just convince her to stay here on the ranch for a while. He grabbed the book he had started to read, but in just a few minutes he had dozed off. He felt Carly sitting down on the other side of his bed. He forced his eyes open and looked over at her.

"Coming to bed?" he asked.

"Is that okay? Can I sleep in here with you again?"

"You can always sleep in here with me," he said with a slow smile creeping across his face.

"I told Christy I was sleeping with you,"

"I hope you explained that it was only sleeping. I don't want her to think I invited you up here to take advantage of you."

"I explained after I teased her a bit and told her how handsome you looked in your hat."

"Did you tell her we could go over to see her tomorrow?"

"I did. I think she was expecting me to come back home tomorrow. I had to tell her I wanted to stay here a little longer. She didn't seem very happy about that. She will probably try to change my mind tomorrow."

"I hope you don't change your mind. We have a whole list of things we want to do together, and you wanted to start working on some of your songs. When we have extra time, I can teach you how to ride. Clearly our calendar is too full for you to think of going back home."

Carly laughed and moved over beside him so he could put his arms around her. "I think I'll stay, Jason. I'm trying to think of ways to put my life back together, and I'm hoping the therapist can help me. If I go home, I know I'll be too frightened to leave my house to get to therapy."

"And you'd probably miss me," Jason said as he reached out and put his arms around her.

"I would," she murmured sleepily.

Chapter 10

Jason walked down the hall and went into the main kitchen. Grandma Gwen and Nettie were sitting there having coffee.
"Still have coffee left, ladies?"
"Of course," said Grandma. "Help yourself, it's right there. Maybe Carly will want some too - maybe save some for her?"
"I just took her some from the other kitchen, but then I decided I wanted more. She's going to start therapy today, so I'm going to take her down to Nashville. She talked to her sister last night, and Christy was hoping she was coming back home today. When she said that, all these terrible images went through my mind about the perp and everything we have learned so far about her kidnapping. I don't want her to go home. I think it's too dangerous, so I hope I've talked her into staying. I guess she thinks she's been here long enough, or maybe she thinks she's in the way. But I hope I've changed her mind for now."
Grandma Gwen looked up, "Well, Jason, we weren't eavesdropping or anything this morning, but we heard you both giggling and laughing down there, so I can't imagine why she'd want to go home after that."
"Okay, Grandma, what are you asking now? Spit it out because I know you're going to."
"We just heard you laughing; it was nice to hear. It made me feel good to know that you were happy, that you guys were having fun – whatever you were doing."
"Grandma, not whatever we were doing. We were laughing, we were joking with each other, and then she said she was going to miss that when she went home, and I was stunned. I hadn't thought about her going home."
He sat down at the table with his coffee. Grandma Gwen looked up at him and said, "You really like this girl, don't you, Jason."
He looked back at her and asked, "Grandma, why do you keep asking me questions about my love life? I don't ask you about yours."
"Well, no, Jason. I'm old and I don't have any love life since your grandfather died. I just have my paintings and my good friends like Nettie. So, since I have no love life, I have to live vicariously through yours."
"Hasn't been much fun lately, has it?"
"No, you haven't given me much to fantasize about in recent years. You don't want her to go home, do you?"

"No, Grandma, I don't. It's been nice having her here."

"Yeah, you have a little company in your bed down there."

"Grandma, it's not what you're thinking, but I still want her to stay. I don't want her to go home where she might be in danger. And yes, it is nice. You wake up in the morning and there's someone there with you. So, we laugh and kid around. We talked about lots of things that we would like to do together."

"No. Don't let her go home. We saw some horrible things on the news today," Gwen lowered her voice to almost a whisper. "I don't know if you have seen it yet, but the news was not good. Nettie and I hoped Carly doesn't see it, but I don't know how you are going to avoid it."

"Oh, Crap! What were they talking about."

"They were talking about the bodies they found and an empty grave. The reporter said they discovered the bodies near the site where Carly was found after the kidnapping. They mentioned that the kidnapper had certainly meant to use that empty grave for Carly."

"Wonderful!" Jason said sarcastically. "Do they ever stop to think about how Carly might feel if she hears that report?"

"I don't think they ever think about the victims. It seems like there are no holds barred when it comes to reporting their stories."

"Oh, crap!" said Jason. He heard Carly walking down the hall and he stopped talking.

Gwen got the hint and started talking about plans for dinner.

"Carly, Jason if you tell us when you will be back tonight, Nettie and I might cook you a nice dinner. Nettie's thinking about doing something Italian. We know it will be delicious."

He looked at Carly, "We could probably be back for dinner, you think?"

"I'm not singing tonight so we can come back whenever you want. I want to pick up some things at my house. I think I'll get some of my music. Maybe some of the songs I never finished. I haven't had a lot of motivation in the last couple of years, but I feel like I could finish some of them now. Maybe I will be inspired by your beautiful piano. Which reminds me Jason, I haven't heard you play it yet."

"Welllll," he hesitated. "I don't really play piano that much."

"You don't play piano? You have this gorgeous piano here. Is it just a piece of furniture?"

"I've been thinking about learning."

"I can teach you – we'll do that tomorrow."

"I'm not sure I could ever learn to move my hands around the keyboard the way you do."

"Oh Jason. You have great piano hands. Look at these fingers!!"

"Would you like more coffee, Carly?"

"No thanks. I'm a little nervous about starting therapy today. I don't want to get too jittery."

He walked over and sat down next to her and put his arm around her. "Don't be nervous. Dr. Mac is a great guy. First sessions are always easy."

She leaned over and put her head against his arm. "I'm trying to be calm. I've been rehearsing all the words in my head that I want to use today to tell him what happened to me. I just hope I can say them out loud when I get there."

Jason thought she might be on the verge of tears. "I'm sure you will, Carly. Anyone who can escape from a kidnapper like that bastard has to have a ton of strength and courage."

"I hope I do. I've never been able to tell anyone this before. I wanted to, but I kept it inside for so many years that it just kept getting harder to say the words."

Jason felt a little confused. At first, he thought she wanted to talk about the kidnapping, but maybe she was going back to the day her mother got killed. He was hoping there wasn't yet a third horrible trauma she had experienced.

He gave her shoulder a little squeeze. "I'm sure you'll be fine. Dr. Mac is very easy to talk to."

"Maybe."

Carly walked down the hall to get ready for her appointment.

"Are you paying for this therapy, Jason? "

"Yes, I am. And we won't need to be selling any horses. I have it covered."

"You always say that, Jason. I have it covered. You know, you still have the settlement money from the lawsuit for your parents. Have you ever used any of it?"

"No. What good was all that anyway? No amount of money could ever bring them back."

"I know," she said softly. "But maybe you'll find a good purpose for it one day."

"Do you need anything, Grandma?"

"No, no. I don't. I was just asking."

Chapter 11

Dr. Mac looked over at Carly, "I'd like to continue our conversation, Carly, but I have another patient coming in now. I'm wondering if you could come back tomorrow. Should we ask Jason if that's possible?"

"Okay. but you're not going to tell him what I told you, are you?"

"No, Carly. Everything you tell me is confidential. Of course, you can tell Jason about it if you want to, or you can ask me to tell him if that would be easier for you."

"No. I don't want him to know. I don't want to tell him."

"That's fine, Carly. There's no reason you need to share this with him unless you want to. Let's see if you can come back tomorrow and we'll talk some more. There are some things I want you to understand about what happened to you."

Dr. Mac used the intercom to summon Jason into the office.

Jason saw the tears in Carly's eyes and immediately sat down next to her. "Are you okay, Carly? Can I put my arm around you?"

Carly nodded silently and Jason slipped his arm around her and pulled her over close to him.

"We talked about some difficult things today, Jason. I'm wondering if it would be possible for you to come back in tomorrow, say about 1 o'clock?"

"Of course. We can do that. Is that okay, Carly?"

She nodded silently and put her head on his shoulder.

"Okay. I'll have some sandwiches sent over and we'll make it a lunch time meeting."

"But it's just for you and me, right Dr. Mac?" Carly sobbed.

"Yes. Carly. But we'll offer Jason a sandwich, okay?"

She nodded again. Jason brushed the side of her face gently with his fingers. "I'm sorry this has been so hard for you, Carly, but things are going to get better. Dr. Mac and I are going to work as hard as we can to help you feel better. You just need to remember that it takes time. Think of this process as taking little baby steps toward your goal."

She nodded again, but the tears were still streaming down her face. Jason brushed the tears away and kissed her cheek. "Okay, let's head out."

They left the office together and Dr. Mac tried to put aside the sadness he felt about her disclosures.

When they got out to the car, Jason asked Carly, "Do you want to go visit with Christy or should we do that tomorrow?"

"Tomorrow would be better. Can you please send her a text and tell her I have a headache and we'll come by tomorrow?"

"I can do that. Do you want to go by your house now?"

"Yes. I need some things there."

Carly was still crying, and Jason squeezed her hand. "Anything I can do? Should we stop for ice cream?"

"No. Let's just get my stuff and go back to the ranch."

"Christy says she hopes you feel better tomorrow."

"Okay."

Carly was deathly quiet for the rest of the ride. When they got to her house, she gathered up some things and gave them to Jason to put in the car. She packed up a small suitcase of clothes which gave Jason some hope that she was planning to stay with him longer. After he put the suitcase in the car, he came back into the house to find her sitting at her piano staring off into space. He sat down next to her and gently wrapped his arm around her shoulders. "I'm not sure what you talked about today, but I'm sorry you're so upset. I'm sure many of the things that happened to you were horrible, and that makes it so much harder to talk about them."

"I'll tell you when we get back to the ranch. I just can't say it right now."

"That's okay, Carly. You don't have to tell me. You can keep it between you and Dr. Mac if that's easier for you."

"I want to tell you, but I don't want anyone else to know."

"Okay. Let's head back to the ranch."

Carly was silent all the way back to the ranch. Jason kept wondering what had happened and what she was going to tell him. He thought maybe they should cancel out on dinner plans tonight. He'd let Grandma know as soon as they got back.

Carly walked back to their bedroom suite as soon as she entered the house. Jason walked off to find Grandma.

"Hey, Grandma, I think Carly and I need to cancel out on dinner tonight. Something happened in therapy that has her very upset, so I'm going to let her stay back in our suite for a while."

"That's too bad," said Gwen. "We can bring you some dinner later if you like."

"Thanks. Let's see how things go. I'll let you know later."

Jason walked back to the bedroom where he found Carly sitting in the armchair sobbing.

He picked her up and just held her in his lap without saying anything. She wrapped her arms around his neck, and he could feel hot tears touching his skin. After her sobs subsided a little, he asked her, "Did you like Dr. Mac? If it isn't a good fit, you can tell me, and we can go anywhere and see anyone you want to see. I want you to be comfortable with any therapist you see."

"I liked him. It was good. He made me look at some things differently. He asked some questions I couldn't answer."

Carly was quiet for a few moments, so Jason just waited to see if she had more to say.

"I told him something I've never told anyone before. I've told you some ugly things, but this was something I've never talked about. He told me what happened wasn't my fault, it wasn't ever my fault. It made me feel better."

"Was that about when your mother got killed, Carly?"

"Yeah, it was. Kind of…"

"You know that wasn't your fault, don't you? You were just a little girl. You were only six years old, weren't you?"

"Yeah. I was little. I told him what my father did."

"You told him he shot your mother, right?"

"Yeah, I told him that, too."

Carly got very quiet again. He just held her and waited. He didn't want to ask her anything or try to make her talk to him.

"I tried to tell him what my father did, but I just kept saying – my father he….my father he…and I couldn't say the words, so Dr. Mac asked, 'he molested you, Carly?' and I just nodded my head and cried."

Jason thought he might be sick. He had a lump in his throat that was choking him. He couldn't think of anything to say.

"He took me out in the woods, and he hurt me. When I heard his footsteps, I tried to hide under my blankets or under the bed, but he found me and carried me out into the woods. He covered my mouth so I couldn't scream, and I could hardly breathe. I begged him to stop but he wouldn't. He made horrible grunting sounds and said that Daddies have to show their little girls how much they love them."

"I'm so sorry, Carly."

"He said if I told my mama what he was doing to me then he would have to shoot her. I didn't tell her, but I was bleeding. I kept bleeding and she saw it and she figured out what he did to me. She told him we were going away, and we were never coming back. I never told her. I told him that I didn't tell her, but he picked up the gun and shot her anyway. I begged him not to hurt her. I never told her that he was molesting me. She just figured it out, so he shot her."

Jason felt like most of the blood was draining out of his head. He was at a loss for words. He felt hot tears stinging the backs of his eyelids. Finally, he looked at her and touched her cheek.

"Oh, my God, Carly. You know it was not your fault, right? He was a horrible man. Only a horrible man could do something like that. It was never your fault. You were only a little girl. Just an innocent child. Your mother wouldn't want you to think it was your fault he shot her."

"That's what Dr. Mac said. He said it was never my fault. I was only a child. He said my momma probably would have wanted me to tell her what he was doing to me. So, when she found out she was going to take me away so he couldn't hurt me anymore, but instead, he shot her. I never told anybody what he did to me. I always thought it was my fault. My father told me it was my fault."

Jason pulled her even closer to him. "I'm so sorry, Carly. Listen to what Dr. Mac is telling you. It was never your fault. He was a horrible man. A horrible man." Jason took a couple of deep breaths and sat very still. His brain seemed to be frozen. *What do you say? What do you say to a little girl who got raped by her father when she was only six years old,* he thought?

Finally, he said, "I'm glad you told Dr. Mac. I'm glad you told me. You've been holding this inside for too many years. All these years you've been thinking it was your fault, but it was never your fault. You were just a child, Carly."

"I told him my father shot himself after he killed her, and I went to live with the neighbors. He asked me if the neighbors were the people who told me my mom had died. But I told him I never really knew she was dead. I kept waiting for her. I thought she was going to come back to get me. So I was waiting for her and waiting for her. I didn't realize until I was much older that she was dead. She wasn't ever going to come back for me. Dr. Mac asked me if we had a funeral service or a burial service for my mother, but I told him no. Then he asked me what happened when the police came, but I didn't remember any police. Then he just said "hmm" and we didn't talk about it anymore."

Jason's brain was reeling. He had the same thoughts as Dr. Mac. *No burial, no funeral service, no police. There was a dead body. Where did it go? Why didn't someone tell this little girl that her mother was dead? How could anyone let a little girl wait for her dead mother to come back for her? He wondered how many nights she cried for her mother. Who was there to comfort her? Maybe only Christy?*

Jason held her and rocked her until she cried herself to sleep. He brushed away his own tears he felt running down his cheeks. *He tried to image what it must have been like for her to see her father pick up a gun and kill her mother. He couldn't even begin to image what it must have been like to have been raped by her father when she was so little. He wondered how she could have kept this hurt inside her for so many years without telling anyone. Did the neighbors know what the father had done to her? Did they know why he had killed her mother? He tried to remember being six years old. He wasn't sure how much a six-year-old would understand about death. He didn't think a six-year-old would understand what the father was doing to her. It was impossible for him to imagine a man who could commit such a violent act against his daughter.*

Grandma texted him to see if they wanted some dinner, but he told her he wasn't hungry, and Carly was sleeping now. She slept in his arms for a long time, and finally he reached down and took off her sandals and picked her up and put her into bed with her clothes on. Jason stripped off his jeans and boots and crawled in beside her and tried to silence the dark thoughts that were pounding on his brain.

The next morning Carly woke up and felt Jason's long limbs stretched out over her, his arms wrapped around her. She laid still and thought about some of the things Dr. Mac told her during therapy yesterday.

"Are you awake, Carly?" Jason whispered softly.

"Yeah, I'm awake."

"Do you need me to move away from you?"

"No, Jason. Don't move away."

"Okay. I'm good with that."

"You don't have to ask me that anymore. I feel safe when you're close to me. I'll just tell you if I need you to move away."

"Okay. I'm sorry about everything you've been through. I'm glad you were able to talk about it yesterday. I hope you will start to feel better in a few days."

"Maybe I will."

"Should we get up and have some breakfast? Would you like to go for an early morning ride on Molly?"

"I would. That would be nice."

"Okay. I'll ask one of the guys over in the barn to saddle both horses up and bring them over to the house for us. Let's get some coffee and a little breakfast."

While they were eating breakfast Jason heard one of the workers arriving with the horses.

Grandma looked out the window. "I see we have ready to ride horse delivery this morning. Are you and Carly going for a ride?"

"I thought Carly might be ready for a short riding lesson this morning."

He was grateful that Grandma didn't try to ask anything about the therapy session yesterday.

After Carly walked down the hall to get ready, Jason told Grandma that they were going back to Nashville for another therapy session in the afternoon.

"Gosh, I hope it won't be as upsetting for her today."

"I think it will be easier today. I hope."

"We postponed dinner last night. If you both feel up to it, you could join us tonight."

"Okay. We'll see what happens today. We're going to visit her sister this afternoon if Carly feels okay. I'm sure her sister is disappointed that Carly isn't coming back to Nashville this week. Don't change your plans or postpone anything on our account, Grandma. I think the next few weeks are going to be a bit rough for her. She's suffered a lot of horrible traumas in her life. There are a lot of things she is going to need to work through. She hasn't had an easy life. It wasn't anything like the life we had here."

"Well, she lost her parents when she was very young, didn't she?"

"Yes, she did. But even that wasn't the hardest part."

"Are you doing okay, Jason? You seem happier, but I worry about you taking on so many of her problems. This could be enough to trigger some of your former demons.

"Honestly, Grandma, when I look at her life, I can only be thankful for the life I had. I lost my parents, but I didn't lose them when I was a little kid. I didn't have to grow up with no one to love me and make me feel secure. Helping her has started to make me feel better. It has given me a real purpose. Yesterday she revealed some secrets she has been keeping for 20 years, and then she told me about them last night. It was hard for her, but I think it will help her heal."

"I hope so," said Grandma. "If you aren't up to having dinner with us in the evenings, I could freeze some dinners for you and Carly. You could just microwave them; or I could make some sandwiches for the two of you."

"Thanks. That sounds good. I don't want her to miss a lot of meals. She seems very thin. Can you order more fruit next time you get a delivery? I think she usually eats a lot of fruit."

"I can do that."

They both heard Carly coming down the hall toward the kitchen. Jason had his hat on, and she smiled at him.

"You're wearing your hat again. Can you wear it this afternoon when we go to see Christy?"

"I can if you want me to. Maybe we need to get you a Stetson, and some cowboy boots. We can turn you into a real cowgirl."

"That's funny. Sean asked me if I was going to turn into a Cowgirl."

"Okay. We'll send him a picture when we get your hat."

Jason and Carly headed out the front door to start their ride.

Chapter 12

Jason and Carly walked into Dr. Mac's office, and he ushered them back to the treatment room.

"We have a little extra time today as one of my patients postponed their appointment until later in the day. Let's have some lunch and you can fill me in on life at the ranch. Jason looks more like a rancher today. Let's eat and then we'll let Jason work on his computer, and you and I will talk. Okay, Carly?"

"Jason can stay. I told him what my father did to me."

"That was very brave of you, Carly."

"I wasn't so brave. I sat in his lap and cried the whole time I was telling him."

"That still counts as being brave. The fact that you kept this secret for so many years makes it just that much harder to disclose now. You have had all those years in between to blame yourself for what happened. That's why I wanted you to come back today. I didn't want you to blame yourself for a minute longer than necessary. That's our mission today. I want you to understand that you were the victim. Your father had a sickness he used to manipulate and blame you for what happened. But first, tell me what you have been doing at the ranch."

"Jason and I went for a ride this morning and I had my first lesson riding Molly all by myself. After our meeting we're going to visit with my sister Christy. That's why Jason is wearing his hat. I told Christy how handsome he looked in his hat when we went on our trail ride this week. Christy is not very happy with me, but I'm going to stay up at the ranch a little while longer. I feel safer up there, and I've been sleeping at night."

"I think that's a wise decision, Carly, but your sister probably misses you. Can you invite her to come up to the ranch and visit with you?"

"Of course, you can. We'll talk to her about that today. Then we are going to go find a Stetson for Carly so we can turn her into a real cowgirl, and we're going to send her picture wearing the hat to Sean and Maia."

Dr. Mac laughed. "Sean was your friend from college, right Carly?" Dr. Mac was careful not to disclose that he knew Sean and was friends with his entire family. Sean's mother, Donna, was a psychiatrist colleague.

"Yes. He was the best friend I ever had. I was very sad when they moved away. I hoped they were going to ask me to go to Utah with them, but they didn't. When I was in rehab,

Sean and Maia wanted me to go to Utah for treatment, but my insurance company refused to pay for rehab in Utah, so I stayed in Tennessee."

"Jason has lots of room at his ranch, maybe you can invite them out to visit you."

"I guess I could. Maia loves riding, and now I'm learning how to ride too."

"It sounds like you are enjoying yourself there, Carly. Are you going to stay for a while?"

"I will if Jason doesn't mind."

"Jason doesn't mind. Jason wants you to stay, Carly. Jason wants you to be safe."

Dr. Mac laughed. "Do you feel safe there at the ranch, Carly?"

"I do. It's been a long time since I've slept all night."

"I think it is a good thing for you to feel safe again and being able to sleep can help with your recovery. Have you thought about going back to the club to sing again?"

"No, not yet. I don't think I'm ready. I know the kidnapper wants to kill me, and I'm afraid he might escape from prison again. He knows how to find me if I'm at the club."

"I guess that's true. Sad, but true. It seems like the best plan would be for the prison system to find a way to keep him incarcerated."

"We're working on that," said Jason. "I'm trying to find a way to get him transferred to a maximum-security prison."

"That should solve the problem," said Dr. Mac. "Well, let's go ahead and talk about the incidents with your father, Carly."

"Okay. I'm going to try not to cry today."

"It's okay if you do. This is going to be a difficult conversation for all of us. Your father is someone we would classify as a pedophile. As an adult now, you know pedophiles are sexually attracted to young children. He was probably a psychopath, a person who suffers from a chronic mental disorder, often exhibiting abnormal or violent social behavior. Psychopaths are generally incapable of love. They are pathological liars, and masters of manipulative behavior. That is how he controlled you, Carly. He threatened to kill your mother if you told her about the molestation. He told you this was how Daddies showed love to their little girls. He said he was teaching you how to be a woman. All of these were manipulative lies."

"I told him I didn't want to be a woman. I just wanted to be a little girl. Then he slapped me. When he raped me and I cried, he would punch me."

"That fits the profile of a psychopath. They are often violent. They rationalize their wrongdoing. They have no conscience, no remorse, no empathy. They feel nothing when someone else is suffering. You were violated by a person you had been taught to trust. We obey our parents, we follow their advice, they tell us they know what is best for us. We assume they are all knowing, caring adults. We are not taught to question their directives. There would have been nothing in your six-year-old past that would have made you think your father was lying to you. He kept you quiet by threatening to shoot your mother. You had no reason to doubt what he was telling you, and in the end, he did shoot your mother, but not because of anything you did. You were just a convenient scapegoat, a way to rationalize wrongdoing. He told you it was your fault, but you were only his victim, just like your mother was. You had no way to prevent him from pulling the trigger. You kept your end of the bargain, but he shot your mother anyway. That's what psychopaths do. In their own eyes they are never wrong. They can justify all their horrible behavior in their own mind. Even if you had told your mother, that wouldn't have been the wrong thing for you to do. It sounds like she didn't know what he was doing to you. He may have drugged her when he was going to molest you. He forced your silence with his threats to kill your mother. You obeyed and kept silent. You never wanted him to kill your mother, but he had probably planned to kill her all along. You couldn't have stopped him from killing her. You need to think about what happened from the viewpoint of a six-year-old, not the viewpoint of the adult you are now. One of the saddest parts of this trauma is you never spoke to anyone about it until yesterday. You have lived all these years with this sadness and never trusted anyone to help you. I'm glad you were finally able to trust me and to trust Jason to help you. When your mother died, did anyone explain anything to you about death? Did they tell you that you could hold your mother in your heart forever or that she would be watching out for you from heaven?"

"No. They never told me where she was. The neighbors kept me in the house, and they wouldn't let me go out to look for her. I didn't know she was dead. Maybe she isn't dead. Maybe he isn't dead. Maybe they just didn't want me. Maybe they never wanted me. Maybe my mother and father just left me there for the men who were going to come to lay inside me."

"What?" said Jason suddenly. "What men?"

"My father said there were men who were going to come to lay inside me and I had to learn not to cry. One day there were two men who came to the farm in an old truck, and I ran and hid in the pantry. Martha found me there and asked me why I was crying. I told her I was afraid of the men who were coming to lay inside me. She asked me what I was talking about, and I pointed to the men outside and told her that they came to lay inside me. She told me that God didn't like men who did that and there wouldn't be any men coming to hurt me. She said Pop would never allow any man to hurt me like that."

"What a bastard," Jason exploded. Dr. Mac gave him a cautionary warning look that stopped him from speaking. Jason closed his eyes and tried to take measured breaths.

"Did the men go away?" asked Dr. Mac.

"Yes. Martha said they were looking for land to buy."

"Did you go out on dates when you were in high school or college, Carly?"

"No. I was afraid that's what the boys wanted to do. I asked Christy if you had to let the boy have sex with you if you went to the movies with him. She said you just had to say no, but I knew that didn't work."

"When you were little did you ever understand what death was? Did you see people die in TV films or movies?"

"We didn't have a TV. I never went to a movie until I met Sean. By that time, I understood what it was to die, but I never liked movies that were violent."

"You said Sean was your best friend. Did you have any romantic feelings for him? If you don't want to answer this question in front of Jason, I understand."

"No. Sean was like a brother. I always wished I had a brother. He taught me how to ride a bike and how to drive a car. He was going to teach me how to swim that summer, but then they moved away. I shared a room with Maia when I stayed at their house. We were like sisters."

"Did you stay with the Bensons often?"

"Yes. Christy was living with Jack, and Mom and Pop had moved out to the retirement home, so I really didn't have a place to stay unless I went to Christy and Jack's apartment. I left things at their place, but it was uncomfortable to stay there. I felt like I was an intruder. At the Benson's it was always fun. I played duets with Sean and Maia, and their family did a lot of things together. They always included me. I even went on some trips with them to visit their relatives. I really liked Sean's grandfather. He even came to see me when I was in the hospital. I always wished I could have a grandfather like him. I never had any grandparents."

"Did you ever meet any of your mother's relatives or family members?"

"No. I asked her once if I had grandparents and she said they were dead."

"How about relatives on your father's side?"

"No. Once I think he said he had a brother. I think he said the brother was a bastard or something ugly like that."

"Someone just like your father. Birds of a feather..." Jason interjected as Mac gave him a look.

"Did the neighbors tell you what happened to your mother? Did you know your father was dead?"

"No. I stayed in their house after they found me in the chicken coop, and I slept with Christy that night. When we got up in the morning my father's old truck was gone, and I thought they both had left. I waited for them to come back for me. Christy said she asked her mother where my parents went, and her mother told her not to ever ask about them again. Martha said I was going to stay there with them, and we shouldn't ever talk about my parents again. She made us promise not to tell anyone my parents had left. She said the Sheriff would send me to an orphanage if they couldn't find my parents. I was scared, and I didn't know what an orphanage was. I thought maybe it was a jail for kids that nobody wanted."

"So you kept going to the same school with Christy and just stayed with the neighbors?"

"Yes. I liked them and I hoped they wouldn't send me away. We had dinner at night at their house. We never had dinner when I lived with my parents. We never had much to eat. My mother said he liked his liquor more than he liked buying food for us. He hit her when she said that. I remember she fell down on the floor, and I couldn't get her to wake up."

"He was a horrible, violent man, Carly. I'm sorry you and your mother had to be subjected to that kind of violence."

"Sean told me he was adopted by the Bensons when he was just a baby. I thought how nice it must have been to have been adopted into a family like that. I wished I could have been adopted and had nice parents like his. They always had plenty of food and they lived in a nice warm house. Everyone there was always smiling. His dad never hit him or Maia. He barely even raised his voice if he was angry. He found a bike for me at a garage sale and cleaned it up so I could ride it to my classes. Sean's mom was like a real mother. She helped me find dresses to wear for the piano competitions. Donna asked me what my mother was like, but I couldn't remember much about her. Martha said my mother was pretty, so that's what I told Donna."

"When the Bensons moved to Utah would you have gone with them if they had asked you?"

"Yes. I loved them, but they just didn't love me." Carly started to cry, and Jason pulled her over onto his lap and tried to soothe her.

"I think you're wrong about that, Carly. I think they do love you. Didn't Sean and Maia come out to help search for you when you were kidnapped?"

"I don't know. I don't think so." Dr. Mac did a mental oops! He only knew that because Donna was a colleague.

"I think they did. They came to see you in the hospital, didn't they? Didn't you tell me Sean stayed at the hospital with you during some of the nights?"

"Yes, he did. I was frightened. I was afraid the kidnapper was going to find me. I was in a lot of pain and Sean let me cry."

"Didn't the whole family come back out after you woke up from your coma?"

Carly nodded her head.

"I think they do love you, Carly. I don't think Sean and Maia ever wanted to move away, but their father had a great job offer in Utah, didn't he?"

"I guess. I just wanted them to be my family. I never had a dad who was always nice like that. Dr. Dan sometimes got up on Sundays and made Belgian waffles for all of us. We ate them with strawberries and whipped cream. That was the first time I ever ate strawberries. Christy and I used to go to the abandoned farm and pick apples, but we never had any other kinds of fruit. I was never hungry when I stayed at the Bensons. We ate breakfast every morning before Sean and I went to class. Sean even packed lunches for both of us when we had a long day of classes. Sometimes he would buy lunch for both of us in the cafeteria. When it rained, he would drive us to class in his car. We didn't have to walk in the rain. He gave me his car when they left for Utah so I could keep going to classes, but I didn't have enough money to continue school."

"I think they all loved you, Carly. They may have assumed you wouldn't want to move away from your sister."

"Maybe."

"Carly, you have people who love you now, and they all want to see you get better and feel stronger. You can invite your sister, or Sean and his family to visit you at the Ranch. I don't think Jason will mind. You can keep in touch with everyone and visit with them. You could even go to Utah to visit Sean and his family. Take Jason with you!"

"We could do that Carly."

"I guess the horrible kidnapper wouldn't find me there!"

"No. He wouldn't. It would be a long walk from a road crew in Tennessee to Utah."

They all laughed.

"Do you understand everything I have told you about your father, Carly?"

"I think so. But why was he such a horrible man? Do you think he's really dead?"

"There isn't an easy answer for that, Carly. He was probably a psychopath. They are sometimes the product of their environment or some type of trauma occurring in their childhood. There are theories that psychopathy can be a genetic or inherited condition caused by the lack of development of parts of the brain responsible for impulse control and regulation of emotions."

"Do you think I will ever be mean like my father? Could I become a psychopath? Can it be inherited?"

"There are some mental diseases that do run in families, but I don't think this is something you should worry about. Little children who exhibit signs of psychopathy often act out with violent or cruel behavior toward animals. There are usually signs, early on, that point toward a mental disorder. One of the signs would be a lack of empathy upon observing someone in pain or an animal in distress. I'm sure you didn't exhibit any of these signs in your childhood, and you didn't spend a very long period of your life with your father, so I don't think there is any possibility you have learned to be cruel."

"God, I hope not. I wouldn't ever want to be like him. I was secretly glad when he went away, but I did miss my mother."

"Those are natural emotions, Carly. He hurt you, so you weren't sorry when he was gone. Your mother didn't hurt you and you missed her. All your emotions seem normal to me."

"Maybe. But I still don't like it when people touch me. I still like them to keep their distance. That can't be very normal."

"That is the result of your kidnapping, Carly. Gradually I think that fear of closeness will go away. You and Jason seem to be able to share a close relationship with each other. You don't feel any fear when Jason is close to you, do you?"

"No. I feel safer when he is close to me. When I go to bed at night, I lie right up against him and then I feel safe enough to sleep. It's odd, really, but when he holds me, I feel comforted. I guess I shouldn't feel that way. After all, I'm not a child. I shouldn't need to be comforted."

"I don't think feeling comforted has anything to do with being a child. Sure, a child looks to his parents for comfort when he is sad or injured, but you have been through a terrible ordeal, and just being able to start to feel safe again and being able to sleep at night are the first steps toward recovery. Feeling comforted by Jason is completely normal, and it is a good thing. I'm sure Jason wants you to feel comforted by his presence. Comforting someone is what we do when we care about a person. It sets us apart from the psychopaths who can feel no empathy."

"I'm sure Jason is never going to be a psychopath. You should see how good he is with the horses and the dogs at the ranch. His horse, Charlie, just loves him!"

"You're good with animals too, Carly. Bandit comes up to the house to sleep on your feet at night because you are so good to him."

Dr. Mac laughed. "I think we are safe in assuming that neither one of you will ever develop any cruel streaks. Most importantly, I hope you have come to realize that what happened to your mother was never your fault. Both you and your mother were victims of a very sick man. I only wish you could have talked to someone about this abuse many years ago. This was a terrible secret to hold inside you for so many years. I hope you will begin to feel better now that we have brought it out into the open and talked about it."

"I do feel better. I even felt better after I told Jason about it last night. I cried for a long time and then I finally fell asleep. So, we both slept there in the chair until early morning. I made Jason miss his dinner."

"Well, there may be other missed dinners as we go through this process. I'm sure there are many more concerns we will need to discuss. But I think this is one of the most important ordeals you needed to talk about. We will surely have some more bumps in the road, but that is all part of the process of healing. I guess you two are off to find that Stetson for Carly now?"

"You bet," said Jason. "We are going to turn her into a cowgirl. Before you know it, she is going to be more popular than Miranda Lambert."

"I'm so glad to see you two are having some fun together. Having fun is a big part of taking your life back, Carly."

"I guess. But sometimes I feel guilty about going out and having fun when I owe money to so many people. Some of the people who saved my life never got paid."

"Trust me, Carly. Everyone in the health care industry knows how long it takes to get paid. I think Jason said he is working with your insurance company and trying to resolve some of the issues. Please don't feel guilty about enjoying yourself with Jason. They saved your life so you could live your life again. In time, everything will get resolved. It's a process that can sometimes take as long as the healing. So go have fun. Visit with your sister and your niece and remember you are still here to enjoy them."

"Okay. I'll try to remember that."

"That's good, Babe. Isn't there a song like that? Girls Just Wanna have Fun?"

Carly laughed. "Yes, Jason. It's a song."

They thanked Dr. Mac and said their goodbyes and headed off to see Christy. Carly was quiet after they started driving.

"Is everything okay, Babe? You're awfully quiet."

"I'm okay. I'm just trying to think of a way to convince Christy that it wouldn't be good for me to come back to Nashville now. She was upset when I told her I wasn't coming back to stay."

"Let's invite them to come up to visit this weekend. Maybe that will make her feel better."

"I can try that."

After they got to the house, they played with Lindsey for a while. Then Carly excused herself to go to her bedroom to pick up some things she needed. Jason watched Christy follow her into the bedroom after a few minutes.

"I want you to come back to Nashville, Carly. I'm worried about you being up there on that ranch. We don't know much about Jason. I don't like having you so far away."

"It's not that far, Christy. Maybe you could come for a visit. I feel safe up there. It's the first time I've felt safe since the kidnapping. I've been able to let Jason hold me when I'm frightened. It takes some of the edge off my pain. I've started sleeping at night again. I don't get up with the chickens like Jack used to say. It's hard to explain, but when you go without sleep for a long time your brain starts to slow down, and it just becomes hard to function. I feel much better now that I'm sleeping. Jason lets me lay right up against him so I can fall asleep. His body is warm and comforting. If I have a bad dream, he wakes up and wraps his arms around me and tells me everything is going to be all right. He makes me laugh in the mornings when we wake up. I like the therapist he found for me. I told him some secrets I've never told anyone before. If I come back here, I know I'll be too frightened to go to therapy. I like Jason. He's been very good to me. He's helping me with my house problems and all the medical bills. He's smart. He's much more worldly than I have ever been. I like everyone there at the ranch. They have a security crew that covers all the property, and the house has a separate security system. You should see the house, Christy. It's huge. I think his parents had planned on having a large family, but they only ended up with Jason."

"So, what price do you think you will pay for all this attention, Carly? What do you think Jason wants from you?"

"So far, nothing. He said he just likes having me there with him. We even talked about sex, which was hard for me. He knows I'm not ready for that kind of relationship. Sometimes Christy I do get some strange quivery little feelings when he is holding me, but I try not to think about them. He looks very handsome in his hat, don't you agree?"

"Yes, Carly. He is a strikingly handsome man. That's part of what worries me. I don't want him to hurt you. I don't want to see you suffer again. If you come back here, I'll take you to therapy any time you need to go. Please think about this."

"I will, but for now I think it will be better for me to stay up there. If that perp breaks out of jail again, I don't want to be where he can find me. I don't want to put you or Lindsey in danger either. Staying here with you could jeopardize your safety. I'm too frightened to stay at my house alone. Jason said if I have to go back to my house he would stay there with me, but I don't want to take him away from the ranch. They need him there. It's a much bigger ranch than I had imagined. The horses are beautiful. I hope you'll come up and visit."

"I'll talk to Jack and see if we can do that."

Carly took her small suitcase out to the family room where Jason picked it up for her.

"Are we ready to go, Babe? Did you talk your sister into coming up for a visit? Did you mention the ponies we have for little girls to ride?"

"Are there little girls on your ranch, Uncle Jason?" Lindsey asked.

"Not yet, but we're hoping to see one soon," answered Jason. "Please come up to visit us, Christy. Carly misses you."

Carly looked at Christy. "Just to show you that I am starting to get better, I need to do this."

Carly walked over to Christy and slid her arm around her sister's back and gave her a quick kiss on the cheek. Then she reached down and gave Lindsey a hug. When Jason looked over at Christy, he could see she had tears in her eyes.

"Thank you, Carly. Thank you. Keep getting better, okay?"

"We'll make sure she does. We are all looking out for her."

Carly was quiet on the way home in the car. After a few minutes she started to cry, and Jason pulled over at a rest stop and put his arms around her.

"You miss her, don't you?"

"Yes. She wanted me to come back, but I feel so frightened there. I don't think she understands what it's like to be that frightened."

"Probably she doesn't. Most people have never been through the kind of horrors you suffered. It's okay to want to feel safe. Like Dr. Mac said, it's okay to want to feel comforted. I want to keep you safe, Carly. Everyone at the ranch is looking out for you. We all want you to be safe."

"She's afraid I'm going to get attached to you and then you are going to send me away. She's afraid I'm going to get hurt again."

"I'm not going to send you away, Carly. I'm fighting to keep you with me. I want you to stay with me. We're going to work together to make you happy again. Let's go get you a hat. I know just the place to go up in Bowling Green."

They drove up to the shop in Bowling Green and when they went in, Carly was amazed by the number of hats all along the walls.

"We're looking for women's hats," Jason told the salesclerk. She took them over to a long wall covered with hats in every imaginable color. Carly started trying on hats and looking at herself in the mirror. After she tried on a few, Jason came over with a gorgeous purple hat with a silver and turquoise broach fastened to a multicolored woven band decorated with a few feathers. He put it on her head as she smiled at him.

"That's got to be the one," said Jason.

Carly looked in the mirror and smiled at herself. "I do love it, Jason."

"Should we take it?"

Carly took the hat off and looked at the turquoise broach and the woven band. Then she caught a glimpse of the price tag. "Oh, no, Jason. This is much too expensive. I've never owned anything this expensive. We should pick out something else."

"No, Carly. It's your favorite color and it looks great on you. I want you to have it."

"I can find something else I like."

"No. We both like this one." He handed it over to the salesclerk and asked her to ring it up. "You can wear it home, Carly."

The salesclerk hesitated for a moment. Then she looked at Jason. "I know you, don't I? You bought your hat here, didn't you? Aren't you the lawyer in town?"

"I think you've nailed it," Jason said. "Could I ask you to please not mention to anyone you saw us here?"

"Sure," she said. She looked at Carly again and suddenly realized who Carly was. "Oh, you're the singer who was kidnapped."

"Yes, and I'm her attorney. We're trying to keep her safe from the kidnapper who keeps escaping from jail in Tennessee. We don't want him to know where she is. Can you help us with that?"

"Sure. I read about the trial. They should have given that monster the death penalty. Men who abuse women don't deserve to ever be free, in my opinion."

"I'm sure we both agree with you about that."

"I went to hear you sing in Nashville. I'm a big fan. I want to go back when you start to sing again. Are you going to sing this weekend?"

"No. I don't think so but thank you. I might be back in a few weeks."

"Okay. Now if you ever want to go for a total country cowgirl look, I can help you with that. Did you see Miranda Lambert on the last awards show when she sang "If I was a Cowboy"? I could help you find an outfit like that."

Carly smiled. "I think I'll just go with the hat for now, but I'll keep you in mind. I'm just learning to ride, so I don't feel like a cowgirl yet."

"I can't tell you how excited I am to meet you. I hope you enjoy your hat."

Jason paid for the hat and picked up one of the clerk's business cards. "We'll try to let you know when Carly starts to sing again. We've got your email now."

"Thanks. I can't wait to hear you sing again. I won't tell anyone you were here. I hope you can stay safe. I love your songs, by the way."

"We're glad we met you," said Jason. "Maybe we will see you at one of the shows."

They left with the hat and started driving back to the ranch.

"You are famous now, Carly. I didn't think about anyone recognizing you in Bowling Green. I purposely avoided shopping in Nashville for that very reason."

"I was surprised she knew who I was. Thank you for the hat. I really do love it."

"That's the most important thing."

When Jason and Carly walked into the house, Grandma was fixing dinner in the kitchen.

"Oh my, my, my! That is one gorgeous hat, Carly. It is perfect for you! Come out to the patio, I want Nettie to see it."

Carly followed her out to the patio where Nettie, Roy and Robbie were having drinks.

Nettie looked up quickly and said, "Whoa, Carly. Where did you get that gorgeous hat? Did you just get it today? I would love to paint you wearing that hat when you have time to pose."

"Yes. Jason bought it for me. I told him it was too expensive, but he bought it anyway."

"Well, it was worth every penny he paid for it," said Roy. "It looks great on you, Carly."

"Yeah," said Robbie, "that's one beautiful hat! You need to let Jason buy you expensive gifts, Carly, otherwise he will go out looking for more horses to buy, and we are up to our ears in horses that need training."

"Isn't that the truth," said Gwen. "I think you are going to have to get Jason to help you start training all these horses, and then maybe he won't keep buying more of them."

"Do you two want to have dinner with us? We made Chicken Parmesan from Nettie's special recipe?"

Jason reached for a glass and poured some wine to share with Carly. He looked at her questioningly and thought he knew the answer. "I think Carly has some song lyrics running around in her head she wants to try to work on this evening, and I have some trial transcripts that I need to read. So we should pass on dinner tonight and go be workaholics."

Grandma smiled. She knew Carly had some tough therapy sessions in the last few days.

"I'll plate up some food for each of you and put it in the warmer and you can just come and get it whenever you get hungry."

"Thanks, Grandma, that sounds great. I'm sure we will be hungry a little later. We had a very early lunch with Dr. Mac today. Okay, cowgirl, let's get back to my music room and let you start writing your next hit song."

They walked off toward their suite of rooms together.

"They look so cute together, don't they?" asked Grandma.

"Yeah. I really do love the hat! It probably cost a small fortune," said Nettie.

"That's okay," said Grandma. "She's such a nice girl. I'm glad Jason wants to buy her nice things. She deserves to have a little more joy in her life."

"I think our Jason might just be a bit smitten," said Roy. "Let's hope he doesn't start buying her horses."

"God forbid," said Gwen. "We don't even have space in the barn for another horse. Maybe we should sell a few."

"Jason doesn't want to sell any right now. He wants to see which young ones are going to show the most promise. I think he has Derby aspirations again."

"That's encouraging. I'm happy to see he's getting interested in the business again. Do you think we can get one of the horses qualified for the Derby next year?"

"I think we have at least three good candidates so far."

"Three? That's wonderful. I guess we should set aside some money for entrances fees. What about the next group of foals coming up behind those three?"

"Again, we have a chance for another three, maybe four. We have a young filly that is really showing some promise."

"I'm excited by this news, Roy. Do you think Jason is going to take more of an interest this year?"

"I hope so. He doesn't think he knows enough about the business, but the truth is, he is so good with animals. He may be better with them than any of us. We have been using him to lead the horses into the practice gates, and so far, that has been easier than usual."

"I'm glad it's working out then. It seems like our Carly just might be giving him a new lease on life. He seems so much happier this week. I know he convinced her to stay longer."

"Where have they been all day?"

"Jason took her back for another therapy session today and then they went to see her sister. Hat shopping after that, I guess."

"I thought they did the therapy on Wednesdays."

"She did go on Wednesday, but I think something rather disturbing came up and they went back today to finish their discussion. She was quite upset last night when they got home, and I heard her crying for a long time down there with Jason."

"Poor thing," said Nettie. "I wonder why she hasn't had more therapy since the kidnapping."

"I think it was a problem with her insurance. I believe Jason said they only allowed her a few sessions with a therapist and then they refused to pay for any additional treatment."

"How is she getting it now?"

"Jason is paying for it I guess."

"Wow. That could add up quickly. These damn insurance companies probably make millions every year and then refuse treatment for someone like Carly who was so traumatized. It's a lousy way to treat people."

"It is," said Grandma, "but luckily, she found Jason, and he wants to help her. She seemed much happier tonight, so maybe things are better. Or maybe it was the hat."

"A hat like that would certainly make me smile," said Nettie.

Jason and Carly went off toward his music room and he got her set up at the digital piano. He walked off to set up his computer and start reading his trial transcripts. In a few minutes he walked back over to Carly and brought her a bottle of water.

"I'm going to get another glass of wine. Do you want one?"

"No, thanks, Jason. Water is fine for now. I don't want to forget the words I'm working on."

"Okay. Let me know when you get hungry, and we'll take a break for dinner."

"I will. I love chicken parmesan. Donna used to make it for us. I should have learned how to make it."

"I'm sure Nettie will be happy to share her recipe with you and teach you how to make it when you have the time."

Jason walked out onto the back patio to pour himself another glass of wine.

"Is Carly doing okay?" asked Grandma.

"I think so. Today wasn't as traumatic as yesterday. Her sister put some pressure on her to come back to Nashville, so we invited her to come up for a weekend and visit with us. I get the feeling her sister doesn't quite trust my motives for helping Carly."

"I guess her sister just doesn't see that little glint in your eyes like your grandmother does," teased Gwen.

"Okay, Grandma, let's not go there, please."

"You can't fool all of us, Jason," said Roy. "Good thought about that hat. We could tell she really liked it."

"We sent pictures of her in the hat to Sean and Maia and Christy. She did seem excited about it. She still has it on her head."

"Good!" said Gwen. "It was nice to see her smile. She looked so sad yesterday."

"Her life has been hard," said Jason. "I miss my parents, but now I feel grateful for the time I had with them. I realize I was lucky to have such a great family. I thought everyone had a family like that. Just so you know, I'm grateful for all of you, too; for all the support you have given me in the last few years. Carly told her sister she feels like she has another family here. So, thank you for that, too."

"Tell her sister we are all watching out for her and so is our security team," said Roy. "Robbie has cleaned his gun just in case that bastard breaks out of jail again."

"She did tell her sister that, but we didn't mention the gun."

Jason walked back to peek in on Carly. He could hear the chord progressions she was working on and didn't want to interrupt her. He settled in with his wine and court transcript. He was reviewing the transcript of the trial with her kidnapper, but he didn't intend to tell her that. He was looking for any clues in the testimony that might point to the presence of a second kidnapper. Having an accomplice might explain the attempted break-ins at her house in Nashville, and the perp's ability to show up at the club so soon after he disappeared from the prison road crew. He wasn't wearing a prison uniform when he assaulted Carly at the club. He looked scruffy and unkempt, but he wasn't in a prison uniform. These were some of the little things that kept tumbling around in the back of Jason's brain.

Chapter 13

The next morning, Jason waited until Carly started working on her song at the piano. Then he slipped away to call Jack at the Sheriff's office.

"Let me speak to Jack Granger, please," he asked.

"Who's calling?"

"Tell him Jason Kingman."

"Jason, are you the guy who took down the perp at the Rosebud the other night."

"Yeah, yeah, that was me."

"Good job, man. When I saw that sucker's head hit the floor, I was hoping he would die of a brain injury."

"We couldn't get that lucky," said Jason. "But if I knew then, what I know now, I would have tried harder. How 'bout Jack? Is he around anywhere?"

"Yeah, he's here; let me get him."

Jason waited a few minutes, finally Jack came on the phone.

"Hey Jason, is everything all right? Is Carly okay?"

"Yeah, Jack, she's okay - as okay as she's gonna be right now. I don't think she's as frightened as she was. She started working on a song last night when we got home, so that's a good sign. But I wanted to talk to you about something. At the court hearing, I told you I heard him slip a couple of times saying 'we' instead of 'I'. I got the court transcript from his trial and had it sent to my email."

"Really?" Jack interrupted, "you read the trial transcript?"

"Yeah, I was looking for other clues. He did the same thing during the trial. Several times he said 'we', not 'I'. There's a part in there where the court reporter said he turned around, to someone behind him in the courtroom and said, "Don't come here. I told you not to come here anymore. Who was he talking to? Are there video tapes of the trial? Is there any way we could see their faces? Maybe it's a second perp. Maybe there were two kidnappers."

"Whoa," said Jack. "I didn't think about looking at that, but you're right. He did. He had a screaming fit and the Bailiffs had to restrain him to keep him from jumping over the railing. They were there a couple of times. I'll find out if there is a video. That's a good call. Who were they? He claimed he didn't have any parents or family. As I recall, there were three of them - a man, a woman, and a younger guy. Not real young but maybe 30ish. I didn't think about that. Ahh! Good call man. Now I know why you are a lawyer. You're looking at all the details."

"The next thing that's bothering me, is how did he walk away from the road crew without being noticed immediately, and why couldn't they find him when they started to search the area? How did he get to the Rosebud Club after escaping from the prison work crew? Assuming they don't use prison crews in the center of town, wouldn't he have had to walk or hitchhike for many miles to get back to the club? I wouldn't think that anyone would pick up a hitchhiker wearing a prison uniform."

"I hope not," said Jack. "That would be an extreme case of stupid."

"When he attacked Carly, he wasn't wearing a prison uniform. Don't they still wear those shirts with big black and white stripes?"

"Yeah, they do. I think the road crews also wear a reflective vest that says 'Prisoner' on the back. I'm going to check on that."

"When he came after her, he looked scruffy and ill kempt, but he wasn't wearing a prison uniform. So, here's my hypothesis, Jack. He had an accomplice or partner in this kidnapping. The accomplice arranges to pick the perp up on the side of the road while he's working on the road crew. That accomplice supplies him with a change of clothes so he can slip into the club without attracting too much attention. He comes into the Rosebud to get Carly and the accomplice is waiting nearby so they can transport her to a site where they can kill or victimize her again."

"That's quite a theory, Jason. but it is plausible. I had questions about the clothing he was wearing that night. I can check his answer, but I believe he said he took the clothes from one of those donation boxes people use to give away used items. Having someone on the road to pick him up makes perfect sense. That's probably how he escaped the first time as well."

"One more thing, Jack, don't hang up yet. I'm hoping you might have photos on file of the injuries to Carly's arms and back. I'm going to file an appeal with her insurance, and I hope they will agree to pay for plastic surgery to restore her arms and back. I might need the photos to prove my case."

"Yeah, I think there were photos. I know there were photos at the hospital. Originally, they were going to repair her arms, and then her back. But that's when the money ran out."

"What the hell does that mean – the money ran out!"

"Her insurance company wouldn't pay for anything else. They labeled it as elective cosmetic work and therefore nonessential. They were claiming the mutilations were not a result of the kidnapping and they called it cosmetic surgery."

"So they thought she mutilated her own back and carved those symbols into her arms?"

"It sounds stupid, I know, but that was their decision."

"Well, I'm contesting that decision and I'm sure they will back down. When I look at her bills, I can hardly believe the number of charges for her hospital care. Her insurance denied payment for a lot of procedures."

"She was in the hospital a long time, Jason, and these damn policies all have limits on how long you can stay in the hospital, how long you can be in rehab, and after that –

everything is on you. That's what they did to her. After she got out of the hospital she had to go to rehab because they were still treating her feet and she couldn't walk yet. At one time we thought she was going to lose her feet, but I think I told you an anonymous donor kicked in $50,000 for some specialized treatments and equipment which turned the corner for her on her recovery. So, thank God she didn't lose her feet. We never knew who the donor was and still don't. The insurance wouldn't pay for anything else, so we started a GoFundMe page – I think I told you that. But it's still not enough."

"I'm going to be appealing many of their decisions, so hopefully this endless list of charges will be somewhat reduced. I had a quick look at one of her arms, and it almost looked like someone had carved letters, or numbers or some kind of symbols into her arm. When I rub her back, it feels like the patterns might be the same as the marks on her arms."

"I think we have photos. I'll look for them. But on her back – I hate to say this – a lot of those scars are bite marks. He bit her. He bit her on her back, on her arms, and everywhere else you can imagine. Part of what you are seeing or feeling are scars from the bites."

"I could tell what the bite marks were. They're kind of circular. But the other marks didn't feel like that. I could be wrong. But if you do have pictures of the bite marks, make sure you hang onto those. Cause bite marks – you know this – are very individual to a person. They are like a thumb print or a fingerprint. If there is another perp out there you might be able to convict him with bite marks."

Jack was quiet for a minute, and then he said, "We went out there on Tuesday. We searched that damn cabin where they kept her, and I wanted to burn it to the ground. We took more DNA samples and fingerprints. The Sheriff thought I was crazy when I asked for cadaver dogs, and he wouldn't authorize the expense. I found a guy with dogs who was willing to donate his time after I told him why we needed them. We took the cadaver dogs out there and we found three bodies. Three graves, three bodies, and one empty grave. I guess he dug that one for Carly. So we called the coroner, and he brought out a team to help us recover the bodies. It has to be the worst damn assignment I have ever had. I hated making our officers dig up those bodies. We found small bits of clothing and jewelry scattered at the top of the graves and small body parts inside the graves with the bodies. We don't know who they are yet. I don't know how we are going to keep it out of the news. There's probably no way to keep it quiet. Carly's going to see this, and she's going to know they were going to kill her."

"I hate to tell you this, but my grandmother already heard about the bodies on the news."

"Crap," said Jack. "Sometimes I just hate these damn reporters. We haven't even had time to identify the bodies and notify the families and they are broadcasting the news to everyone."

"I'll try to keep Carly away from the news programs, but she already told me the perp had planned to kill her. That was why she ran that night even though she wasn't sure she was going to survive in the cold and snow. He put a chain around her neck that night, and she thought he was getting ready to hang her. Another thing that she told me..."

"You guys have been doing some talking," interrupted Jack. "This is the most she has talked about this since it happened. She wouldn't even talk to us."

"That's shock, Jack. That's what happens when you are in shock. The first night she was here she cried and talked to me almost all night. So, here's the other thing. She said sometimes the perp called himself "Evil Twin". He told her he was the Evil Twin and when he said that he was more brutal. He would slam her around and kick her. She said he would put the gun to her head. He'd put the gun in her mouth and tell her he was going to blow her brains out. She said whenever he called himself the Evil Twin, he was much more violent. He raped her more violently and he would shove the gun into places we don't want to describe."

"Oh God," said Jack. "I think this keeps getting worse and worse. But maybe it's good that she's talking. Do you think that helps, or makes it worse?"

"I know this is hard for her. But she doesn't know me too well. Maybe that makes it easier. Usually, it helps to talk things out. When you go through therapy, they almost make you talk about what happened. When you're holding everything inside it can make you crazy. I think she's got more to say. It was 4 days. Four days of terror."

"Yeah! It's a miracle she survived!"

Jason was quiet for a minute. "Please don't tell Christy these things. I don't want Carly to know I am sharing her confidences, but you have three bodies now. We need to use every clue we can to see if there is another killer out there. She's not safe if there is another one. If you tell Christy, she might tell Carly everything. Carly feels ashamed, so it's hard for me to tell you all this, but I hope by keeping it just between us we might fill in the missing pieces – or missing perp as the case might be."

"Yeah, I'm not telling Christy about the graves, or about the bodies we found. If I told her, then Carly would know. Maybe later, maybe when she's stronger. Maybe we don't have to ever tell her. I don't know. I don't know what the hell to do. We're looking for another kidnapper. We couldn't find any other names related to this God Damn felon. But you had a good thought about the court incident. He had a screaming fit. He didn't want them there. Maybe because the other guy was one of the perps. It's a good thought, Jason. Thank you. Give Carly my best. I'd say give her a hug for me but that's not going to fly. I just hope that one of these days she will let us try to comfort her. But if she will let you put an arm around her that's good. It's a step forward. Little baby steps... Treat her nice. Give her our love – love from all of us."

Chapter 14

Jason's phone was ringing, and he saw the call was coming in from Dr. Mac. He walked outside onto the patio to take the call.

"Hey, Dr. Mac, what's up?'

"Jason," he said, "Can you talk? Are you somewhere we can have a private conversation?"

"Yeah, sure. I'll go into my office. Is everything all right?" Jason asked.

"Yes, I just wanted to check on Carly to see if she is feeling okay, and then I have a few questions for you."

"I think she is doing as well as can be expected under the circumstances. We stopped to see her sister after we left your office, and her sister made a real attempt to get Carly to stay in Nashville, but she came back to the ranch with me. We stopped off to buy her a Stetson, and that seemed to cheer her up a bit."

"So maybe she took my advice about letting herself have some fun?"

"I was glad you said that. When we went for a trail ride this week she started crying because she felt guilty about having a wonderful day when so many people had not been paid for saving her life. I assured her I was working on all her medical bills, and everything would be resolved soon. I want her to feel free to enjoy her life and her talents again. We can't let that bastard take all these things away from her."

"No, he shouldn't get to do that to her. Please keep encouraging her to have fun, to start singing and writing songs again. It sounds like that was a big part of her life before the kidnapping. If you do some research about children who lose a mother at a very young age, Jason, you learn that they lose the feeling of being loved unconditionally because that parent is gone. Unless someone steps in to take the place of that parent they can have a void in their life that is never quite filled again. When Carly was little, she had her mother, but her mother got killed. And did her mother really love her if Carly was getting molested by this horrible father? What was her mother doing? Why couldn't she protect her? That's part of what you do for your children. You love them, you protect them from harm; you don't let anyone, not an uncle, a brother, an aunt, or another parent abuse your child. You don't let them molest your little daughter. Did she really love her? Or was she just so scared of this man that she couldn't protect her? With good reason, obviously, because he did kill her mother. Carly did say that Christy, her sister, really loved her - and I got the drift – they're not really sisters.

They were both children and they did love each other and probably still do. Other than that, she never had anyone to love her or protect her. When this happens, people can think they aren't worthy of love. No one loved them then, why should anyone love them now. Then we talked a little bit about you, Jason, and you know she likes being with you and likes being up at your ranch. She mentioned your grandma and how fun she was. We have all heard the stories about your grandma, and I heard that she carries a gun. So we should all be careful about that, huh?"

Jason started laughing, "I don't think she'd shoot you, Dr. Mac. You're a nice guy. But yes, my grandma is kind of a hoot."

"Then she mentioned Nettie and that's your aunt?"

"She's not really my aunt but she's my grandma's friend."

"But she lives at your house, right?"

Yes, she came to live at the house quite a long time ago, maybe 2-3 years ago. She asked me if she could stay with my grandma for a while, so she came over and moved into a bedroom. I built an art studio for my grandma so they could take all their art supplies over there and have a place to paint. They're both artists. Now they have this great studio with lots of light, lots of glass and beautiful views, and they go over there and paint and do their thing. They both love to troll the internet, which makes me a little crazy but I'm learning to live with it. Anyway, I digress. So yes, there are 3 of us here and now Carly."

"I get the feeling that she likes it. I think she likes it more than she wants to admit. It seems to give her a sense of family and that is something she always wanted when she was little. She lived with the neighbors, so I guess it was like a family, but it seems there was never anything official about it. They didn't adopt her, but even if you don't formally adopt a child, you could have a little ceremony saying welcome to our family, you are going to be our daughter now, and we're sorry about what happened to your mother. But it seems like nothing was ever said. They didn't have a funeral for her mother, or a burial. She said she kept waiting for her mother to come back to get her. But her mother was dead. She didn't know until she was older that her mother was dead. I thought that was strange. These were adults. You would think they could have handled this much better. I believe she always viewed the mother as Christy's mother, and she was just waiting for her own mother to come back for her. Then she talked about you, Jason. She describes you as the giver, and herself as the taker. I tried to explain to her that it is okay to let someone help you. It doesn't make you a taker, it just means someone cares about you. She talked a bit about how you like to help people. She said she feels guilty because she keeps taking and taking and you, Jason, just keep giving and giving. I asked her if that didn't feel nice for a change, and she said it was nice, but then she said, "Maybe I'm just another one of his projects."

I latched onto that word 'projects', Jason, because I've heard about all the things you do, and I know right now you said you were working on one of the Campaign for Justice cases trying to help a prisoner who went to jail when he was very young. I have to tell you I really admire you for that, and I'm sure nobody pays you to do it. You can't get paid by these people who have been in jail for 20 years. They don't have any money."

"No, they don't have any money and that's not why I do it. If someone has been in jail for 20 years and they shouldn't have ever been there in the first place, then it's time for someone to step up and get them out of jail."

"Yeah, I couldn't agree with you more, and I also agree that we should leave the guys there who really deserve to be there." They both laughed.

"I told Carly she could ask you if she was just one of your projects, but she said she couldn't. So I told her I would ask you if she wanted me to find out, and she said yes. So that is the real reason for this call. She wants to know if she is just one of your projects. I know you brought her to me for therapy and you are paying for her sessions, so I assumed there was some kind of relationship between the two of you. But I don't think you have known her very long, have you?"

"No. I just met her at the club the night when the kidnapper showed up to grab her."

"I guess what I'm asking you, Jason, is that if she has feelings for you, if she can start to trust again, is it going to be safe for her to trust you, to try to find the kind of love she needs with you. That you aren't going to help her and then turn around and say "Okay, I'm done. You're healed.""

"Oh, God, no! I would never do that!!"

"So, you have feelings for her? She's not just someone you want to help. She's not your project?"

"Oh, God no, no, she's not a project. This may sound strange to you, Dr. Mac, but I felt something for her almost immediately. I always thought it took a long time to develop real feelings for someone - to fall in love. Much longer than a single weekend. But something about her just spoke to me, and it goes way beyond the fact that she is very beautiful. There's just something special about the way we interact with each other, the things we can talk about, and laugh about. She is interested in exploring and learning things she never had a chance to learn before. She has an amazing talent, and she has dreams and goals, and ambitions. I like the fact that she is ambitious, and she always wants to learn new skills. Not every woman I meet has such lofty goals. She's not just waiting around to find someone to support her and make her life a walk in the park. She even gets upset when I try to do anything for her to make her life easier. She calls herself a 'taker' and calls me a 'giver'."

"I think we talked about that today, Jason. She called herself a 'taker' and I reminded her again that it is all right to let people help her. Remember we talked about this with you when we all got together for a session. It sounds to me like you have been meeting too many women from the country club set, Jason. Are those the women with no ambition?"

"Sadly, it seems to be that way. Carly is so different from those women. I admire what she has done with her life with so little help or support from anyone."

"It's very sad to know she had the strength to survive a horrible childhood only to be victimized by this vicious kidnapper."

"She started to talk about going back to her house in Nashville yesterday and I felt panicky. I would really miss her if she left the ranch, but there's another reason I don't want her to move back to her house. You've probably heard about it on the news."

"Are you talking about the graves they found out in the woods?"

"Yeah, that. The three graves and the empty grave."

Dr. Mac was silent for a moment, then added, "Is that where the kidnapper held her?"

"Yeah, that was it. She was supposed to be in the empty grave."

"Oh, jeez! Does she know about the bodies they found?"

"No. Jack's been leading the investigation, and he and I talk. I'll tell her if I have to, but so far, she hasn't heard about the bodies."

"He really was going to kill her?"

"Oh, yeah. He told her over and over that he was going to kill her."

"Do they know who the other victims were?"

"Nope. They don't have any identities for them yet."

"But the kidnapper is in jail, right? Or on his way back to jail?"

"Yes, but here's the second part. Please don't share this, but Jack and I think there was more than just the one kidnapper. There might have been 2 or 3 of them taking part in the kidnapping."

"Two or three perps that kidnapped her?"

"Possibly."

"So they – like - gang raped her?"

"Yeah, something like that."

"They just found these graves recently, right?"

"Yeah. After I subdued the perp at the club, I told Jack about the cadaver dogs we used in the army that go out to search for bodies. I asked him if they had taken any cadaver dogs out to the location where they found Carly. If this perp was as vicious as it appeared, there could be other victims who had been killed. They went out with dogs and found three bodies and one empty grave. Today or tomorrow, they are going out with the dogs again to do a wider search parameter to see if there might be more bodies out there. Then there was something else Carly told me yesterday, that when she escaped..."

"And how the hell did she do that, anyway? How did she escape from this perp? I wanted to ask her about her escape, but I thought it might be too painful for her to talk about it."

"It's a real story of courage, Mac. They gave her pills to knock her out at night, and she held them in her mouth until they weren't looking, and then she stuffed them into a little hole in the mattress. She planned to take them herself when the pain got unbearable and hoped there would be enough of them to kill her. The night she escaped she stuck the pills into a binding around her wrists that they used to tie her to the bedposts. She said he put a chain around her neck, and she thought he was going to hang her. But he took her into the kitchen, chained her up to a table leg, and told her to fix him something to eat, so she did, and put the pills into his food and his beer."

"Whoa! That was smart."

"Yeah, except it was about 20 degrees outside. But he did fall asleep, and she got the chain off her neck and decided to make a run for it. When he kidnapped her, he made her drive her car to this place. She thought her car was outside and she knew she had a "Hide a Key" hidden on it. But when she got outside her car wasn't there. The perp was knocked out in the cabin, so who was driving the car?"

"You have really thought this through, haven't you? There had to have been another kidnapper because someone else was driving her car, right?"

"Sad but true. So she ran through the woods in the snow. She had no clothing, no shoes, nothing. It was snowing. It was 20 degrees out there. When she was running, she started to hear people calling to her, so she kept running toward the voices. She was afraid to call out because she thought the perp woke up and was behind her, coming back after her, and she didn't want him to know where she was. She said she probably fell down or passed out and that's where Jack found her. Almost buried in the snow. Her body temperature was so low she probably lost consciousness. When they got her to the hospital, they had to run her blood through a heart lung machine to warm it and return it to her body."

"That took a lot of courage – a lot of guts to do that. Thank God Jack found her in time – well I guess just barely in time."

"That's why we think there might be another kidnapper. One of them may have been following her in the woods."

"I'm glad you told me this, Jason. She shouldn't ever go back to her house, should she?"

"Oh, no. Especially if there are one or two more of them. She's got big guard dogs in her house and in her yard. They bring them over every night, but people can shoot a dog."

"That's true."

"It's not safe and I don't want her to go back there. I want her to stay up at my place. I don't think they can find her here."

"Well, Jason, now I have to tell you something. You know people love to gossip about you. Even in this town, and in Kentucky. I saw a little blurb in the gossip column about you."

"Oh no. Not again. I thought I was done with this."

"It said 'rumor has it Kentucky's most eligible bachelor, Jason Kingman, has been seen around town with singer Carly Styles."

"Oh, shit!! Who the hell wrote that?"

"I don't remember. My wife pointed it out to me. She said, 'Oh you know Jason, don't you?' and I said I hadn't seen you in a long time. She said, "It looks like he's dating this cute singer."

I asked my wife if she knew who she was and she said, "Oh yeah. The girls and I went to the Rosebud one night."

I looked at her and I said, "Really, you girls went to this club?" She said, "Yeah. We've been there a few times. She's real cute and a great singer. Everybody loves that club. They have tons of people there."

"I asked her if she planned to go there again if she could please take me with her, so that's how I knew this. She told me yesterday."

"Damn" said Jason.

"I was just thinking that if there are more of them – now they know where you are."

"Well, they can always find me. I'm Jason Kingman and it's Kingman Ranch. My ancestors should have come up with a more obscure name. I just don't want anyone to come poking around looking for her."

"You've got good security up there, don't you Jason? With all those pretty horses?"

"We have 24-hour security. But it's a worry. Oh crap! Why can't these people mind their own business? Why do they have to write about me? What is it that motivates people to do that?"

"Well, Jason, all those young ladies in Kentucky keep hoping they might have a shot at finding a place in your life. You know they call you "the guy with the pretty eyes.""

"Come on, Mac, stop that!"

"Well, that's the truth, Jason. That's why they write about you. Everybody wants to be a busybody. Now with the internet, Facebook and all this social media, it is only getting worse."

"Jeez, I hadn't even thought about that happening. I'm surprised my grandmother hasn't told me about it yet."

"She probably will."

"I guess we have to keep our eyes open at the ranch. I'll be calling Roy in a minute."

"Roy is still with you, right? I met him at a fundraiser your parents hosted. I liked your parents, by the way, and I'm so sorry about what happened to them. That had to have been a real shock."

"It was," said Jason. "It was a horrible shock. I was flying over the Atlantic on my way home, and they were getting killed by a sleep deprived driver. When I got home, they were gone. I had a very hard time with it. I had been in the military all those years, and I thought I was coming home to enjoy my time with them, and they were gone. Everything was gone except the ranch. We still have the ranch and we're still doing well. I think we have some promising horses coming up that you might end up seeing in the Derby."

"That would be great. We could bet on them. My wife loves to go to the Derby."

"Well, if we get a horse in the Derby, you can come sit in our box."

"Really? You have a box? "

"We're owners. All the owners have boxes."

"My wife would be all over that. She would have to buy one of those fancy hats."

"It's possible we may get a horse in the Derby this year or maybe next year. I'm not one of the trainers, as you can tell. I never thought someone could track me down and look for her at the ranch."

"It didn't say she was up at your ranch. It just said you had been seen around town."

"And where the hell did anybody see me? Except for the night I was at the Rosebud when I knocked that guy out. She did dance with me a little, so maybe that's what they saw."

"Okay, Jason, I'm going to let you get back to your work. I just wanted to make sure she wasn't just another one of your projects, and I will tell her that, if it's okay with you. So, you're all in, I'm all in, I'm sure her sister's all in. So, we're all there for her, right?"

"Oh yeah," said Jason. "And my grandma and Nettie. They're going to be all in. They really like her. Everyone at the ranch likes her. I think we are all amazed by her talent."

"Well, who knows, Jason. Maybe this will grow into something for the two of you, and in the meantime, we'll all work together to help her heal."

Chapter 15

Carly was chatting with Grandma and Nettie while Jason was busy with phone calls in his office. Carly looked up suddenly and saw Jason pausing in the doorway to the kitchen.

"Oh, oh, my! I wasn't expecting that," she gasped.

"These are my 'lawyering duds'" he said, tugging gently at the lapel of the suit he was wearing. It was a gorgeous shade of blue violet, and he had paired it with a lilac shirt and purple patterned tie that almost matched the color of his eyes. It fit over his tall muscular frame like a custom-made glove. Her coffee cup clattered a bit onto the table as she tried to put it down.

"He is a handsome devil in that suit," quipped Nettie. "It almost takes your breath away!"

Jason slid into the chair next to Carly. "So, you like a man in a suit, huh?"

"Wow - I definitely like <u>That Man</u> in <u>That Suit</u>," she said softly.

"Wish I had known. I could have been in one, and out of one a lot earlier," he whispered in her ear.

"Jason! Isn't it a bit early for that talk?" asked Grandma with a bit of a scolding tone.

"I like to see her smile." he replied and ran his fingers up through her golden curls and pulled her gently toward him and kissed her. "You look gorgeous Babe, so gorgeous." He kissed her again. He glanced across the table at Nettie and Grandma Gwen and made a quick signaling motion using his finger to close up his mouth.

"Okay ladies you can stop gaping. I'm sure your man kissed you at the breakfast table a time or two."

"Lord, I don't think any man kissed me like that. Ever!" said Nettie.

He wrapped his arms around Carly and kissed her again. "You smell so nice. Kind of like bubble bath," and they both laughed. "It's always nice to see a gorgeous woman in my bathtub," he whispered.

"Do you have meetings today?" Carly asked.

"Yep. Today is my meeting with the President of the bank that holds your mortgage. The best news yet is that I know the guy. He was a friend of my dad's, and I know he came to the funeral. I really don't remember him very well, but I'll pretend I do."

"I wish you didn't have to do this for me, but I appreciate it and hope it won't take too much of your time. I guess it is a bit of a trip to Louisville."

"Not by helicopter. It's just a short hop."

"Helicopter? Where would you get a helicopter?"

"Easy. We just take it out of the hanger. Robby and I love to fly the chopper."

"You have a helicopter here? You know how to fly a helicopter, Jason?"

"I do. That's why I joined the Army. I wanted to learn how to fly. I thought I was going to be an airline pilot."

"You are just full of surprises, Jason. Not quite the boring lawyer you claimed you were."

Carly started rocking her body back and forth in her chair and Jason put his arms around her and kissed her on the cheek. He recognized her reaction as fear of being alone and felt a pang of pain in his chest at the thought of leaving her for a few hours. He had kept her with him constantly since the first night they met when the kidnapper had shown up at the club. "I won't be gone too long," he assured her. "Grandma and Nettie will be here at the house with you, and all the alarm systems will be turned on. I promise you will be safe here. Roy and Robbie are just minutes away if you need them. This is just the start, Carly. Remember I told you I am not going to let you drown in all this debt. It's something I can help you with, and I can work some deals to get you some relief. While I'm gone, why don't you show Grandma your GoFundMe page. My grandfather was a prominent surgeon here in Bowling Green. Grandma knows lots of wealthy doctors, don't you, Grandma?'

"I do. Nettie and I can send out some emails today. Nettie has a lot of connections with the health care community as well."

"I feel guilty about asking for donations. I wonder how people feel about being asked for money."

"Well, one generous donor saved your feet," Jason reminded her. "I think that people who see what happened to you during this kidnapping realize how unfair it is for you to be slammed with hundreds of thousands of dollars in hospital bills. Even small donations can help you work your way out of this. It doesn't hurt to try everything we can. Okay?"

"Okay," she said softly. He could see her eyes filling up with tears.

"It'll be okay, Carly. Trust me."

When Jason got back from his meeting, he slid in alongside Carly on the piano bench.

"Did I startle you?" he asked, as she stopped playing.

"No, I heard the helicopter overhead. I thought it had to be you. Did the meeting go okay?"

"Yes. It was fine. I'm sure you won't have to pay any of those penalty fees, and I asked him to give you a one-year grace period so you could get back on your feet."

"That would be good. I hope I can get back into singing at the club again."

"I'm sure you can. Are you working on a song?"

"Yes, it's a song I'm writing for Mike to sing. It's more of a guy kind of song."

"Can you sing some of the words for me?"

Okay. Here's the first verse and chorus -
I've been here listening to the radio, Trying to get you out of my mind,
But they keep playing the same old tunes, all the Won't you come back to me kind.
Honey if I'd only known, you could walk right out of my life.
I would have written a love song, just to play it on the radio tonight.

"I like that! Did you just write that today?"

"Most of it. I had the idea in my head for a few days."

Grandma appeared in the doorway. "I have so enjoyed hearing you play while we were working. Nettie and I found some Victim's Advocacy Groups you can petition for benefits, and we have sent out almost 100 emails to individuals and groups we have in our contact files. Nettie just said she saw some new donations already. We are going to put some food out for lunch, and I thought we could eat out on the patio if that's okay. A package came for you, Jason, and I put it on the desk in your office."

"Thanks, Grandma. I'll get with you about the groups we should contact. I'll get out of this suit and help you take things out to the patio. Maybe we can get Carly to play her new song for us again. Any chance of that, Carly?"

"Maybe."

Jason set a small box on the patio table and went in to help carry out the lunch trays. Robbie and Roy appeared on the patio as they were sitting down to eat.

"Just in time," said Gwen. "Did you open your package, Jason?"

"No, not yet. I think this is something for Carly."

"You're not supposed to buy me any more gifts, Jason."

"Sorry, but you heard what Robbie said. I can't spend any more money on horses, so I have to buy you expensive gifts. This isn't an expensive gift. It's just something you need."

Jason slit open the box with his knife and set it in her lap. Carly looked at it hesitantly.

"I really don't need anything, Jason. You shouldn't buy things for me."

"I think you might like this. Open it up."

Carly reached into the box and pulled out a beautiful multicolored purple, pink, and green one-piece bathing suit. She looked up at Jason with a question in her eyes.

"You said you wanted to learn to swim but you didn't have a swimsuit," he answered.

"But…But… Well, I guess I could…I could…" He knew she was thinking about all the scars on her back and her arms that everyone would be able to see.

"Keep looking. There's more in the box."

Carly reached in and pulled out a short coverup jacket with long sleeves. She smiled at Jason, and he knew what she had been worried about.

"That's really beautiful," said Nettie. "I like the way the jacket matches up with the swimsuit. That was a great choice, Jason."

"One more piece in there, Carly."

She reached in again and pulled out a long wrap-around coverup in a matching flower print. She stood up and wrapped it around her waist and smiled.

"Wow. This is gorgeous. Thank you, Jason, but no more gifts, okay? This coverup print looks like it could be from Hawaii."

"We could go to Hawaii, if you would like." said Jason.

"That's Jason for you, Carly. He's always ready to go somewhere on a moment's notice."

Carly reached over and gave Jason a hug.

"Thank you," she whispered. "I didn't want to get in the pool where everyone could see my scars."

"I figured that out. Try it on after lunch, and if it fits, we can do your first swimming lesson." He saw tears flooding her eyes and he hugged her closer so nobody would see the tears. "Shh, it's okay. We're going to find a way to get rid of your scars. We just need a little time to figure it out."

He held her close until he felt her start to relax, and her breathing slowed back to normal.

"Jason, I think you're developing a fondness for Amazon. You teased Nettie and I about all the things we order from them, but now I think you're beginning to like them."

"I've got to admit, it's an easy way to shop, and it's fun to find things Carly might like."

"No more presents, Jason. I don't need anything else. After you bought me my gorgeous hat you promised you wouldn't buy me anything else."

"You said that, Carly. I never promised. Don't spoil my fun."

Chapter 16

The next morning, Jason rang Jack up on his cell phone, and he answered right away.

"Hey, Jason, is everything okay? Is Carly okay?"

"Sure. She's fine. She's doing great. She's in the family room playing the piano."

"Oh, you have a piano?"

"Well, we do now. Let's put it that way."

"So, what? You bought her a piano?"

"Not exactly. I rented one to see if she liked it, but I think she likes it, so I'll probably buy it."

Jack started laughing. "Okay, what's up then?"

"Did you ask Christy about Carly's parents?"

Yeah, I did. She remembered her parents told her not to talk about Carly's parents or the Sheriff might come and take Carly away."

"Okay. That should be enough to scare a little kid. That's all she remembers?"

"Yeah. But she was only seven. What does anyone remember from when they were seven?"

"But that was a rather traumatic event."

"Traumatic for Carly. Maybe not as traumatic for Christy. When she asked her mother if Carly's mother was going to come back to get her, Martha told her not to ever ask about Carly's parents again. Christy said they never talked about it – ever. When she was much older, Martha finally told her that Carly's father shot her mother and then killed himself."

"Well, that sheds a little light on things. Here's my next question. Any chance we could go out and visit with Christy's parents?"

"Why do we want to visit them?"

"I'm assuming you go visit them anyway, right? Why can't we go ask them? They have to know."

"I think we know already, don't we? They're dead. He killed her. He shot himself."

"Did he?" asked Jason. "Did he shoot himself? Carly has wondered if he might still be alive."

"Well, yeah. They said he killed himself."

"Maybe we could see what else Christy's parents might remember."

"You want to go all the way out to this retirement home to ask them what they remember? It's about an hour's drive out there."

"What if I can get you there in about 20 minutes? Do you have a helipad at your building? Can we land a chopper on your roof?"

"Yes. We have a helipad. Sometimes the State brings a chopper over."

"Yeah. Like that. Is it open? Is it empty?"

"Yeah, there's nothing up there. Where are we going to get a helicopter today, Jason?"

"I have a helicopter."

"You have a helicopter? You own a helicopter?"

"Yes, we have a helicopter here."

"Do you know how to fly a helicopter?"

"Yes, I do, but we'll bring Robbie. Robbie is a great helicopter pilot. He can land the chopper on a stinking dime. We can land on your helipad, you guys can run out, we'll put you in the chopper, and we'll fly out to the retirement home. Send me the location, and Robbie will see where we can land close to the home."

"Are you going to put the helicopter down in the front yard of the retirement home?"

"Well, possibly. Is it big enough?"

"Hell, yes. It's like a park out there."

"But we don't want to scare any of these old people, Jack."

Jack was quiet for a moment. "Holy shit, Jason. We're going to take a helicopter out to this retirement home just to see what Christy's parents have to say?"

"Yeah. That's the plan. Can we do that today? Can you get away?"

"I'm off duty today, so it could work."

"And Christy is there? Can she come?"

"Yeah, she can. Are we sure we want to do this, Jason? I don't know if Christy has ever flown in a helicopter. I have, of course."

"Well, she might get a kick out of it. It's kind of fun."

"Does this guy Robbie live on your ranch, too?"

"Yeah. He lives here. He's one of our trainers now. He does both jobs. He flies the chopper with me, and he works with the horses. He's a retired Army guy. That's all he did for 10 years in the Army is fly helicopters. In the Rangers we all had to learn to fly the choppers. If you were on a mission and your pilot got shot, you didn't want to sit there on the ground and wait for the insurgents to kill you off. We all knew how to fly in case there was an emergency."

"Oh my God. Did that ever happen that your pilot got shot?"

"Yeah, but that's a story for another day. Let's look at today. We can leave here in about 10 minutes. We have the chopper warmed up already. I just need to let my grandma know that we are taking off, so she can keep an eye on Carly while we are gone."

"Carly won't want to come with us, will she?"

"No, she's playing the piano and working on some music. I think she really likes this piano I picked out."

"What did you buy her Jason? A Steinway?"

"Something like that, but let's get going."

"Christy and I can go to the office. How will we know when you get there? Will you text me?"

"Oh, you're going to know when we get there. You're going to hear us coming overhead when we land on your roof. So just run out. and we'll put you in the chopper. I've got helmets and protective gear for you."

"Oh my God, I can't believe we're doing this."

"Well, why not? Let's go. See you in about 20 minutes. Robbie said the spot in front of the retirement home is big enough for the chopper, so can you let the retirement home know we'll land there. We don't want to scare the residents."

"Guess I better do that. You know they're all going to want to come out and go for a ride. Some of these older people love to have company and they love any excitement."

"They can come out and see it if they want, but we're not taking them for any rides."

Christy looked nervous when she got into the chopper. Robbie looked over his shoulder and said, "It's going to be okay. This will be a very short hop."

"Are these things safe? We have a daughter, you know."

"You'll be safe. Short hop there and a short hop back. This is an easy one. And if anything happens to me, you've got Jason. He's a great pilot."

"Really?" asked Christy. "Jason, do you know how to fly a helicopter?"

"Yeah. I was in the Army. You learn to do these things if you want to stay alive."

"Does Carly know you have a helicopter?"

"Yes, she knows. We flew the chopper when I went to Louisville to talk to the Bank President about her mortgage."

"Was she surprised?"

"I think she was a bit surprised, but I explained it was something my dad bought before he died."

"Carly told me you had a plane. She didn't say it was a helicopter."

Robby looked back at her. "We got a plane, too!"

"What! You have a plane and a helicopter?"

"Ahh, yeah. My dad loved to buy things."

"But why would you have a plane and a helicopter?"

"When you have racehorses, you need to travel around the country to the various racetracks. Once you make a little money you get past the stage where you need to travel in your motor home and park it out in the pastures. So, my dad bought a plane, and we just flew into all those places. Then if it was a short hop like going up to Louisville, he liked to take the helicopter. This all started when I was a kid, but then shortly before he died, he bought a newer plane and a new helicopter. So, this chopper is fairly new, and we haven't used it all that much."

"Not nearly enough," interjected Robbie.

"You know, Jason, I remember when Carly tried to flirt with you at the club, and you told her you were a boring lawyer."

"Yeah, I think Carly and I have covered that again a time or two. I asked her if she would have wanted me to say 'Hey, Babe, I have a plane. Let's go for a ride.'"

"Well, no, Jason, but boring lawyer doesn't really seem to describe you. How is Carly?"

"She's doing better, and I don't think she feels as frightened as she did before."

"No, Jason, she told me she doesn't feel so frightened. She told me some other things, too."

"Well maybe we won't go there today, Christy. Maybe we'll just stick with this discussion about your parents. Okay?"

"Yeah, Jason, you don't want me to embarrass you, huh?"

"I don't know if it's embarrassing or not, but I'm guessing it might be kind of personal, and sometimes personal things are best left – UNSAID!"

"Okay. We'll focus on – What are we asking my parents?"

"We're asking them exactly what happened to Carly's parents."

"I think we already know that. He shot her mother. He killed himself."

"Did he? Did he kill himself? Did you know Carly has always worried that he might still be alive?"

Christy looked at him. "No. I never heard her say that."

"Okay, let's see. Let's find out what we can learn about her parents today."

Within a few minutes Robbie set the chopper down gently in the park-like setting in front of the retirement home. It caused quite a commotion among the residents. Groups of them came streaming out the doors to get a look at the people who were arriving by helicopter. Some of them hustled out using canes or walkers, curiosity overcoming any disabilities. Robbie stayed with the chopper so he could let some of the residents look at it.

Christy's mom and dad were happy to see her. Her dad was excited about seeing her come in out of a helicopter. They sat down at a small table in the kitchen. Christy started explaining the visit.

"Jack and Jason want to ask you some questions to see what you might remember. It's okay if you don't. It was a long time ago, so you might not remember many details."

"I know you think I have old age memory loss, Christy, but I pretty much remember everything. Your dad is having a hard time, and he might not be able to answer your questions."

Her dad, Harold, looked up from the table, "Yeah, yeah, you all say that, but I can remember stuff. I can remember when Red here was just a little bitty girl. Red used to sneak out at night and go partying, but not little Blondie. She didn't do that. She'd be home in bed and Red would be out sneaking around."

"Okay, Pop. We're not going to talk about that today. Jack and Jason have some questions for you."

Jack started explaining to Harold and Martha. "We're trying to learn something about Carly's parents. Carly has had some rough times since the kidnapping. You heard about how she escaped, right?"

"Yes, Jack," said Martha. "Thank God you were there. Christy said you found her in the woods and saved her life. Thank God for you!"

"Carly is a bit troubled about some things from her past, so we're trying to find out exactly what happened to her mother."

Martha looked up, "Well, Carly's father shot her mother, and then he killed himself."

Harold looked up quickly from the table, "Nah, he didn't shoot himself. He was too God damn mean to shoot himself. I shot that sucker in the back."

Everyone was suddenly silent. Christy's eyes were as round as saucers as she stared in disbelief at her dad.

"No, you didn't, Harold. You don't know what you're saying. See that's what happens. That's the dementia talking," said Martha.

"Stop, Martha. You know what I did. You know I shot that bastard. I heard a loud bang and I saw Blondie running from the cabin like her feet were on fire. I went over there to see what happened and I could see her mother was lying on the floor, and most of her face was gone. So, I asked him, 'What the hell have you done, Bobby?' and he said, 'I told that little brat if she told her mother what I was doing that I would shoot her mother, so I shot her.' I asked him, 'what are you talking about, Bobby? Why would you shoot her mother?' And he said, 'I warned her. If she told her mother what we were doing, I told her I would shoot her mother. She went and told her mother, so I shot her.' What do you mean? What were you doing, Bobby? 'I was teachin' her how to be a woman,' he told me. So, I asked, 'You were raping your daughter, Bobby?' He said, 'I guess if that's what you want to call it. But I was teachin' her how to be a woman.' I looked at him again and I said, 'She doesn't need to be a woman. How could you rape your daughter? She's six years old.' He said 'Hell yes, and she's not going to get any older. When I find her, I'm going to put a bullet in her head too."

Harold paused and sighed heavily. "He turned around and picked up one of the guns from the table, went walking to the door, and I picked up another gun, and I shot him in the back."

The room became deadly quiet again. Everyone at the table just stared at him.

Finally, Martha said, "He didn't do that, Jack. He's just making it all up. It's something that happens to you when you have Alzheimer's. Her father shot himself."

"He shot himself in the back, right Martha? That's hard to do."

"Harold just be quiet. This isn't something we want to talk about."

Christy looked at Jack and said, "Jack, this isn't going anywhere, right?"

"Harold, be quiet. You know Jack is a deputy. He's with the Sheriff's office, so just be quiet."

"Hell, no! That was 20 years ago. He was a rapist! He was going to kill that little Blondie girl, so I shot him in the back. He laid on the floor and he begged me to help him. He begged for his life, and I was so angry about what he did to her, I shot him again. He was nothing but a pervert. I left him there to bleed out on the floor."

Christy looked at Jack. Her face was pale, her eyes were pleading. "Please tell me this isn't going anywhere."

"No, this isn't going anywhere. It was a long time ago. There's no way to prove this story." He looked at Jason, "This is just a family matter, okay, Jason?"

"Yeah," said Jason. "It's all family."

The room was deadly quiet for a few minutes. Finally, Jason asked, "So you knew. You both knew what he did to her? Did you talk to her about it?"

Martha just shook her head.

"You never tried to help her, or talk to her?"

"I didn't know what to say," said Martha.

"You couldn't even tell her you were sorry about what he did to her? Did you tell her you wouldn't let anyone hurt her again? Did you tell her she was safe?"

"I didn't think we should talk about it. She was so little. I thought she would just forget."

"She didn't. She never forgot what he did to her. There are things you can never forget and never forgive. She could stand here right now and tell you every gruesome detail about what he did to her. She used to count the number of bruises she had on her arms and legs. And yet, nobody noticed. He choked her when she cried and beat her when she tried to get away from him. Sometimes he taped up her mouth or gaged her so she couldn't cry out while he was raping her."

Jason gritted his teeth and tried to stem the anger he felt rising up and taking over his whole body. He shoved his chair back and walked over to the windowsill and slammed his fist down onto the sill. He tried to keep breathing. He heard Christy say something to her mother, but he couldn't focus on her words.

Finally, he said, "She used to hide under her blankets and hide under the bed so her father couldn't find her, but he grabbed her and dragged her out to the woods and held his hand over her mouth so she couldn't scream or cry for help. Sometimes she heard his footsteps coming for her every night."

"Oh, God!" Christy cried out. "She used to sleep under my bed at night. One night it was so cold I got my jacket and wrapped it around her legs, and I found one of my dad's old coats and covered her up. I gave her my pillow because she was crying. She was hiding from her father! She asked me one day if Pop ever hurt me. I thought she was asking about spankings. I told her that when I did something wrong Pop just told me not to do it again. Then she said, 'But that's how Daddies show their little girls how much they love them.' She said it in a low growling kind of voice, and I thought she was just being funny. She was telling me what happened, wasn't she? Is that what he told her?"

"Yes. That's what he told her."

"Oh, God! She was telling me what happened, and I laughed. I thought she was trying to be funny. Oh, Carly! I'm so sorry! So Sorry!" Christy burst into tears and Jack wrapped his arms around her.

"You couldn't have known, Christy, you were only a little girl. You didn't know what he did to her."

"They did. They knew," she whispered and kept sobbing. "They knew."

Jason walked back to the table and sat down "So what happened after you shot him? You never called the police?"

"Hell no. I didn't want to go to jail. He hurt that little girl, and he was going to kill her. He had the gun in his hand. You don't go looking for a kid with a gun in your hand unless you're going to shoot them."

"I'm sure that's true," said Jack.

"What was I going to do? Stand there and watch him shoot her? Maybe he would have killed all of us. We would have been witnesses. We didn't mean anything to him."

"Probably so," said Jack. "You did the right thing. The only thing you could have done."

"She's always had doubts about what happened to her mother. Whether her mother was dead or not," said Jason. "She spent a lot of years thinking her mother was going to come back to get her. I don't know when she finally realized her mother was dead."

"I told her," said Christy. "When we graduated from high school, I told her that her mother was dead. She wanted her mom to come to see her graduate. She asked me if I thought her mom would be proud of her, and I told her 'Of course, Carly,' I told her then. It was hard, but I knew her mother was dead. I told her that her mother was looking down from heaven and smiling because she was so proud of Carly. Proud of her because she finished school and got such good grades. That's when I told her that her mother was dead."

"Yeah, she did say you told her, Christy. She said you were the one person who loved her, and even though you were only a little girl, just like Carly, you were always looking out for her. You brought her food, and you shared your lunches with her, so she didn't go hungry. You brought her little sweaters to wear when it was cold, you brought her socks, and shoes, and even a winter jacket. She said she was always hungry, but you always shared with her, and sometimes you gave her practically everything you had for your lunch."

"She was always so hungry, and I wasn't ever that hungry. Some of the other kids shared with her too. They gave her cookies or desserts their mama's baked for them."

"So, she never brought a lunch to school?"

"No. I don't remember that she ever did."

Jason looked at the other people around the table. "Where were the adults in her life? Where were the teachers? Didn't she have teachers who saw she was hungry, that she wasn't properly clothed, and she was cold? Where were the adults in this whole scenario? You were at school..."

"Yeah, Jason, this was probably not the kind of school you went to. They lived way back in the woods, and probably most of the children were poor, and nobody ever noticed."

"God," said Jason, "it's hard to wrap your head around a scenario where nobody would notice that a little girl was going hungry and was cold. How can you not notice that?"

"After she lived with us, I always gave her my jackets when my mama made me a new one. We shared our clothes and shoes, so she always had warm clothes then. I wish she could have told me her father hurt her like that."

Christy looked at Jason and said, "You weren't surprised were you? I saw it on your face when my dad said that. You weren't surprised. You already knew her dad molested her, didn't you?"

"Yes," said Jason. "She told me."

"She told you! She never told me, but she told you her father was molesting her when she was six years old. She told you this?"

"Yeah, she told the therapist the first day she went to him. She said she never told anyone before because she was afraid no one would believe her. Her father thought Carly told her mother what he was doing to her. She never told her mother because she was afraid her father would shoot her mother, but she was bleeding, and her mother noticed it and figured out what was happening to her. Carly said she heard her mother scream at him, 'I know what you did. I know what you did to her, and we are going away and never coming back.' Carly said he reached for the gun and Carly tried to run to her mother, but her mother yelled, 'No, Carly no! Run Carly run!' Then he picked up the gun and shot her mother.'

"Jason, I can't believe she told you this. She never told me."

"She never told anyone until she told the therapist, and then after her therapy she told me."

"Why did she tell you, if she already told the therapist?"

"I don't know Christy. She's told me a lot of things."

"I can't believe she's telling you all this stuff. After the kidnapping we tried to get her to talk to us and she wouldn't even tell us what happened. Now she's telling you everything. Why is that, Jason? Why is she telling you everything? I'm her sister."

Christy started to cry again.

Jack comforted her. "Come on, Christy. Maybe she was ashamed. She didn't want to tell you this."

Jason looked at Christy. "You know, Christy. Carly really loves you. She might have been afraid to tell you about her father. Think about it in context. You were both little girls. Could she really have understood what he was doing to her except that it hurt. Probably terribly! He was hurting her, and he was threatening her. He was telling her he was going to kill her mother. And as little girls, even if she had told you, you wouldn't have understood what he was doing to her – I hope. You were both so young when this happened. Then she held this inside her all these years, thinking she got her mother killed. She told her father that she never told her mother what he was doing to her. But he shot her mother anyway. When she started to run toward her mother, her mother said "No, Carly, no. Run Carly run." Carly and her mother had a secret code. When she said that, Carly would know she had to run and hide. There's a nice thing for a six-year-old, huh?"

"Jason, I don't see how you know this! She told you all this?"

"Yes, Christy."

"I don't understand why she's telling you all this."

Jack put his arm around Christy. "Just let it go, Christy. Let's be glad she's telling somebody. She's talking to her therapist, and she can talk to Jason. Evidently, he's won her trust and she's telling him things that she shouldn't have been keeping inside all these years."

"I thought she trusted me," said Christy.

"She trusts you, Christy. But I think there are certain things that were just too painful for her to say to anybody she knew. Now she's telling me because she feels safe with me and knows I'm not going to let anything happen to her. I was shocked when she told me about her father. Remember she was just a little girl. Even if you are an adult, it's not something you want to tell people. Think how hard that is. She was so little. She didn't understand what was happening to her. How could she? She understands now what he was doing to her. She's told me a lot of things that have surprised and shocked me. But it has to be good to let it out. The therapist said to let her tell me anything she wants. Like the story about her father. She was always afraid to tell anybody, so that's just one more thing she's not keeping inside now."

Everyone was quiet for a moment.

"So, what is it about you, Jason?" asked Christy. "She's telling you things she never told anybody before. I'm her sister. She didn't tell me. But you walk into the club one night, you sit down next to her, and she flirts with you! She hadn't spoken to a stranger in over 3 years, and yet she turns around and starts flirting with you. She can't even go to the grocery store. She has a meltdown if people get too close to her in line. Then you put your arm around her, and later she gets up and dances with you! At the end of the evening when the band plays the song for her, she has both arms wrapped around your neck and you're holding on to her with both arms like she is about to fall off a cliff! What is it about you, Jason? She hasn't touched anybody for over 2 years. You walk into the club one night and you can just put your arm around her and touch her and she's fine? I don't get it!"

"I'm not sure, Christy. We just seemed to make a connection. I felt terrible when I realized what that psycho was trying to do. Why he was trying to grab her."

"Yeah, and it only took you about 5 seconds to practically knock the guy out. What's with that?"

"I was an Army Ranger, Christy. You learn these kinds of moves. I couldn't sit there and let some jerk manhandle a woman. That's ridiculous. He was way over the line!"

"Yeah, and he wasn't there long, was he?"

"Did you want me to wait until he hurt her? Come on, Christy, you saw what happened."

"I know, Jason. Then at the end of the evening she still didn't want to let you go, so you went back to the house with us. Carly went to bed to try to get some sleep, she had one of her nightmares, and you picked her up and took her out into the family room, and she sat on your lap sleeping for the rest of the night. She doesn't even like to touch people and she's sitting on your lap for the rest of the night. Even when she woke up, she wasn't panicky."

"Well, she was a little. She didn't know where she was."

"Yeah, but then she looked up at you, I saw her, and she wasn't panicky. I don't get it. The next night she went into her room to sleep but then she went out to the couch where you were and laid down and snuggled up to you. This is a woman who wouldn't let me do more than just touch her hand. She couldn't stand to have anyone even close to her and suddenly she is snuggling up to you on the couch. In the morning, I heard her laughing. I go to look in her room and she's out in the family room with you and Lindsey and you are all laughing. She's laughing! I hadn't heard her laugh in 3 years! Then I take Lindsey away and I go back into the kitchen. When I start to come out of the kitchen, I see you are both still lying on the couch and she's kissing you. She's kissing you! Not just a peck on the cheek kind of kissing, but passionately kissing you! I had to go back in the kitchen and close the door."

"I can't explain it, Christy, we just felt a connection to each other. It surprised me as well."

"Now she keeps telling you all these things about her life that nobody else knows. Suddenly she talks to you about everything. Why is that?"

"It hasn't been as easy for her as you might think. Most of the time when she talks to me about these horrible things, she will come over to me and bury her head in my chest and start talking. She doesn't look at me, we don't make any eye contact, and she will just lay there and talk. Sometimes she'll cry, and sometimes she'll let me hold her when she cries, and other times she won't. She'll roll over to the other side of the bed and doesn't want me to touch her. That's pretty much how it has been. The first night she was at my house, that's what she did. She just cried."

"She cried all night?"

"Yes, til about 6 o'clock in the morning. I just let her cry. I didn't try to stop her. When she would let me, I would just hold her in my arms and let her cry. She's got to let all this come out. She needs to talk about it. Think about what she's been through. It's horrible."

"Well, we tried, Jason. We tried to talk to her. We tried everything. She went to a therapist. But she wouldn't talk to us."

"It might have been harder for her to talk to you than to talk to me. It doesn't sound like the therapist was the right fit for her. He gave her pills, but that doesn't usually work."

"So, you know all about this therapy stuff too, Jason. Then you said she had PTSD. Nobody else said that."

"Well, she does have PTSD."

"How do you know this, Jason? Is this your diagnosis?"

"No. It's what her therapist told her. It's obvious what's happening when you have these night terrors. Memories are coming back to you at night that you have tried to suppress. The images from her kidnapping are returning and it's frightening for her. That's why she shouldn't be alone. Think what it's like to be alone and have this happening to you."

"I suppose you know all about this, too, Jason."

"Well, Christy, I had a bit of a breakdown after I came back from the war, and I learned my parents had been killed. I had terrible flashbacks, but I don't have them anymore because I did a lot of therapy. Usually that's the only way to get rid of them. Now I try not to think or talk about anything related to my military career."

"I don't know, Jason. It just seems strange to me that suddenly, she can do all this talking. Talk, Talk, Talk. Sometimes we couldn't even get her to speak to us."

"Well, that's shock, Christy. Don't you think she was in shock about what happened to her? Shock about being kidnapped, being tortured. From what you all said, she was barely alive when she got to the hospital. You said they ran her blood through a heart machine to warm it up and then put it back into her body. It sounds like she was lucky to have even survived."

"She was in terrible shape," said Jack. "It was awful what he did to her."

"Along with all the trauma she went through, she said she thought she was going to lose her feet. She had to be in shock most of the time. That's what happens. You can't talk. You can't believe these things are happening to you. I think she's getting better. She talks and I just listen."

"So do you tell her things about yourself, Jason?"

"A little bit. If she asks me something, we talk about it."

"So only what she asks you about. You don't really tell her about yourself."

"I'm not sure what you mean, Christy, but from the way you are saying it I have to wonder what you're getting at."

"You don't tell her they refer to you in Kentucky as 'Kentucky's most eligible millionaire bachelor'. You don't tell her that, do you?"

"No, Christy. I don't."

"And you don't tell her about all the women who are following you on social media and making suggestive offers to you. Do you tell her she has a lot of competition up there in Kentucky?"

"Christy, that's ridiculous. Come on, now. I don't read any of that stuff."

"Oh! You don't read about yourself on all these little Twitter postings?"

"No, I don't. And I wonder why you're reading it."

"Because I don't want you to hurt her, Jason. I don't want you to suddenly find there is someone else Twittering about having casual sex hookups with you and Carly ends up out the door."

"Christy, that's not going to happen. I don't have any other relationships. I'm not dating anyone. I didn't have a girlfriend when we met each other. I don't read any of that stuff because it is all a bunch of Crap! I'm not sure why you're reading it. This is what has happened to our world since all this social media nonsense started. There are people out there who just can't mind their own business. Maybe their own lives are horribly boring."

"Okay, Jason, but do you tell her that you have millions of dollars? Have you told her that?"

"Do you think she really wants to know that? Do you think she's interested in money?"

"She might be. Obviously, you haven't told her that you are one of Kentucky's richest bachelors."

"Christy, where are you going with this? What's the problem?"

"Well, I don't know Jason, you're flying around in your own plane and now it turns out you also have your own helicopter, and she said you bought her a very beautiful German piano. Then she refers to herself as the taker and you are the giver. She doesn't want to be a taker, but you just keep giving her all these things. You're paying for her therapy, I guess, because I know she doesn't have any money."

"Yes, Christy. My foundation is paying for her therapy. Don't you think it's worth it? He's an excellent therapist, she seems to like him and seems to be getting better. Every day I see a little change in her, a little more spunk, a bit of playfulness. She kids around with me a little more and teases me a little."

"She was always like that, Jason."

"Really? Since the kidnapping or before?"

Christy paused. "Before the kidnapping she was like that."

"That's my point. Before. Not since. If that means she is getting back a part of her old self, isn't that good?"

"Of course it's good. I just don't want you to hurt her, Jason. From what I read you have millions and millions of dollars."

"Christy you are making this sound like I have a contagious disease I haven't disclosed to Carly. My grandmother and I own a large thoroughbred horse ranch. It has been in the family for about 5 generations. I don't know the actual value of the ranch and neither do all the people who write comments. I also received a wrongful death settlement when my parents were killed, but that was supposed to be a confidential settlement. Sadly, the money couldn't bring them back or help with the grief we all felt over losing them. I don't know why you think my having money means I would hurt Carly. I would only use the money to help her with her recovery. Having money doesn't make me some slime ball who wants to take advantage of Carly and victimize her again. If you read something beyond the Twitter pages, you would have seen that I am a lawyer who does a fair amount of pro bono work. I have a foundation I created to help veterans and people like Carly who have been gravely injured by other people in our society. I work to free prisoners who have been wrongfully and unjustly convicted of crimes they didn't commit."

"But you do have millions of dollars, right Jason?"

"You seem upset about this, so what is it about the money that offends you, Christy?"

"Well, you're giving her all these things, but she told me that the two of you do not really have a relationship."

"What does that mean, Christy? Are you talking about a sexual relationship?"

"Yeah, I guess I am."

"You guess you are, or you are?"

"I am."

"Okay. Is there something about that that bothers you?"

"Well, I'm guessing it's because of what she went through."

"Yeah. Do you think so?" he added somewhat sarcastically. "That would be it, Christy. She's suffered a terrifying trauma. It may take her a long time to recover."

"What if she doesn't ever recover? What then? Are you just going to walk away?"

"I'm not going to walk away, and I think you are getting into territory that is a little too personal here. Whatever happens between Carly and I, we will work it out together just like other couples do. She needs time, a lot of time to heal. It's not something that is going to happen in 6 months, or a year. It might take a long time."

"So, you are going to wait around all this time to see if she gets better?"

"That's the plan, Christy, if it's all right with you."

"Then why is she sleeping in your bed if you know she can't have that kind of a relationship with you? That makes it seem like you are expecting that from her."

"She's sleeping in bed with me because she is frightened. I had another room ready for her, but she couldn't sleep in there alone. She may not admit this to herself, but she wants to be comforted when she cries, and when she is frightened. Even when she falls asleep on the far side of the bed, she is always right next to me when I wake up in the morning. I love seeing how peaceful she looks in the morning when she is sleeping. It seems like all the hurt has drained away from her body during the night. Her face is just soft and beautiful."

"So I guess you are just the ultimate giver, Jason. What can't you give her now?"

"Well, Christy, I can't give her back all the years she spent waiting for her mother to come back to get her because no one told her that her mother was dead! I can't give her back the childhood innocence her father stole from her when he started raping her when she was only six years old. I can't give her back the nights she spent hiding in a chicken coop, cold and alone, because her mother told her to run for her life. I can't give her back these things, but I can give her some new memories. We can make better memories together. She wants to go to Paris, so we are going to go there and make new memories to try to blot out some of the old, horrible things she lived through. We need to find a way to get her a passport, so

I have some other questions to ask if we are finished with all this. Okay, Christy? Are we done here?"

"I just don't want to see Carly get hurt, Jason. I think she's been through enough!"

"Don't you think I know that Christy," he said softly, "after everything she's told me?"

"Well, I guess, Jason. It seems you know more than anyone here. Did you know my dad shot her father?"

Jason was silent for a minute. "I didn't think he shot himself, because Carly said when she was in the chicken coop, she heard a shot and then a little bit later she heard a second shot. Suicides only get one shot, not two."

"That's very true," interjected Jack.

"Oh, my god," said Christy. "You weren't even surprised by that."

"No, not really."

"Oh, my God. And then you knew all about her father molesting her?"

"Yeah, she told me."

"Of course, she did!"

"Listen, Christy, don't take this out on Carly. It's been so hard for her."

"I guess," she answered with a shrug.

Martha reached over for Christy's hand and pulled it over toward her side of the table.

"Christy, honey, stop this! Stop this now! Carly's your sister, and she's always going to love you. When you got married, Carly knew you were still going to love her, but you were going to love Jack, too. Isn't this the same thing? Maybe Carly needs someone to love her, the way you and Jack love each other. Maybe Jason is that person and he and Carly will love each other, but you are still going to have your sister if that happens. He looks like a nice person. He's got nice eyes, and he smiles when he talks about her. It looks like he loves her. What's wrong with that? Why are you so upset?"

"I just don't want him to hurt her!"

"Well, no one can ever guarantee how things are going to work out, but I don't think he wants to hurt her. I don't think he would be doing this today, coming here to find out this information if he wanted to hurt her. Do you think??"

"I don't know, Mom. I just worry about her."

"Why don't you give it some thought," said Martha. "Then try to feel good for Carly. Maybe she's found something she has been looking for. You know how hard it was for her when she lost her mother, remember? It was hard. She was so little. Then you girls developed this great friendship, and I think that's one of the things that pulled her through – your friendship. If she falls in love with Jason don't begrudge her that. Just feel good for her, knowing that she is happy. If it doesn't work out between them, you should be there to comfort her. Okay?"

"I'll try, Mom. I just don't want him to hurt her."

"I know you don't, baby. But I don't think he's going to hurt her."

Nobody knew what to say next. Christy put her head down on Jack's shoulder and cried.

"Come on, Christy, come on." whispered Jack. "Don't be so angry. Let's just hope Carly's happy. Jason's doing nice things for her. She said he bought her a beautiful piano. Does that sound like he wants to hurt her?"

"Christy, why don't you come up to the ranch and visit with Carly. I don't think it's safe for her to spend much time in Nashville."

Jack shook his head. "No, let's not bring her to Nashville."

"Why don't you come up to the ranch and see how she is. Bring Lindsey. We have lots of extra bedrooms. Plenty of room for you. I think you'll see she's getting better, and she's not as frightened as she was. Come and visit anytime. Bring Jack. She's learning how to swim, and we've been doing riding lessons. We have ponies for Lindsey to ride and new little foals that are amazingly cute! Robbie could even come down and pick you up in the helicopter."

"I don't know," said Christy. "Maybe."

"You can do that," said Jack. "Take Lindsey and go visit with Carly. We could all go up on a weekend. I'm sure Lindsay would like to go for a pony ride."

"I'm sure she would."

"We'll plan on that," said Jack.

"Okay", said Jason. "I have another question for you now. Carly wants to go to Paris, but she doesn't have a passport, and we need to find a birth certificate for her. Do you know if there might be a birth certificate for her anywhere?"

"I don't know," said Martha. "I don't remember anything like that. Harold burned that cabin down, so if it was there, it's gone now."

"Well, what is her birthday date?" asked Jason.

Martha and Christy looked at each other. Finally, Christy said, "We celebrated our birthdays on the same day."

"You were born on the same day?" asked Jason.

"No. We just celebrated both our birthdays on my birthday."

"Oh," said Jason. "But that wasn't her birthday?"

"No," said Martha. "It wasn't. We just decided that we'd bake a cake for both girls and celebrate their birthdays on the same day."

"So, you don't know what her real birth date was?" asked Jason.

"I don't think I do," said Martha. "Doesn't she remember?"

"Well, no," said Jason. "She was 6. That was a long time ago."

"Do you remember, Christy?"

"No, I don't remember. We just always said it was OUR birthday and we shared our birthday.

Mom always made us a nice cake and we called it OUR birthday."

Jason was feeling somewhat annoyed by this answer. He was thinking – no mother, no father, and no real birthday.

"How old was Carly when she and her parents came to live in the little cabin on your property?"

"I think it was when Carly was about 4 years old, because she and Christy started Kindergarten together. Carly was a little young for kindergarten, but it was time for Christy to go, so they both started and that was why they were in the same grade."

"Do you have any idea where the family lived before that?"

"I don't think so, but I think somewhere in Tennessee."

"So nobody has any idea where she might have been born? I wish I knew how to figure this out. I guess if she wasn't born in a hospital there might not have been a birth certificate."

Jack looked up at him, "You're a lawyer. Don't you know these things?"

"I guess I should. I think you can petition the court to issue a birth certificate. The biggest obstacle right now is trying to determine the exact name that was used on her birth certificate. I didn't know it was going to turn into such a problem. I have a few more questions now," said Jason. "Carly told me she didn't remember having a funeral service for her mother, or a burial. You had two bodies in that cabin, where did they go?"

Martha looked up at him with a big sigh and said, "We buried them down by the creek. I wrapped her mother up in a nice quilt that was in the cabin, and Harold carried her down to the creek and we dug a grave for her. Then we dug a different grave for the father. I begged Harold not to put them together. She didn't want to be buried with her murderer. Not too long after we buried them, Harold burned the cabin down."

"Oh," said Jack. "That explains a lot."

"Do you have any idea what her mother's maiden name was? Or her first name?" asked Jason.

"Her first name was Bonnie."

"Was it Bonnie Carl?"

"I only remember Bonnie," said Martha.

"What about her father. What was his name?"

"Bobby"

"Last name?"

"I'm not sure, let me think..."

"What about Carly? What name did she use?"

"Carly Lynn," said Martha. "Carly Lynn Miles. At school, she used our family name."

"So right in the middle of her school career you just changed her name to Miles?"

"Well, we didn't really change it. We just told her she should use our name."

"So she was Carly Lynn Miles going through school?"

"Yeah, Carly Lynn Miles."

"Any memory of her dad's name?"

"I'm still thinking about that," said Martha. "I think it started with an "S", but it wasn't Styles."

"Do you know how old her mother was?"

"Her mother came over for coffee one day when the girls were at school. This wasn't too long before she died. She said it was her birthday and she was 21!"

"She was 21. 21 years old? And Carly was 6? So she had a baby when she was 15 years old?"

"Yeah, I guess so, but sometimes that wasn't so unusual in that part of the country back then. I hope it is now. I probably didn't blink an eye at that. She was turning 21 that day. She kidded about it and said she could vote now if we lived anywhere close to a city."

"Did she ever mention the name "Carl – Bonnie Carl?"

"No," said Martha. "Why? Who was that?"

"I'm not sure, but I think that was her name – Bonnie Carl."

"I know her name was Bonnie – that's for sure. Didn't Carly remember what her mother's name was?"

"I didn't ask her," said Jason. "I pretty much just listen to anything she wants to tell me, and I don't ask her a lot of questions. I just listen."

Martha laughed. "Wow! A guy who can listen. How did she find you, Jason? A man who can listen. Wow! That's a good trait, right Jack?"

Jack laughed. "What are you trying to tell me, Martha?"

"It's good to have a man who listens. I'm glad she has you to talk to, Jason. You seem like a nice person, and I'm assuming you must have a helicopter, right?"

"Yes. It's mine. It was my dad's chopper, actually. You don't remember the father's name?"

"I don't know. It started with an "S". Slater, Slater. His last name was Slater."

Jack's head popped up quickly. He exchanged looks with Jason. "Slater? Are you sure?"

"Oh, yeah," said Martha. "I had the "S" part, but I kept thinking Styles. But no, it was Slater. Don't you think that was it, Christy?"

"Maybe."

"Bobby Slater is the name of the kidnapper. Are you sure that was her dad's name?" asked Jack.

"Do you think he was related to her father?" asked Jason.

"There's a good question. We know her father is dead, and the kidnapper claimed he had no family. I think we need to take another look at this felon."

Jason looked over at Jack and his face was pale. "Okay, I think we've really learned some things here. One more thing, though, did Carly's mother ever mention having any family?"

"She did one time, and she said all her family was dead. She had a mother, a father, and a little brother. She said they were all dead."

"What about Carly's father? Did he have any family? Did anyone come to visit them?"

Harold piped up, "Oh, yeah, that son of a bitch, that brother came out there looking for him. We told them they moved away. I think it was right after I burned the cabin down. He wanted to know if that was their cabin. I told him, 'Yeah, it burned down so they moved away.' He was just like the brother, Bobby. A real jerk! I told Martha to keep Carly out of sight when he was there. We didn't know what he might do, and we weren't about to let him take her away."

"Interesting," said Jason. "But he did show up there looking for the brother?"

"Yeah. It seemed like he wanted something from the brother, not like he just came for a visit. It was like the brother owed him something. He was angry, and he wanted to know where the brother went. So I told him, 'how the hell would I know? They just moved on in the middle of the night. The cabin burned down, and they left.' He was a nasty guy."

"Real nasty guy with a bad attitude. We couldn't wait until he got off our property and left. We prayed he would never come back."

"Well, I think we've shed a lot of light on things today. We can head back if you're ready. Christy, do you want to stay and have lunch with your parents before we leave?"

"No, I think I'll come back another day. This has been hard, and I should get back to Lindsey."

"Okay. We can take off then, I guess."

"Hey, Red," said Harold, "you didn't tell me how your little friend Blondie is doing. We didn't talk about her. What's going on with Blondie? What is she doing?"

Martha looked up and smiled. "This is how it goes with him."

"Oh, she's good, Dad. She's doing a lot of singing."

"Singing? I didn't know she could sing, but she was a hell of a little piano player. I used to tell her to play a little louder so I could hear it. So she still plays the piano?"

"Yeah, Dad, she plays the piano, she sings. She's a good singer."

"Never knew she could sing. You tell her Mom and Pop said hello."

"That's kind of how it goes, folks," said Martha.

"Okay," said Christy, "I'm going to come back and see you later this week."

Harold's head popped up, "Are you going to bring that little whirlybird back with you?"

"No, Dad, I'm going to drive in my car next time. That's Jason's helicopter."

"A man with a helicopter, huh? Maybe you should marry this man, Christy."

"No, Pop. You know I'm married to Jack. You remember that I married Jack, right?"

"Yeah, sure. Good looking guy with blonde hair, right?"

"That's him." She looked at Jack and smiled. "Yeah, Pop. Good looking guy with blonde hair. That's Jack. I'll come back later next week and bring Lindsey out to see you."

"Lindsey? Is that like Blondie?"

"No, Pop. Lindsey is my little daughter. Remember when I brought her out to see you?"

Martha just smiled. "He'll remember when he sees her, Christy. He'll remember her."

"Okay. I'll come back and bring Lindsey and we'll do lunch or maybe a picnic."

Her mom smiled. "That'd be nice Christy. We love to see you and we wish we were closer to you, but we just couldn't find a way to live somewhere closer."

"That's okay. I like to drive, and Lindsey is pretty good in the car now."

"Well, whenever you can come, we always want to see you."

"Okay, Mom, Pop we're going to take off now. Do you want to come outside and watch us take off in the chopper."

"Hell, yes," said Pop. "I want to see if this man can really fly that helicopter."

He looked at Jack and said, "How about you? Are you the pilot?"

"No, Pop. This is Jack. Remember Jack – blond haired guy. Jack's not flying the helicopter. Jack came with me because he's my husband."

"Oh, okay. So you don't know how to fly a helicopter. "

"No, no. Not me. We'll leave that up to Jason."

They walked down the hall saying their goodbyes and went out to the helicopter. Her mom and dad were standing there with a lot of other residents. They were all watching them take off.

"Well, that was good, I guess. I think we learned a lot, right?"

"Yeah," said Jack. "I think we learned more than what we were expecting to learn. I wasn't expecting to hear that her dad shot Carly's father. I thought the dad killed himself."

"Well," said Jason. "It's rare that nasty people kill themselves. They really have no remorse."

"I can't believe my dad killed somebody."

"Think about it," said Jack. "He was going to kill Carly. He told your dad he was going to put a bullet in her head. What would you do if someone told you that? I would have shot him. You couldn't stand there and let him kill a little child. I say – Good for him! But I think your mom was worried we were going to start something – like we were going to turn him in. But the fact is: Who cares? We care that he killed her mother. She was probably a nice young girl. But he was not! And he is probably why she had a child when she was only 15. He probably raped her, too. Think about it."

"That thought flashed through my mind, too," said Christy.

Jason looked back over his shoulder and asked, "I guess you were surprised to learn her father's last name was Slater. When her mother said Slater, your jaw dropped about a foot."

"Yeah," said Jack. "Didn't you ever recognize that name during the trial, Christy?"

"I guess I didn't. Maybe little kids don't pay any attention to last names. I don't think I even knew her father's name was Bobby. I don't remember seeing him very often. Carly and I were only six when he died. We never played together over in the little cabin."

"Yeah. The name was a shocker."

"I guess that gives me another name to look for on a birth certificate. Carly isn't sure what happened to her driver's license, but she thought she used the name Carly Lynn Miles on her license," said Jason.

"She probably did," said Christy. "I'm sure that was the name she used in college. Sean might remember. He took her to get her driver's license. She must have used her school records as her identification. Jack, do you remember if any of Carly's personal items were recovered from the kidnapping scene? Anything like her wallet, her purse, her cell phone, or clothing?"

"No. I don't think any of those things were ever recovered. I'm sure that's what happened to her Driver's License. Jason, you should probably have her apply for a new License, but I'm not sure if she can get a copy of it without proving her identity. Maybe our office could provide proof of identity since she was a crime victim, and her License was stolen during the crime."

"Okay, I'll have her look into that," said Jason. He turned around and put his headgear back on. They landed at the Sherriff's office, and no one had said anything else. Jason got out of the chopper and walked inside with Jack and Christy.

"I'm kind of blown away right now," said Jason. "What are you guys thinking?"

"I'm thinking I'm not so proud of my parents right now. I can't believe they knew what Carly's father did to her and they never tried to help her. I never knew why she wanted to sleep under the bed."

"I think they did the best they could, Christy. I think they were frightened about the killing of her father, but they took her in and provided for her all those years. Everyone in Tennessee had heard the horror stories about Georgia Tann's Children's Home and the children she sold and the 500 children who died in her care. I'm sure your parents wanted to keep her out of the foster care system."

"I think they were too afraid to say anything. Oh, hell! I just got a text. They found more bodies out there. Further back in the woods. They are digging right now. They have 3 cadaver dogs and they have found 3 more sites."

Christy looked up and said, "What are you talking about?"

Jason and Jack each looked at each other and just sucked in a little air.

Jack looked over at Christy and said, "Christy they have cadaver dogs out where we found Carly, and they're looking for bodies."

"Oh, I saw that on the news. They found bodies. Is that where they were?"

"Yes, Christy, but we don't want you to tell Carly this yet. We'll tell her when we have to, but please don't tell her yet. Can you do that?"

"I can do that if you think that's best for Carly."

"It's definitely best for Carly. You saw it on the news then?" asked Jack.

"Yeah. They unearthed 3 bodies and there was one empty grave."

She looked up at Jack and said, "Oh, no. no, no." She just stood there for a moment. "No, no Jack."

"Yeah, Christy, the empty grave was for Carly. They told her they were going to kill her."

"Oh, my God. So that was her grave? That was where they were going to put her?"

"Yes. And that's why I didn't tell you this, and why we don't want to tell Carly, although she knew they were going to kill her. They told her they were going to kill her."

"They did? They told her they were going to kill her? How do you know this?"

"She told Jason."

"Of course! Once again! She told Jason!"

Jason looked at her and said, "Look Christy, listen to me. Carly loves you. You're her sister. She loves you unconditionally. You're the only one who has probably ever, ever really loved her and she knows that. It's hard to tell these things to someone you love. When I came back from the war, I learned my parents had been killed. I came back to a big empty house. I still had my grandma, but I couldn't sit and tell her all the horrible things I saw. The friends that I watched die. I couldn't do that to her. I couldn't tell her those things. I loved her. I didn't want to share those horror stories with her. But when I went to therapy, I shared it with my therapist and that's what Carly's doing right now. She's sharing with him, and she has been sharing with me. The first night we were up at the ranch she talked and cried all night. The next night she talked to me again almost all night long. She didn't really know me that well. We were lying in the same bed together, but she only knew me for 3 or 4 days at that point. Sometimes it's easier to talk to someone you don't know all that well. So that's why she can do this. She can open up and talk about these things. This is good for her."

"I just wish she felt comfortable talking to me."

"She does feel comfortable talking to you, Christy. She tells you almost everything, from what I've learned," he said with a smile. "And you probably know all kinds of things she's telling you about how we interact, although there's really not that much to tell right now."

"Oh, I don't know about that, Jason. She's told me a few things."

"Well, I'm not sure what she has told you, but it is mostly fun stuff, right?"

"Yeah. She said you make her smile, and you make her laugh in the morning. She said sometimes when she wakes up," she looked up at Jason kind of shyly, "that you have your whole body all wrapped around her."

"Okay," Jason laughed. "I think that's enough information."

"But that's good for her, Jason. For 2 years she wouldn't let me do anything more than pat her hand. She wouldn't let anybody hug her. If people came up to shake her hand, she would practically have a meltdown. This is good. She likes being with you. She said that's her favorite part of the day – when she wakes up in the morning and you are all wrapped around her."

Christy started laughing.

"Okay, Christy. I think we can stop this now."

She looked at him and said, "No, good for you, Jason. Good for you. I don't know why I'm feeling and acting almost like a jealous boyfriend. But good for you. She's really suffered these last two years, and we just haven't been able to find a way to make things better for her. She lost interest in her music; she lost interest in playing with the band. She likes to come see Lindsey. She likes her little dog, Charlie. But she's lost interest in most of her life."

"I think we are uncovering some of the truths about her life and about the kidnapping. Together, we are going to get her life back for her. We can't let this bastard take everything from her. She had a promising career she created for herself. She has an amazing talent and obviously she had a tremendous will to live. I want her to have everything she struggled so hard to attain. I'm not going to let the bastard ruin her life, and I know you will be with me 100% on this."

"We will," said Christy. "We will be with you every step of the way. No one deserves help more than Carly does. When I witnessed what she went through to recover, I swore that I was going to do everything I could to help her. I never realized how hard it was going to be to jump through all the hoops that would be thrown out in front of us. I think you were right about her need for legal help. I think you are making a big difference in these negotiations now. Sadly, I just couldn't get people to listen to my pleas."

"That is the sad part, but together I think we are making a difference, and the idea you both had for the GoFundMe page was a good one that is going to provide a lot of help to her. I have my grandma and Aunt Nettie sending out emails to get additional donations. They know a great many doctors and healthcare professionals who are likely to make donations."

"Carly is extremely concerned about paying the doctors and nurses who saved her life. She doesn't want them to feel like they have been forgotten."

"Yes. We have discussed this, and she also talked it over with Dr. Mac. He told her that it is still okay to have fun and enjoy her life, even though there are still professionals that need to be paid. He told her to let me handle that part of her life and resume working on her professional goals."

"Good," said Christy. "It may take some time to resolve all the financial issues surrounding her case. She can't put her career on hold that long. She seems to like and respect her therapist's advice. I'm glad he told her to get on with the business of living. I'm glad you found someone like that to help her, Jason."

"Yes. He is a good man who really cares about his patients. I think he and Carly are developing a nice trust. I think she will emerge from this with his help, and because she has such internal strength. I never let her forget she has all of us to help her."

"Amen," said Christy and Jack together.

Chapter 17

Jason woke up slowly and thought he heard voices coming from the kitchen. He looked at his phone and it was only 6am so he wondered why anyone was in the kitchen this early. Suddenly there was a persistent knock on his bedroom door. Carly woke with a start and grabbed hold of Jason.

"Jason I need you to come out to the front gate with me."

"What's going on, Roy?"

"We have a bit of an emergency."

"What is it? Is it Grandma? Is she okay?"

"No, it's not Gwen. She's fine, but I need you to come with me."

"Just tell me what's wrong."

"I'll text you."

Jason looked at the phone and said, "Oh, crap! Really Roy?"

"Yeah. We need you. I need to send Carly down to the Safe Room with Gwen and Nettie."

"What's going on? What's a safe room?" asked Carly.

"It's a fortified room. Grandma is going to lock you in. Don't open the door for anyone except me or Roy. If you don't hear one of us, don't open the door. Okay, grab your shoes and run down the hall and find Grandma."

Jason was putting on his boots and grabbing a shirt. He opened the door for Roy. "Who's the trespasser?"

"I think it's one of the kidnappers you've been looking for."

"Are you kidding me?"

"No. Security nailed him, and they have him on the ground near the gate."

"Crap. Hurry up Carly. Run down the hall and go with Grandma."

"Okay, but you're scaring me."

"I promise you'll be okay. Grandma and Nettie will take you downstairs to the Safe Room in the basement. Take your iPad. There's plenty of food and drink down there for you."

Carly went running down the hall, and Jason and Roy ran out the front door. Jason clicked on the security seal for the whole house. "When did they find this guy, Roy?"

"About ten minutes ago."

"You really think it's one of the murdering brothers?"

"Yeah. He looks somewhat like the picture you gave to security."

"I gave them a picture of the guy who's in prison already. Bobby."

"He looks like that but maybe a little thinner, and a little younger. I'm pretty sure he's one of them."

"Carly thought there might have been two or three of them during the kidnapping."

"Maybe we just found the second one."

"How the hell did he get in here?"

"We don't know that yet, but he was right here on the grounds near the main gate."

"Damn!" said Jason. "It's a good thing Security saw him. I don't want to think what might have happened if we didn't know he was here."

"They nailed him right away. He started to run from them, but they were in the vehicle, and he was on foot, so of course they caught him."

"He didn't bring a car in here, did he?"

"No. He couldn't have gotten a car through the gate."

"How did he get in?"

"I don't know, but we need to figure it out, so it never happens again. Okay. Get in the cart. Let's go look at him."

"Do you think they will be okay downstairs? I'm wondering if there might be two of them here on the property already."

"Oh, hell yes. In that room? No one's going to get in there. That's the first thing your grandma thought about – getting Carly and going to the Safe Room. Second thing she thought of was her gun."

"Do you think she would really shoot someone?"

"Hell, yes. If she felt threatened she would shoot. I'm not sure she would take a kill shot, but she would wound the poor bastard til he couldn't move. I've done target shooting with her and she's good with that gun. I think her dad taught her how to defend herself ever since she was a little girl."

"I guess the ladies are safe then. How did this guy find us? I guess I won't feel secure up here anymore. I promised Carly she would be safe here on the ranch."

They got out to the spot where Security had the guy down on the ground. Jason jumped out of the cart and sat down on top of the trespasser. "Who the hell are you and what are you doing here?"

"I don't have to tell you," answered the trespasser.

"Well, I'm going to slam your head against the ground until you tell me, so there's something for you to think about."

The trespasser didn't say anything, so Jason grabbed him up by the shoulders and thumped him back down against the ground.

"Tell me who you are, and what are you doing here?"

"I'm just looking around."

"This is private property not some damn public park and all the signs say, 'No Trespassing' so what the hell are you doing here?"

"I didn't see any signs."

"Look over there. There's one sign only 10 feet away from your nose. Do you think we have big fences around the property because we want people to come in? Who are you and what are you doing here? How did you get in here?"

He didn't answer, so Jason grabbed him up and slammed him back down into the ground.

Roy could see the raw anger on Jason's face. It was almost frightening.

"I followed you from Nashville yesterday."

"You followed me from Carly's house?"

"Hey, Jason, take it easy. The Sheriff is coming."

"Hell no! I'm not going to go easy on this loser." He looked down at the trespasser and said, "If you are one of the bastards who raped and tortured Carly you are going to be sorry for the rest of your damn life."

"I didn't rape nobody."

"Then why do you look just like the picture we have of this felon, Bobby Slater? What is your name? Is he your brother?"

He still didn't answer. Jason gave him a good thump. "The next hit is going to be a lot worse. What's your name?"

"I'm Ryan."

"Ryan, what?"

"Ryan Slater."

"Oh, so you are part of this murderous family. Are you Bobby's brother?"

He didn't answer, so Jason started twisting his arm until he started screaming.

"Who are you? Are you his brother?"

"I'm his brother."

"Oh, good! Another member of the family of murderers and rapists. So, you're a rapist too, right?"

Ryan didn't answer again.

Jason grabbed him by his jacket and started shaking him violently, and Roy saw the look on his face and thought, *Oh, my God, Jason is going to kill this guy. I can't let him kill the guy.*

"Okay, Jason. The Sherriff is close by now."

"I hope he gets here before I have to kill this bastard."

"No, Jason. We're not going to kill him."

"I might." He looked at Ryan. "If you're Bobby's brother then you are one of the guys who raped Carly. You raped and tortured her, you bastard."

"I didn't do nothing to her."

"Yeah, I heard all about the 'nothing'. We know what you did. She remembers everything now. You were the one who raped her when she was blindfolded, right?"

He didn't say anything.

"Right? Did you hear me? They put a blindfold on her when you came in to rape her, right?"

"Maybe," he said.

"Yeah maybe. Did that make you feel like a man, Ryan? Do you feel like a man when you tie a woman down to a bed and rape her? There were three of you, weren't there? You fractured her skull, and you broke her jaw! Did you need to show her how tough you were?"

"That wasn't me. That was Evil."

"Who's Evil?"

"Evil Twin."

"What kind of a name is that? Evil Twin? Is that a name?"

"Yeah. Evil Twin did that. I didn't hurt her."

"Oh, you didn't hurt her, you just raped her, right?"

"Yeah. But she liked it."

"She didn't like it, you bastard. Women don't like being raped."

"She said she liked it."

"Yeah, she might have said anything after you tortured her and beat her. I'll give you an example of how much she liked it." Jason pulled his leg up and kneed the trespasser in the groin until he screamed in agony. "How did that feel? Did you like it?"

"I didn't beat her. That was Evil."

"So Evil is the one who fractured her skull?"

"Yeah. He did that in the shower."

"And broke her jaw?"

"Yeah. In the shower."

"All the same day?"

"Yeah."

"And what did you do to her?"

"I didn't hurt her, and I didn't beat her. That was Evil and sometimes Bobby."

"So Evil is the one who beat her up and broke her cheekbone? And what about you? Are you the one who choked her?"

"No. That was Bobby."

"So, Bobby is the choker, Evil is the beater, and you are just the rapist? Is that your claim to fame? You don't beat up these women, you just rape them and then you kill them, right?"

"I didn't hurt her. I didn't beat her."

"Yeah. You just raped her and stood by and watched your brothers beat and torture her. You think that was okay, right? Are you too stupid to understand what an accessory to murder is? Why did all of you hurt Carly?"

"It was all Bobby."

"What does that mean?"

"Bobby did it."

"No. There were three of you. It took all three of you to rape a woman."

He slammed the trespasser's head back down against the ground.

The perp looked at him and said, "You can't do this to me. You can't beat me up like this."

"So, you don't like violence when you're the victim, huh? It's okay when a woman is the victim, right? Do you want to take a swing at me? Do you want to try to hurt me and see what happens? Got any weapons on you? Got a knife? Got a gun with you?"

"We took the gun," said Security.

"Good. Who were you planning to shoot, Ryan? I bet you have a knife on you. Maybe on your leg."

Jason ran his hand down Ryan's leg. "Oh, sure enough. I can feel it." Jason grabbed the knife out of its holster and brought it up to Ryan's face. "How about if I put this up against your face and every time you say something I don't like I'll cut something off your face."

"Jason, Jason," said Roy. "We don't want to kill anybody here. The sheriff is coming to pick him up."

"Yeah. I hope they put him in a strait jacket so he can't ever escape. That's what they do with crazy people, isn't it? What we have here is a real psychopath. Grab my phone and take his picture and send it to Jack. Please message Jack that we have this bastard. Tell him that there is one more psychopathic brother out there that they call Evil. Where's Evil? Where is he?"

"Probably out in the woods somewhere."

"Is Evil up here on this property? Did he come up here with you? If he's up here, we're going to shoot him. Security is going to radio the other cars so they will know to shoot him on sight. What does Evil look like, Ryan?"

"He looks like Bobby. He's a twin."

"And you call him Evil?"

"That's his name. Sometimes he's slow."

"What does that mean? He's not a fast thinker like you? Is he mentally handicapped?"

"It's like he's not all there."

"He's not all there, but he knows how to torture people and cut them up and burn them and bite them? Or maybe you did that!"

"No. That's what Evil does."

"And you just sit and watch him torture people, huh? You don't mind watching Evil cut somebody up and burn them and bite them, right? How about you? Did you do some biting? You know we are going to check your teeth and look at every tooth mark on every single body we find. Did you bite Carly? Were you biting her?"

Jason grabbed him by the shoulders and threw him down against the ground again.

"I might have."

"Great. So you aren't just a rapist, you're also a biter. You were biting her like a rabid dog. Should we shoot you like a rabid animal?"

"I didn't do it all. It was mostly Bobby."

"What about Evil?"

"Yeah. Bobby and Evil."

"Who killed those other people out there? You know we found graves out there. Nice young girls that didn't get to live very long. Lots of graves. That makes you serial killers. All three of you."

"It was Bobby. He killed them. I didn't kill them."

"Bobby killed all those people?"

"Uncle Bobby killed the Carl family."

"Uncle Bobby? Bobby Slater? Carly's father?"

"Yeah. Uncle Bobby did that."

"Uncle Bobby killed the Carl family? But not Bonnie, right?"

"No. He kept Bonnie. He raped her and then she got pregnant."

"Big surprise! He raped her, and was she only about 14 years old when he killed her family?"

"Yeah. She was just a girl."

"So he raped her and he kept her, right?"

"Yeah, and they moved away."

"Then she had a baby and that was Carly. So you decided that you would go after Carly and kill her too, right?"

"And Bonnie. We're going to kill Bonnie too."

"Bonnie is already dead. She and Bobby are both dead."

"Shit! Uncle Bobby is dead? He's not dead!"

"He is. He got shot for being a murderer and a rapist. Too bad that didn't happen to you."

"Shit! We're trying to find Uncle Bobby."

"Uncle Bobby is very dead. He's been dead for a long time. He's been dead since Carly was six years old. He was a rapist and got rewarded with a bullet. Seems like that's what all of you should get too."

"Shit. Uncle Bobby's dead?"

"Is that such a big surprise to you?"

"He was supposed to…."

"What was he supposed to do?"

"He was supposed to bring the kid when she was seven, and then we couldn't find him."

"What do you mean, 'bring the kid'?"

"After Bonnie had the kid then Bobby was going to kill her, and we were going to take care of the kid."

"You were going to kill a little girl?"

"No. We weren't going to kill her."

"What were you going to do with her?"

"My dad was going to sell her."

"Sell her? You were going to sell her? Sell a little girl?"

"Yeah. There's good money in it."

"Who was he going to sell her to?"

"It depends. If they're old enough he sells them into prostitution. If it's a baby, he sells them to a family."

"I think you are making me feel a little sick right now. Your father sells young girls into prostitution?"

"Sometimes. It's easy money."

"Your dad is where?"

"Don't know."

"So that's who was at Bobby's trial. Your dad, your mother and you. You were at the trial. We have video footage of all of you. So, your parents traffic in children. Who do they sell the children to?"

"Pimps and old men always want little girls. You can make good money if they're cute."

"You are just a family of bastards, aren't you? You would sell little girls into prostitution to make money? Hey Roy, send another message to Jack. He needs to go find the mother and the father of this psychopath and arrest them. Evidently, they traffic in children. We have an entire family of psychopaths here. Where do they live, Ryan?"

"Nashville."

"Where in Nashville?"

Ryan didn't answer, so Jason thumped his head against the ground again.

"They live out in the country."

"Near the property where you kept Carly?"

"No. I can't tell you."

"Don't worry we'll find your father and mother and arrest them."

"Why would you arrest my mother?"

"Child trafficking, murder, assault, accessory to murder, accessory to kidnapping, accessory to rape. Do you want me to continue? She knew what you were doing, didn't she?"

"No. She didn't know nothing."

"I'm sure she did. Your family might not be very popular with your new friends in prison. Even felons have families and little girls. You just might not live very long in prison once they find out you sold little girls into prostitution."

"I didn't do that! That was my dad and my mom. I didn't sell the girls."

"What did you do, just kidnap them?"

"Sometimes."

"So sometimes you killed them and sometimes you sold them. Do you know how many graves we have uncovered out there? How many people did you kill? How many?"

"I didn't kill nobody."

"So, you're not one of the murderers, right?"

"No. That's Bobby. Sometimes it's Evil. He gets carried away."

"He gets carried away, huh? Where are we going to find Evil?"

"I don't know where he is. He lives underground."

"He lives in a hole in the ground? Like a snake? Or does he live with your parents?"

"No, he doesn't live with them. They won't let him live there."

"Why? Is he too evil?"

"I told you. Sometimes he's slow."

"What does that mean? Is he mentally challenged? Is that what you mean by slow?"

"He doesn't know about some things. He doesn't understand everything."

"But he knows how to torture people. He knows how to kill people. Did you teach him to do that?"

"No. I didn't do that. It's only Evil that does that."

"Not Bobby? Bobby doesn't kill people or bite people? You do. You bite people. How about Evil. Does he bite people?"

"Yeah. Sometimes."

"We saw what you did to Carly. You don't deserve to live after doing that to another human being."

"Well, she got away. She didn't get killed."

"Oh, yeah. She got away. She was half frozen, but she got away. She almost died, but yeah, she got away because she doped up your brother with sleeping pills. She ran through the woods on the coldest damn night of the year. Were you following her in the woods? You wanted to grab her and take her back to that filthy cabin, didn't you?"

"No. That was Evil."

"Once again, you didn't do anything, it was only Evil."

"That was Evil. He was following her, but he couldn't get to her. There were too many police cops out there. Then one of the Troopers found her."

"Dumb luck for Evil, right? He couldn't take her back to kill her. You had a grave ready for her, didn't you?"

"Yeah, we did. We dug it before the ground froze up."

"So, you were planning to murder her for quite some time, huh? Well, you are going to jail for a long time Buddy. Probably forever if they don't decide on a lethal injection for you."

"I didn't kill nobody. They can't do that to me."

"Sure. How are you going to prove that? There are a lot of graves out there. Surely your DNA is going to turn up on some of the bodies. Do you know how many dead people they have found so far?"

Ryan didn't answer and Jason slammed his head down into the ground again. "Do you know how many people are dead out there?" Jason shouted.

"Five."

"Just five? Are those the five people you killed?"

"No, but Uncle Bobby killed all of the Carl family."

"How many were in the Carl family?"

"There were four, but Uncle Bobby didn't kill the girl."

"No. Uncle Bobby just raped her. She had a great life with him. He raped her and he beat her and then he shot her in the head. She was 21 years old, and he killed her. Then he got killed too. Same day!"

"No, he didn't. He moved away. They weren't dead. My dad and I went out to that farm."

"Joke's on you, buddy. They were both lying in a grave down by the creek. He was dead in the grave by the time your father went looking for him. So was Carly's mother. Carly was still there. You all missed her, didn't you? You didn't see her there, did you?"

"No. that farmer told us they all moved away."

"Yeah. They moved down to the creek to a grave. That's where they were. Uncle Bobby was there, dead in the grave, but Carly was still there. She was with the neighbors. They saved her from you. They saved her from your murderous family. What a bunch of psychopaths! Why did he kill the Carl family?"

"Uncle Bobby didn't like the Carl family. I think they were squatting on our land."

"So that's a reason to kill them? Why didn't he let them move away?"

"I don't know. He hated the Carl's."

"Why did he hate the Carl family?"

"I don't know. I was only a kid."

"But you got to grow up, huh? Nobody killed you. You got to grow up and become a murderer. Too bad. Someone should have killed you."

Jason heard the sirens in the distance. "Sounds like the Sheriff is coming for you, Buddy."

"You can't hold me for anything. Just trespassing."

Jason started laughing. "Oh no, Buddy. We are going to get your DNA and match it up to every corpse we find. Then we can charge you with rape and assault on Carly. Oh, and don't forget about the biting. Every little thing you have done in your whole life is going to come back to bite you in the ass, which is very appropriate since you, yourself, are a biter."

"You can't do that. I didn't kill no one."

"If we find Evil up here, we'll just put a bullet in his head. He doesn't deserve anything better."

"You can't do that. You can't kill Evil."

"No? Why not? That's what you do. You kill people. Evil kills people. The Slater family serial killers. Seems like it's your turn to be at the wrong end of a gun. How many more graves are we going to find? How many more people have you killed?"

"You're not going to find them. You'll never find all of them."

"I guess we need to keep looking then. I guess there are more graves out there for us to find. We have big cadaver dogs out there searching for bodies. They even found the Carl family and your Uncle Bobby murdered them a long time ago. How many bodies do you think we found so far?"

Ryan was silent. "You're not talking now, huh? Do you know what happens to serial killers?"

"They go to prison."

"If they don't get the death penalty. I've never met anyone who deserves the death penalty more than every member of your family. There's a special place for serial killers. Do you know where that is?"

"Jail."

"Not just jail. There's a Maximum-Security Prison in Colorado you can go to. You get to stay in solitary for 23 hours a day. No one has ever escaped from it. It is known as the worst prison in America. Sound fun? Something you can look forward to."

"I didn't kill those girls."

"Which one didn't you kill? Your brothers killed them all? And your dad?"

"Jason, I'm opening the gate for the Sheriff."

The Sheriff pulled up and got out of the car. He had a deputy with him. "Roll him over, Jason so we can cuff him."

Jason got off him and rolled him over. He pulled Ryan's arms up behind his back and the perp screamed.

"That hurts. You're twisting my arm."

"Oh, too bad. That's what happens to rapists."

The Sheriff looked at Jason. "Who is this? I thought you had a trespasser."

"He's a trespasser all right. But he is also a murderer and a rapist."

"What's going on here, Jason?"

"Remember the flyer I sent you about the Slater family? Meet Ryan Slater, brother of Bobby Slater. He's a rapist too. And a murderer. He was part of the kidnapping of Carly Styles."

"Shit. This guy was in on that? He kidnapped the singer?"

"Yeah. And there's one more brother. They call him Evil."

The Sheriff looked over at Jason. "There were three of them? All three of them assaulted her?"

Jason nodded. "Sadly, yes."

The Sheriff moved over closer to Jason. "Is she up here now? Is that why he came here? How did he know she was here?"

"He said he followed me from Nashville."

"So we know he has a car up here somewhere."

The Sheriff looked down at Ryan and asked, "What's your other brother's name?"

"Evil. We call him Evil Twin."

"What's his real name?"

"Just Evil."

Sherriff looked over at the deputy and said, "Get this guy's picture and send it in to face recognition. Run his name in the criminal database and look for priors. See if we can find a match anywhere."

"I think the brother Bobby is going to be a close match. He's the perp already in jail. I think Bobby and Evil are twins."

"Are they twins, buddy?" asked the Sheriff. "Bobby and Evil, are they twins?"

"Yeah."

"What's his real name?"

"That's all we call him. Evil. Evil Twin."

"Great," said the Sheriff. "So here we have kidnapping, rape, murder, trespassing…"

"Assault and torture," said Jason. "He came up here fully armed with a gun and a knife, so there's no telling what he was planning to do here."

"So, everything except the trespassing happened in Tennessee, right?" asked the Sheriff.

"Right." Said Jason.

"What were you planning to do here, Buddy? Why do you have a gun with you and a knife?

Do you have a permit to carry a weapon? We're checking your record right now, so don't lie to me. Who is the gun registered to?"

"I don't know."

"Why are you here with a gun?"

"To get Carly."

"To do what with her?"

"Take her."

"Take her where?"

"Take her back."

"Buddy, did you think this man, Jason, this former Army Ranger was just going to let you leave this ranch with Carly? He would have killed you first. Are you too stupid to realize that?"

"I dunno. That's what Bobby told me to do."

"Bobby who's in prison? I guess he needed you to join him. Well, he's going to get his wish. Where is your car? How did you get up here? Did he get his car in here?"

"No," said Jason. "He couldn't get his car in here. We're not even sure how he got in. Where is your car, Ryan?"

"I dunno."

"I'm sure we can find it," said the Sheriff. He started ordering an APB for the missing car. Ten minutes later a message came up on his phone. "One of my deputies found a car with Tennessee plates about a mile from here. He's running the plates now. There might be lots of evidence in that car."

"Where is Robbie right now, Roy?" asked Jason.

"Over in the barn I think."

"Ask him to take his gun and go over to the house and keep patrolling around it just in case Evil is up here. This might be a diversion tactic. Tell him to shoot if he sees him. Get Grandma on the phone and tell her to let us know if she hears any noises in the house. Tell her that Robbie is going to be right outside. Try not to scare her, okay?"

"I have my gun with me. Do you want me to go with Robbie?"

"Yeah. Please do that. Let's send security back out to continue patrolling the grounds. The Evil bastard could be up here. Make sure all the security patrols are looking for him. Message all the employees to be on the lookout for any strangers. Tell them to look in every stall and every stinking corner of every barn. Let's bag up his gun for the Sheriff."

A few minutes later the Sheriff saw the message that the plates did not match the vehicle.

"Big surprise. The car has stolen plates. Guess we need to run the VIN number now to find the owner. Did you steal this car, buddy?"

"No."

"Who owns the car?"

"Don't know. It's not my car."

The Sherriff reached down and pulled a set of keys from Ryan's jacket pocket. "Are these the keys to that car?"

"It's not my car."

"No. It's probably stolen."

The Sheriff tossed the keys to one of his deputies. "See if these are the keys for that car. Wear gloves and don't touch the steering wheel or anything inside. Check the trunk too."

"We checked the trunk already. It was empty."

The Sheriff looked at his phone again and started swearing. He pulled up a picture of a young girl and shoved the phone into Ryan's face. "Did you kill this girl, you bastard? Did you kill her?"

"I didn't kill nobody."

"You're driving her car. Your ID is in the car. Where is she? Did you kill her?"

Jason looked at the picture on the Sheriff's phone. The Sheriff explained to Jason.

"She's the daughter of a friend. She's been missing for about a year. Thought she took off with a loser boyfriend. We were never able to find even a trace of her. Till now."

Jason sighed. "Sorry Sheriff. That's what they do. They're killers. Send her DNA to Granger and he can see if there is a match. They still have unidentified bodies."

The Sheriff grabbed Ryan by the neck and started screaming at him. "Tell me where this girl is Buddy. Where is she? Did you kill her? Is she dead? Start talking!"

"I dunno. I don't remember."

"I want to know, and I want to know now." The Sheriff was tightening his grip on Ryan's neck.

"She was pretty. I think my dad sold her. I can't remember."

"You sell so many girls you can't remember? Who did you sell her to?"

"I dunno. There's some old guy in Kentucky who buys them, I think."

The Sheriff released him and threw him back down on the ground. "How do we end up with psychopaths like these? Do you want me to bring in another patrol car to help you search the grounds for the other bastard, Jason?"

"It might help," said Jason. "We have a lot of buildings to go through. He could be hiding anywhere."

The Sheriff walked over and pushed Ryan hard enough with his foot to roll him over.

"Is your brother up here on this ranch? Did you bring him with you? Everyone up here is armed now, and I'm going to authorize them to shoot him on sight. You're armed and dangerous serial killers. You came up here to kill Carly. We'll shoot him if he's here. Is that what you want?"

"He's not here. I didn't bring him."

"We don't believe you. The only thing we believe is that you are a dangerous killer."

Jason heard the Sheriff radioing for additional patrol cars to come to the ranch. Jason's stomach churned when he thought of what this monster had planned to do. He took a minute to call Grandma on her phone and asked to speak to Carly. He just needed to hear her voice. He needed to know she was okay. "Are you ladies okay there?" Jason asked.

"We're playing cards," said Carly. "I can't believe all the food and supplies you have down here. We even made coffee. I wish I could bring you some. How long are we going to be staying here? Are you okay? Have you seen Bandit? Do you think he's okay?"

"Sure, we are all okay," said Jason. "The Sheriff is here now for the trespasser. Don't worry about Bandit. He could outrun any trespasser on the planet. Dogs are smart. They run from danger."

"Are you coming to get us?"

"Not quite yet. We're making sure there isn't anyone else up here."

"Who was the trespasser?"

"I'll let you know later when we know for sure," Jason lied. He didn't want to frighten her. He'd tell her when they were together again. When he could hold her and tell her she was still safe. He remembered how he had promised to keep her safe on the ranch.

"Let me speak to Grandma again for a minute." Carly passed the phone back to Gwen.

"Grandma, if Roy told you who the trespasser is, please don't tell Carly yet. I want to tell her when we finish looking for the third brother. I promised to keep her safe up here. I never thought something like this could happen. I promised her she would always be safe."

"We're all safe here, Jason. Don't beat yourself up about this. It's not your fault, and we are perfectly safe. Go look for the other guy and we are going to play Scrabble."

Jason smiled and ended the call. He heard the sirens from police cars in the distance. He walked back toward the main gate and saw two more patrol cars entering.

Jason walked over toward the Sheriff. "Reinforcements are here, Jason," said the Sheriff. "I'm going to take this guy back to the jail and lock him up nice and tight until Granger gets here tomorrow to pick him up."

"You can't hold me for trespassing, it's only a misdemeanor," Ryan started shouting. "You can't hold me. I want a lawyer."

"Went to law school, did you?" the Sheriff asked. "Jason here is a lawyer, maybe he could help you."

"Not in this lifetime," said Jason. "I want to see him prosecuted for every last thing he has ever done."

"You can't lock me up for trespassing," Ryan yelled.

"Son, I'm going to lock you up for trespassing, possession of a stolen car, stolen license plates, carrying a firearm without a permit, possession of a stolen firearm, and attempted kidnapping. Those are just charges in Kentucky. Then we have a whole laundry list of charges from Tennessee. You are never going to be free again. All your new best friends are going to be inmates. And I guarantee you that some of them are going to be a lot friendlier than you might like. You won't be able to rape and torture them like you did with all those young girls."

"I'll make sure that Carly comes to testify at your trial, Ryan. Hopefully all three of you will be awarded the lethal injection and the state of Tennessee will be finished with you."

"I didn't kill nobody."

"Should have talked to a lawyer sooner, Buddy. You have been an accessory to every kidnapping, rape, and murder that either you or your brothers committed. You're all finished."

Jason walked away from Ryan; disgust blazoned across his face. He looked over at the Sheriff. "What a waste of a human being he is. I'm sorry about your friend's daughter. I'm sure the FBI will be looking into the child trafficking. With any luck they might be able to find her. Did they ever find the boyfriend they thought she left town with?"

"No. He was never found either. It's possible he might be in one of those graves they are excavating. Or maybe they sold him along with the girl. I guess there might be a market for young males."

"Anything is possible. I'll tell Jack to let you know about any unidentified bodies. Okay, let's start our search out by the Hangar. That's the furthest outbuilding on the ranch. I'm going to keep Roy and Robbie over by the house just in case he turns up there."

"Can they both handle a gun, Jason?"

"Oh, yeah. Robbie is ex-Army, and Roy grew up here and learned to shoot when he was a kid. Even my grandmother can handle a gun, and she's a crack shot!"

"This guy was armed, so I'm sure the brother would have a gun as well. Do you have a gun, Jason?"

"No. I don't do weapons anymore. I did enough of that in the Army."

"If he shoots at you, you might wish you had one." The Sheriff walked over to his car and took a gun from the glove box. "Take this with you. Just give it back to one of my guys at the end of the search if I'm not back here."

Jason headed out to the hangar with the Deputies. He made calls to all the ranch hands on duty to see if anyone had noticed a stranger walking around. They searched every building on the ranch before ending the search. The Sheriff was back just as they were finishing up. Jason gave the gun back to the Sheriff.

"Luckily, I didn't need to use this. We didn't find anyone. I think I should go back to the house and get the ladies out of the Safe Room."

"Safe Room? You have a Safe Room in that house?"

"Oh, yeah. My dad put it in when he had the house built."

"Not very long ago I wouldn't have thought anyone in Kentucky would need a Safe Room. Now I wonder where all these sorry-ass criminals are coming from. I blame some of it on the drugs, but that can't be the only reason for psychopaths like these brothers. At least we took one more of them off the streets today. That Sheriff down in Nashville better get busy and find that third 'Evil' guy if he wants to get re-elected."

"When they find him, I think Carly will finally feel safe again. She has nightmares about being taken away and killed by these bastards."

"With good reason, evidently. That's exactly what he said he came here to do - to take her back. What a horrible feeling that must be. They need to find that Evil brother and put him away!"

"Soon, I hope! Thanks for all your help here, Sheriff. If we happen to find him later, we'll be calling you. Let me know what evidence you find in the car. I hope they can find the girl and her boyfriend. If they really did sell her, they may have killed the boyfriend. Usually, they only snatch girls who are alone, so maybe they only stole her car."

"I'd like to believe that, but we'll see where the evidence leads us."

Jason went down to the Safe Room to retrieve the ladies. He knocked at the door and identified himself.

"I think we know your voice, Jason. But just to make sure, tell me who is your favorite girl?"

"Carly, you know you are my favorite girl."

"Okay. Now what do you call me?"

"Babe. Stop teasing me, Carly. Open the door now. You can all leave, and we need to get some lunch."

She opened the door and wrapped her arms around Jason. "Who was the trespasser, Jason?"

Jason put his arms around her and held her close. "It was Ryan Slater. Turns out he is the youngest of the murdering Slater brothers. I'm so sorry, Carly. I promised to always keep you safe here. I never thought one of them would find their way up to the ranch or come onto the property."

"It's not your fault. I'm glad you caught him. He'll go to jail now, won't he? He won't be able to come after me again, will he? Is that why he was here? Was he going to take me back to that filthy cabin?"

"I think he wanted to do that. He said Bobby told him to come and get you."

"Oh, God!" she shivered. "When does this end? Is there another trespasser you were looking for?"

"Yes. I'm sorry. There's one more brother they call Evil."

"Evil Twin. That's what he called himself. I thought he was the same guy, Bobby. It was another brother? He was truly Evil. He was the most violent one. He fractured my skull in the shower and left me to bleed out on the floor."

Jason hugged her closer. "We're going to find him. He's going to pay for what he did to you. He's not going to come here and hurt you. I'll kill him if I have to. I already alerted Jack, so he knows there is one more brother down there in Nashville. Let's go see what we can fix for lunch."

"I'll do that," said Gwen. "Where are Roy and Robbie?"

"Outside the house with loaded guns."

"Oh, good," said Gwen. "Can I take my gun and go out with them? Who are we going to shoot?"

"Evil. The Evil Twin."

"Perfect," said Gwen, and she went running up the stairs to go out with the men.

"Looks like I'm going to fix lunch while Annie Oakley goes out with her gun," said Nettie.

Chapter 18

Jason looked up from the notes he was reviewing and saw Carly standing on the other side of the bed. She was wearing a soft, silky lavender shirt which covered her arms and back. Her pajama shorts were a lavender and purple flower print edged with lace trim. He could see her eyes were brimming with tears she was desperately trying to hold back. "Ready for bed?" he asked.

"Can I sleep here with you again?"

"Of course, you can." Jason lifted the covers with one hand and reached out to her with the other. Carly slid under the covers and moved over toward Jason.

"I just need to hold onto you for a few minutes if that's okay." Carly reached across him and wrapped her arms tightly around him.

"It's always okay. What's wrong, Carly? Do you feel frightened?"

She nodded her head without speaking. He could feel her feet twitching, which was always a sign that she was upset or frightened. Her hands were trembling, and her body was shaking.

"What's happened? Can you tell me what you're thinking about?"

"I'm as good as dead, Jason. That's what he said. But I'm not ready to die now. I like being here with you. I like it here on the ranch. Everyone has been so good to me. When he was raping me, I wanted to die. I prayed that I would die. When I was going to lose my feet, I asked Sean if he would help me die. He said he couldn't do that, and he would take care of me, but I just wanted to die. I didn't want to live without feet. I didn't want to be a burden to anyone. Now I want my life back. I think I could finish some of my songs. I'm not ready to die. Not now."

"I'm not going to let anyone hurt you, Carly. He's not going to kill you. He's in prison. I know who he is now. I'll never forget his face. There's no way he's going to come here and hurt you. Remember I promised you I'd keep you safe here. I promised you that no one was ever going to hurt you again. Don't you remember?"

"You can't promise that Jason. He's a vicious felon who wants to kill me. How can you promise that?"

"Because he's no match for me. I had years of training in the Army. If you want to stay alive you don't forget that training. Your life is on the line every day in a war zone. You learn to react quickly to every possible threat. I had combat experience and I'm still here. I'm bigger and stronger than he is, Carly. I would recognize him in a heartbeat, and if I ever see him near you again, I'll know what I have to do."

"But he has guns, Jason, and knives and he is a vicious psychopath. His desire to kill me is stronger than his wish to be free. When he escaped, he could have run, but instead he came back to kill me. I feel like I need to be watching for him every minute of the day."

"So, there's proof he is not a smart felon. I know how to disarm men with guns and knives. I've had plenty of practice, Carly. He has no experience dealing with men like me. He preys on women and young girls he can subdue easily. He's basically a coward who searches for young women he can torture and kill. He wasn't even a match for you, Carly, you drugged him and escaped. That must be eating away at him every moment he spends in prison. Now he knows he needs to deal with both of us. I don't think we will be seeing him again. Jack said his sentence was extended after his escape and assault against you. My friend Donnie has sent documents to the Warden to assure that he cannot be placed on any crews outside the prison walls."

Carly started to sob, "I wouldn't ever want you to get hurt because of me, Jason. That would only make everything so much worse. I would never forgive myself if you were injured. Oh, God! I can't believe I'm crying again."

"It's okay, Carly. Your tears are just washing away some of the pain. I'm not going to let him hurt me, and I'm not going to let him hurt you. We have too many things to look forward to. Too many things we want to do together. You're starting a new chapter of your life. In this chapter you are going to become a big star and write a hit song. We're going to go visit places you have never seen and learn new things together. Maybe you can even teach me how to play the piano."

"I'm sorry. I don't want to keep crying like this. I'm sure your family thinks I just cry all the time."

"They don't think that. They think you have survived a terrible trauma, and you are the bravest woman they have ever known. Everyone thinks that, Carly. Remember the tribute your band gave you the night we met? They said you were the bravest and strongest person they had ever known. And you survived this trauma all on your own, Carly. You were the one who had the strength to pull through and survive all your injuries."

"I didn't really do it all on my own, Jason. If Jack hadn't found me, I would be dead now, and if Christy hadn't coaxed me back to consciousness I might never have woken up. Without Sean, I probably would have lost my feet and never gotten through the treatments. His whole family gave me so much strength and encouragement I will never forget what they did for me."

"I'm glad they were all there for you, but you were still the person who had the strength to pull yourself through. You had the courage to escape before he could kill you, and without that courage, we would not be here talking about this."

"I'm sure that's true. I believe he did mean to kill me. He talked about different ways to kill people. Maybe he's killed other women. Do you think that's possible, Jason?"

"Yes. I believe he has killed women before." Jason didn't want to tell her about the other bodies that Jack and his deputies had already found. That would only add to her fear. "I see him as a very vicious, dangerous psychopath. Thank God, your escape took him off the street and put him in prison where he belongs. You made Nashville a safer place for women, Carly."

"I'm glad I could do that, and I'm glad he can't kidnap anyone else and hurt them the way he hurt me. I just wish I could forget now, and I wish I could stop crying."

"In good time, both of those things will happen. Dr. Mac will help you find ways to push some of those horrible memories away and then we can fill your life with new, happier memories. It's okay to cry. You need to release some of the pain you're holding inside. Think of your tears as a way to wash away the pain. Keep talking to Dr. Mac about your memories. You shouldn't hold all that pain inside and never talk about it. No one is judging you, Carly. Nothing that happened to you was your fault. That's the most important thing to remember. None of this was your fault. After you told Dr. Mac about your father, didn't you feel better?"

"I did – a little. I always felt guilty about my mother. I never wanted her to die. But I forgot that I was only 6 years old, and there wasn't anything I could do to stop him. Dr. Mac said that I was blaming myself as if I were a full-grown adult back then, instead of looking at it through the eyes of a little child. We talked about what it is like to be a 6-year-old child. He had me pretend to be six and then he asked me if I knew how to read, if I knew how to use a telephone, or get on the computer and use the internet, or drive a car. I told him we didn't have a telephone, or a computer or even a television set. I never even saw my mother drive a car. It made me realize how dependent I was on my parents. We talked about how young children can be victimized if they don't have loving parents to protect them. It made me realize how vulnerable I was and how easy it was for my father to hurt me, living way out there in the woods in the middle of nowhere."

"Yes, Carly. You were his victim, and he was a horrible pedophile. You couldn't have saved your mother. I think you were lucky to have survived that abuse yourself. I'm sorry you lost your mother when you were so young, but it was never your fault. I'm sure you missed her terribly. Can you tell me something about her? Do you still remember things you did together?"

"I don't remember too much about her. Martha always said that my mother was very pretty. My mother used to call me her pretty girl. Then she was gone, and I was Nobody's Girl. I was Nobody's Pretty Girl ever again."

"Do you remember some things you and your mother used to do together?"

"I remember she would come to get me from the chicken coop and walk me to school when I stayed out there all night. She would always brush my hair and help me get dressed for school."

Jason cringed at the thought of her memory. He couldn't reconcile his own privileged life with the thought of a little girl spending the night in an old chicken coop all alone. He wondered what kind of a mother could expect a little girl to spend the night alone in a cold, abandoned chicken coop. It saddened him to know this was what she remembered about her mother.

"I want to tell you something, Jason. You might think this is crazy, but the first night you stayed at Christy's house with me when you wrapped that blanket around me and kissed me on the forehead, I thought someone had finally come to comfort me. I kept waiting for my mother to come back. I wanted her to say I was still a good girl, and she wasn't angry with me. I wanted her to forgive me. I wanted her to love me. I wanted to be her pretty girl again. I waited for her to comfort me. I waited for someone for so long, and finally I felt like you were the one who came. I felt like she sent you to comfort me. That's crazy, isn't it?"

Jason watched as tears escaped from her eyes and rolled down her cheeks. He felt her arms wrapping around him even tighter, and he kissed her cheeks and wiped away the tears.

"Maybe not, Carly. We can never really know about things like this. Maybe she did send me. I felt such a strong pull toward you the night we met. After you went to bed that night I stayed and talked to Jack. I kept hoping he wouldn't ask me to leave. I wanted to go to your room and lay down next to you and just hold you and let you know you were safe, you could go to sleep, and I would stay there to protect you. I did want to comfort you. Your mama would have come back to comfort you if she could, Carly, but she died. There was nothing for her to forgive, Carly. You were a little child who was victimized and abused. You were still a good girl. I'm sorry you waited for her for so long."

"Do you think she was angry with me, Jason?"

"No, Babe. I think she was probably horrified when she discovered what happened to you. Remember she said she was going to take you away and never come back? She never wanted you to be hurt like that. She couldn't have been angry with you. You were just a little child."

"I hope not. I never wanted her to die so I never told her what he did to me. I was so afraid. I didn't know what to do."

"Of course, you didn't. You were just a child. You were his victim, but you're safe with me now. You can hold on to me as long as you want, and I'm not going to let anything happen to you tonight or any night. I've fallen in love with you, Carly," he whispered. "I'm not going to let anyone hurt you. You can be my pretty girl."

Carly started and pushed herself away from him. "What did you say, Jason?"

"I said I've fallen in love with you."

"No, no, you can't be in love with me. My life is a mess, Jason. I'm broken. I'm not even sure who I am anymore or where my life is going." She started sobbing.

"This isn't the reaction I had hoped for. I'm sorry. Maybe I said this too soon. Did that frighten you?"

"No. No Jason. How can you love me? I'm so broken. I'm nobody's pretty girl. How can you love me?"

"Easy! You're beautiful and so talented. I love everything about you. You're not broken, Carly. You're recovering from a horrible trauma. Don't you feel like you're getting better every day?"

Carly kept sobbing and Jason rocked her in his arms.

"I thought you just felt sorry for me, Jason. I didn't think you would ever love someone like me. I'm too ordinary. I'm just the little orphan girl no one ever wanted. I'm not educated and sophisticated like you are."

"Those things don't matter. You have a very special gift and a wonderful talent. There are people who would give anything to be able to play the piano the way you do. Our education is different, but that doesn't make one better than the other. You have an amazing gift that few people possess."

"I don't hear the music in my head anymore, and I don't hear the words like I used to, so I don't feel special now. I haven't heard the words or the music since I was kidnapped. I just didn't want to tell anyone. I always thought of that as my special gift but now it's gone."

"Those abilities will all come back when the stress of this trauma comes to an end for you. You have a beautiful voice and an amazing ability to play the piano. You have tons of fans at the Club who are waiting for you to return. You said you have songs you never quite had a chance to finish. Maybe this would be a good time to work on them."

"I don't know what to do, Jason, I need to go back to Nashville. I need to start singing again, and Christy wants me to come back home, but I love you, I want to stay here with you on the ranch. Sometimes I feel like I have a family now."

Jason hugged her tightly. "That's the best news I've ever heard. I want you to stay here with me. You can go to the club and sing. It's not that far away. We can visit Christy in Nashville, and she can come here to visit you. I think Jack will tell you that returning to Nashville is not a good idea."

"Okay. I want to stay if you want me, and I'm going to try to stop crying."

"I don't want you to worry about the crying. You can't hold all this pain inside forever. Crying is one way of releasing the pain. Letting go of the pain will help you heal. Let's see if we can think of something fun we can do tomorrow and then we'll try to go to sleep."

"Okay. We could do another piano lesson tomorrow, Jason. Did you practice?"

"Ohhh, let's not talk about that right now." Jason kissed her on the cheek and grinned. "I do have a surprise for you tomorrow. We are going to have a date night."

"We're going to go out on a date? I thought we had to be careful not to be seen here in Kentucky."

"It's going to be a bit of a private date. We're going to have a catered dinner in an art gallery, and then we're going to do some dancing."

"Really, Jason? I can't wait. I'm so excited."

"I wasn't going to tell you until tomorrow, but you might want to pack some jammies and a toothbrush."

"We're staying all night? In an art gallery?"

"Yes. It has a very beautiful bedroom with skylights."

"Oh, we're going to your grandma's studio, aren't we?"

"Yes, Carly. You figured it out. You will be safe there and no one will be able to gossip about us. I alerted security, and the gallery has a state-of-the-art alarm system just like the house."

"I love this idea, Jason. I wanted to go back to see all the paintings again. I can't wait!"

"I have a few other surprises for you, but I'm not going to tell you about them now."

"Jason, no more surprises, and no presents. You are not supposed to buy me anything else."

"Sure, Carly, I remember," he lied. "Let's get some sleep now and think about how much fun we are going to have tomorrow night."

"What are we having for dinner?"

"I'm not sure. I was going to hire a caterer, but Nettie said she knew what you would like, so she is doing the dinner and she's not talking."

"She likes to keep things a secret, doesn't she?"

"It appears that way. Are you feeling better? Can I kiss you now?"

"Ummm, yes!"

Chapter 19

Carly was almost giddy with excitement the next day. She tried on all her dresses and agonized over the decision on which dress to wear. "You're being ridiculous," she told herself. "Jason will probably wear blue jeans and boots. and not even notice what I am wearing." But he told her he loved her last night, even though she had been crying again. She wanted him to think she was pretty. She wanted to feel like someone who deserved to be loved. She didn't want to feel like 'Nobody's Girl'. She didn't want Jason to be staring at her ugly, mutilated arms, so she finally chose a long-sleeved purple wrap dress. Jason was working in his office on one of his Innocence Project cases, so Carly went into the piano room and started trying to finish some of the songs she had started a few years ago.

"That sounds beautiful," said Gwen as she walked into the piano room.

"Thanks," said Carly. "I'm trying to finish some of the songs I started before the kidnapping. It seems so much harder now, but I'm hoping to finish at least a few of them."

"What I heard just now sounded great. I hear you and Jason are planning a date night this evening."

"Yes. I'm excited about it, and thanks for letting us use your art studio."

"Well, you can use it any time you like. I thought it was a great idea when Jason mentioned it. I know he would like to take you out and show you the town, but I guess it's just too risky. Unfortunately, people always seem to want to Twitter about Jason every time they see him somewhere. He never seems to be able to escape this unwanted attention."

"That's because he is just so darn handsome," Carly said with a smile.

"Maybe. Maybe it's just the way people try to make themselves feel important. We never used to have to deal with problems like these. There was a time when people could have a private life without everyone prying into their personal business. I don't think George and Lexie ever had to deal with all this unwanted notoriety. George was a handsome devil, much like Jason, but George didn't have the beautiful eyes Jason has. He got those from his mother. She was a beautiful woman. She came from a wealthy family in Chicago and when I first met her, I just couldn't believe she would want to marry George and spend her life on a horse ranch. But they were very much in love, and she really embraced this lifestyle and made her mark in the community as well."

"I wish I had met Jason's parents. They sound wonderful. Did Jason live here on the ranch when he got married?"

"Oh, no! Lisa was not fond of horses, and she was not fond of Lexie. I think she knew his mother was against the marriage and wanted him to wait until he finished his time with the Army before thinking of settling down. Lisa pursued Jason like he was a Grand Prize, but then when he joined the Army, I guess she moved on to greener pastures. Just a little ranch sarcasm here."

"That must have been very hard for Jason. He doesn't like to talk about her, but he let me ask him some questions about his marriage. I hope he doesn't read all the Twitter postings you are talking about. I don't know much about social media, but I've heard it can disrupt lives and become very addicting."

"I don't think you have anything to worry about, Carly. I would say Jason only has eyes for you, and he usually gets angry when I tell him about things that have been posted about him."

"Well, I'm going to try not to read anything like that. When we bought my hat, the young girl in the shop recognized me, and she remembered who Jason was because he purchased his hat at her shop. We were afraid she might post something about meeting us in Bowling Green, but Jason asked her not to tell anyone she had met us there and we promised to let her know when I was going back to the club."

"That seems like a good trade off. I don't think she posted anything about meeting you. If she did, I never saw it. I guess I should let you keep working on your songs. I hope you and Jason enjoy your special date night. Jason has had fun planning it for you, and Nettie is enjoying making your dinner."

"You have all been so nice to me. I want you to know how much I enjoy being here. My sister has been asking me to come back to Nashville, but Jason convinced me that it is safer for me to stay here."

"I think that's a good decision, Carly. There's no reason to put your life in jeopardy. You can invite your sister to come up here and visit you. We have plenty of room for visitors."

"That's what Jason said."

I'll bet he did, thought Gwen. She wondered about the ring Jason had found in his mother's jewelry collection. Perhaps all the planning Jason had made for this evening was leading up to a marriage proposal. It was wonderful to see him happy and excited about life again.

Carly got back to work on her music, but her thoughts kept drifting away to the coming evening. She thought about writing a song for him, but the words just didn't fly into her head like they used to. She messaged Jason to see what time she should be ready for their date.

"How about 6 o'clock?" he texted.

"Perfect. I think I might go take a little nap right now."

"Good. I think I might join you in a few minutes."

Carly was almost asleep when she felt Jason getting into bed with her and then wrapping himself around her. "I've got you," he said.

She smiled. She always felt safe when he said that.

When Carly woke up Jason was gone. She looked at her iPad and saw he had sent her a message. "I'll come pick you up at 6, okay?"

She messaged him back. "Where are you?"

"Down in my old bedroom taking a shower. I didn't want to wake you up yet. See you soon."

Carly smiled and jumped out of bed to get ready.

At 6pm she heard a soft knock on the door. "You can come in Jason. You don't have to knock."

"I'm picking you up for a date. It's only polite to knock."

Carly laughed and opened the door. Jason was standing there in his gorgeous violet blue suit with a purple shirt, holding a beautiful bouquet of flowers.

"Oh my gosh, Jason. I wasn't expecting flowers!"

"Good. That means maybe I am staying one jump ahead of you. You look gorgeous, by the way."

They rode out to the art studio in Jason's golf cart, and he helped her out and walked her to the door. "What should we do first, some dancing or move right to dinner?"

"Let's look at some of the displays. I wonder if your grandmother or Nettie have added any new paintings."

"I think they have hung some new pictures recently."

Carly walked over to a group of photographs and looked over at Jason quizzically.

"That's odd, Jason. I think I have a photo of this exact same place. I wonder when your grandmother took this. This sunset looks like one of my photos too...." Her voice trailed off.

"Those are your photos, Carly. Look at the name plaque on the wall. I showed Grandma your photos on your website, and she liked them so much she had them printed and framed and then we hung them up here in the studio. Grandma thought your photos were quite professional and one of the owners at a gallery in Bowling Green offered to take them on consignment if you want to sell any of your work."

"Really, Jason? He thought he could sell my photos?"

"Yes, and with a hefty price tag. I'm not sure if you should do that right now since we want to keep your location a secret, but it is something you could think about in the future."

"Wow! I feel so flattered. I love the way she had them framed. I've never had any of my photos framed or printed before. You are just full of surprises tonight, aren't you Jason?"

"This was really my grandma's doing. I only helped with the hanging when they told me exactly where to put the nail."

Carly reached over and hugged Jason. "Your grandmother is such a wonderful artist. I'm so flattered that she liked my photos. Your family has been so good to me Jason. It seems like you all never stop doing nice things for me."

"That's because we love you. We are your new family now. Let's go see what Nettie has cooked for us and let's have some wine."

They went into the little kitchen and Jason poured them each a glass of wine while Carly took their plates out of the warmer.

"Oh, salmon! I love salmon!"

"Nettie said she knew what you would like, so I guess she did. It looks wonderful. Let's eat."

During dinner, Jason was fidgeting around in his pockets as Carly looked over at him. "Did you lose something Jason? You put the golfcart keys on the hook when we came in the door."

"Oh, that's right. Thanks!"

They finished their dinner and Jason picked up their plates and took them to the kitchen.

"I can do the dishes while you check on dessert," Carly offered.

"No, no. We're not doing dishes. That will all be taken care of later. This is our date night, and you never do dishes in a restaurant. I have something I need to ask you before we start dessert."

"Okay. Is anything wrong?"

"No. Nothing's wrong." Jason pulled a small box out of his pocket, got down on one knee and took Carly's hand. "I want to ask you to marry me, Carly. I love you. Will you marry me, please?" He opened the small box and put the ring into her hand.

Carly was silent. She just kept staring at Jason.

"You're not saying anything, Carly."

"I don't know what to say. I wasn't expecting this. I don't know if I'm ready to get married. I feel like I still have a lot of issues to work out with Dr. Mac. Sometimes I still feel broken."

"I know you do, but really, you are getting so much better. You don't have to stop working with Dr. Mac. I want you to see him. I just want you to know that I love you more than I could ever imagine was possible. I want to spend the rest of my life with you. You can take some time to decide if you need to. I'm not rushing you and you don't have to decide tonight. I just couldn't wait any longer to give you this ring and let you know I am ready to make a commitment to you."

"I do love it. I think it's the most beautiful ring I have ever seen, and I love vintage jewelry like this. Where did you ever find it?"

"It was my great grandmother's engagement ring on my mother's side of the family. It is truly a family heirloom. I got Grandma to fill me in on as much history as she could remember. My mother told her the ring had been created especially for her grandmother and they had a happy marriage, a wonderful life, and two children."

"I'm speechless. I don't know what to say, except I love you, Jason."

"That's enough for now. I think it's time for some dessert and some dancing."

After dessert, Jason turned on the music and took Carly in his arms. He held her gently and he loved the way she nestled her head right into his shoulder. He could feel her breath warm and soft against his neck. He thought this was the most perfect date he could ever remember. He wondered why he hadn't thought of this plan sooner. She was so beautiful it almost took his breath away. He wanted her in a way that he knew wasn't possible just yet, but the longing was there in every fiber of his body. He swung her around off her feet and she started laughing until he put her back down. He loved to hear her laugh. He knew it was a sign she was getting better. Sometimes she could just give in to being playful and even a little sassy. When he held her and she told him she felt peaceful, he just knew that they belonged together. His goal was to create a peaceful paradise for her on the ranch. He wanted it to be a place where she would always feel safe and protected. A place where no one could come to hurt her or frighten her. He didn't want her to ever have to hear the kidnapper threatening to kill her again. He didn't want her to have to be strong and brave any more. She had done that all her life. He felt her body relax and he hoped this was one of those moments when she started to feel peaceful and free.

Carly reached up and kissed Jason on the neck and whispered in his ear. "Yes!"

"Yes?" he answered. "Is that a 'yes' you want to marry me?"

"Yes, I want to marry you, Jason. I love you."

Jason swung her around off her feet and she started laughing again. "You've made me so happy, Carly. We're going to have a wonderful life together. I promise to always keep you safe and make you happy. Let's try on the ring and see if it fits."

"I did try it on when you were in the kitchen. It's a great fit."

Jason smiled. "Well, I still get to put it on your finger now."

He reached for the ring and pulled her down onto his lap and slid the ring onto her finger. "It looks perfect on you!"

"Are we going to tell everyone we are engaged?"

"Of course, we are."

"I'm not sure if I know how to be a good wife to you, Jason. I guess I can talk about this with Dr. Mac. He's married. He should know something about how to have a good marriage."

"Carly, we are both professionals with busy careers, and we will only have to make time to enjoy being together. I don't expect you to change anything. You're perfect just the way you are."

"But maybe I should learn to cook, Jason."

"We have Nettie. She loves to cook. You're a singer/songwriter, Carly. That's much harder than cooking. Let's not worry about that until Nettie decides to move back to her house. Grandma likes to cook, too. I think we have that covered for now."

"You're making this sound so easy. I'll have to tell Christy. I'm not sure that will be easy. She's still asking me to come back to Nashville, but it wouldn't be very practical for us to live there."

"No, it wouldn't, but Christy and Jack can always come here to visit with you. We can turn Lindsey into a little pony riding cowgirl."

Jason kissed her again. "I think it's time for bed. You look tired."

"I am – a little. This has certainly been a night of surprises!!"

Chapter 20

Jason and Carly walked out onto the patio where Grandma and Nettie were setting up lunch.

"This looks great," said Jason. "Can I help with anything?"

"I figured that since you were still enjoying your date night you both might have missed breakfast," she paused and gave Jason a bit of a teasing smile, "I thought you might be hungry for some lunch."

"We didn't miss breakfast. We had a wonderful breakfast, thanks to Nettie. It was Carly's favorite – Belgian waffles with strawberries and whipped cream. Thank you, Nettie, for all the wonderful food you prepared for us. You managed to choose all of Carly's favorites, and everything was delicious."

"I was happy to do it, Jason. I'm glad you both enjoyed it."

"We did. We had a wonderful time, didn't we, Carly?"

"Oh yes. I'm hoping we can do it again if it isn't too much trouble. It was fun, the food was amazing, and Jason was full of surprises, weren't you, Jason?"

"Well, there were a few surprises. Carly's talking about her photos you had on display. That was really my grandma's surprise, not mine."

"I was shocked when I saw my photos on the wall in your gallery. You are both such wonderful artists, so I felt honored to be a part of your displays. I never printed or framed any of my photos, but I loved the way you had them displayed. I didn't know they could look so good!"

"You had some beautiful photos on your website, Carly. You are quite an accomplished photographer. Jason said you are going to teach him how to handle a camera. We could use some new photos for our ranch website when you both have the time."

"Thank you. I haven't taken any photos recently. I haven't done any since the kidnapping. I just don't feel safe when I go out alone."

"Well, there's another part of your life you can take back now, Carly. Take Jason with you and teach him how to take wonderful photos like you do!"

"We have that on our calendar, along with many other things we plan to do together. After lunch, Carly is going to teach me how to write a song, right, Carly?"

"I am," said Carly and she leaned over, and she kissed him. He put his arms around her, and he hugged her and kissed her back. Grandma gave them a smile.

She started thinking about the beautiful vintage ring Jason had found in his mother's jewelry collection and wondered if he had given it to Carly last night. She tried to look at Carly's left hand without being too obvious. But Carly had her hand locked into Jason's and it just wasn't possible to see if she had the ring on her finger. She didn't want to ask for fear of spoiling the surprise just in case Jason hadn't given it to her last night.

Jason sat down and Carly plunked herself right down onto his lap, wrapped her arms around his neck and started kissing him again. They both started laughing again. Grandma looked over and smiled.

"Oh, gosh, you two, you are reminding me of George and Lexie. Jason, did you remember to look at that letter that came for you?"

"Oh, no, I totally forgot about that. Get up a second, Carly. I need to go get this. I think this is actually for you."

"What's actually for me? What are you talking about?"

"Let me go get it. Let's look at it." Jason went running back into the house and came back with a large envelope he was tearing open. He looked at the papers inside and pulled out a big, long, legal looking document.

"What is it?" asked Carly.

"Whoa! It looks like the bank sent you the deed for your house."

"I guess I don't understand. What does that mean?"

"I'm not sure. They don't usually release the deed until the mortgage is satisfied. But it's marked paid in full."

"It can't be paid. I still owe money for the house. I thought you were going to help me get rid of all the late fees and fines. I didn't want you to pay the mortgage off. I told you not to do that." Carly started to cry.

"I didn't do that, Carly. I didn't pay it off. You told me you didn't want me to. I would have. I didn't want you to lose your house because of what that bastard did to you."

"Jason, you've already done too much for me. I can't let you do this."

Grandma and Nettie looked at the two of them, trying to figure out what was going on.

"Carly, Carly, listen to me. I didn't do that. I wanted to, but you asked me not to, so I didn't. Let's read the letter and see what they said, okay?"

Jason took the knife off the table, slit the envelope open quickly, and pulled out the letter.

"This is addressed to you. It says Dear... Well, I'll let you read it."

"I can't read it, I'm too upset."

"Don't be upset, Babe. Let's just read it. It says, 'Dear Ms. Styles, on behalf of the Western Central Bank of Kentucky we want to say how sorry we are about your recent ordeal, and the long recovery period you had to endure. It is always sad to hear about citizens who are victimized by other members of the community. We are sorry we did not respond to you in a more prompt and timely manner. As a respected member of our community, you certainly deserve our support, so we want to make amends, and we have credited back all the late fees and penalties that were assessed to your account. After we did that, we found you had a final mortgage balance of $25,565. We have a fund set up here at our bank, which we can use for emergency relief purposes. We have used the money from this fund to pay off the balance of your mortgage. We are sending your attorney the deed to your house, so he can keep it on file for you. We have also used these funds to pay off the last two years of your property tax and insurance assessments that were a part of this mortgage. Your taxes and insurance coverage are now up to date. Please accept our apology for not giving you better support in your time of need. We have also enclosed a check for $10,000 to assist you in your recovery. We are glad your attorney brought your matter to our attention. I hope you will soon be singing again at the Rosebud Club, and my wife and I would like to come down to hear you. I have asked Jason to let us know when you will be performing again. We wish you a speedy recovery.'

Carly got up and sat in Jason's lap and put her arms around his neck and kept crying.

"It's okay, Carly, those are happy tears, right?"

"Yes."

"You were just surprised, weren't you?"

"Yeah. I was."

"They sent you a nice check, so you can use that for some of the other bills you have. You can open a new bank account. That'll be nice, right?"

Carly kept crying and Jason started rubbing her back.

"It's okay. Just let it out. It's okay, you can cry."

She kept crying. In a few minutes Roy and Robbie came around the side of the house and Roy said, "Oh, dear, what's wrong?"

Grandma looked at him, "We think they're happy tears, Roy."

"I hope so," he said quietly.

Jason looked up at him, "Hey, Roy, can you get us a bottle of Champagne? And some glasses?"

"Are we celebrating?"

"Yeah, we're going to celebrate, in a few minutes…"

"Okay. I'll go get one."

Carly kept crying. "This is a good thing, baby," Jason said, as he rocked her back and forth. "It's one less thing you have to worry about now."

Carly sobbed and choked a little. Jason started rubbing her back very gently.

"C'mon, Carly. This is good for you. It's a good step up. It's going to give you a little breathing room. Isn't that a good thing?"

"Yeah, Jason. It's good. You just keep doing everything for me."

"I like doing things for you. It makes me happy to be able to help you."

"But you shouldn't have to do all this. I feel like a big rock around your neck. You're always doing things for me, and what do I do for you?"

"You love me. You told me that this morning. That's all I need, okay? I want you to be free of your debts so you can concentrate on your career again. You didn't deserve to be saddled with these medical bills. You shouldn't have had to spend the past two years recovering from your injuries. You deserve to have a normal life now, Carly - free of worry and free of debts."

"That sounds like a dream that might never come true."

"I think we can make it come true. We just need to keep working on it."

"I can't ask you to spend all your time with my problems, because I don't do anything for you. I want to, but I don't know what I can do."

Grandma Gwen looked up and reached over and patted Carly on her hand. As she did it, she remembered she wasn't supposed to do any touching, but Carly didn't yank her hand away, so she just patted Carly softly on the hand and said, "Listen to me, Carly, and I am going to tell you what you've done for Jason, okay? When you came here to the ranch, this is not the same Jason we had here. The first night you came here I saw a little light in Jason's eyes, that I hadn't seen for a long time. After his parents died, Jason did a lot of grieving and he had to work through some of the bad memories from his service in the military. He started to get past that and got better, but he still wasn't the Jason we used to know. He was sad, and he was in a dark place. We tried, but we didn't know what to do for him. Then one night he came back to the house, and you were with him, and I thought, 'Wow, I wonder what's going on here.' He told us who you were and told us a little bit about what happened at the club two nights before. He told us about the guy who came after you and he said you were terribly frightened. He thought this might be a good place for you to stay for a while until the authorities could get the felon back to prison where he belonged. So I thought, 'Okay, good. Jason does a lot of nice things for people.' But it wasn't quite the same. I could see in his eyes that this wasn't like one of his veterans, not like one of his projects that he takes on. I could see this was just a little bit different. Then you stayed here a few days, and I kidded him a little about how he had never brought a girl home before. He said, 'It's not like that, Grandma. She's been a victim of a terrible, terrible trauma. I'm not trying to romance her. She's been terrorized, and I want to try to make her feel a little safer. She told me she is frightened every minute of the day, and she's too frightened to sleep at night. I thought she might feel safe up here with all our security, and I'm not going to let anybody hurt her. So that's why she's here. It's not what you're thinking, Grandma.' I thought, okay, Jason if you say so, but I could still see that little light in his eyes. And every time I saw you together, I saw a little bit more light in his eyes. In the last two months you've been here, Carly, you've changed Jason. He's not the same Jason we had here 3 months ago. So that's what you've done for him. You brought him out of the gloomy world he was living in, and you've done that for all of us. Now we hear him laughing in the morning, we see him kissing you, we see you both having fun, and that's what you've done for him. So, this has not been a one-sided thing. You've done as much or more for him as he has done for you, and you have done it for all of us, believe me. We didn't know how to help gloomy Jason, and now, what do we call him guys?"

"Jason in Love," they answered. Even Jason laughed.

"Oh, no, you guys. Don't do this to me."

"That's what we call him now," said Roy. "He's Jason in Love."

Everyone was laughing.

"Okay, I'm ready to pop the cork on this Champagne, so I need to know what we are celebrating," said Roy.

"Just pour the champagne, Roy," said Grandma.

Roy started pouring Champagne into the glasses and Carly was still crying a little bit. Grandma reached over and touched Carly's hand again.

"Do you understand what I'm telling you, Carly?"

"I guess. Maybe."

"I want you to understand, because we couldn't find a way to bring him out of that dark place he was living in. That's what you did, Carly. So don't think you haven't done anything for Jason. You've done plenty for him, and you did what none of us were able to do. Maybe he didn't tell you that, did you, Jason?"

"No, Grandma. I didn't want to scare her away."

"But now you're happy, right?"

"Yeah, Grandma. I'm very happy. I have Carly. Thanks for asking." Jason rocked Carly back and forth in his arms. "I'm happy, Carly. Don't cry. I want you to be happy, too. This is a good day. It's been all good things today, right?"

"Yeah, I guess. It just wasn't what I was expecting."

"That's okay. This is good news. We have some other good news. Do you want to tell everyone?"

"What do you mean? What are we talking about?" Carly asked.

"I'm talking about the ring," Jason whispered. "Show them the ring."

Grandma looked over at Carly's hand. "Oh, my, it even fits your finger."

"Yeah, it fits great."

Everyone was looking at the ring. Robbie looked over at Jason, "So this is a significant ring, right?"

"Yeah, Robbie. It's an engagement ring."

"That's what I meant. Significant."

"Yes. I asked Carly to marry me, and she said yes."

"No wonder you have such a big smile on your face today. It is the Jason in love."

"Okay, guys, I think I've heard enough of that now."

"Oh, Jason, we can't help it. We're just glad to see how everything has changed for you. It's so good to see," said Nettie.

"So we are celebrating the engagement, right?" asked Roy. "Get your glass and drink up, here's to Carly and Jason and a happy, happy, happy ever after."

"Come on, Carly. Are you going to drink some?"

"I'll just drink some of yours."

Jason held the glass up for her. He drank some and then she had a little more.

"Okay, now we have one more thing we are celebrating."

Everyone looked up with a question in their eyes.

"Do you want to tell them, Carly?"

"No. You should say it, so I won't cry again."

"Okay. Here's the other thing we are celebrating. Carly has a house down in Nashville, and while she was trying to recover from her injuries her mortgage company was not sympathetic to her, and they kept adding fees and penalties to her mortgage. Then they wanted to foreclose on her house because she couldn't bring everything up to date within 30 days. So Robbie and I flew up to Louisville and I went in and talked to the President of the bank. Turns out he was a friend of George's, and I told him what had happened to her and why she wasn't able to keep up with her payments. I asked him if he could waive all the penalties and fees and give her a one-year grace period so she could get back on her feet and start working again. We opened his letter today and discovered they had sent the deed for her house to her. She started crying because she thought I had paid off the mortgage, but I didn't. They have something at the bank they call a relief fund, and they used it to pay off her mortgage balance and they sent her a check for $10,000."

"Wow," said Roy. "You did some kind of negotiating there, huh Jason?"

"He said he admired the courage she displayed when she escaped from the kidnapper. He said he was sorry about what happened to her, and they certainly wouldn't make her pay all the penalty fees. Then he remembered he had seen a clip of the incident on TV, and realized I was the guy who subdued the kidnapper. He said my dad would have been proud of me and would have laughed when he saw me take that guy down. So, end of story. Now she has the deed for her house, and they sent her a check! So, I need to write him a letter and thank him. He told me he wanted to come down to hear Carly sing when she gets back on her feet and feels like singing again, huh Carly?"

"Maybe," she said.

"You will. You'll start feeling better."

"Should we tell Jason about our news?" asked Roy.

"What news is that?" asked Jason.

"You tell him, Gwen."

"Lady Allison had her foal last night. A very cute little filly."

"What? You didn't call me?"

"We didn't want to interrupt your date night. You spent so much time planning it."

"Is she okay? Is the foal okay?"

"They are both doing great. Thanks to your attention to her and our wonderful vet, she came through it like a champ."

"This is exciting. We have to go see her, Carly. What does she look like?"

"She is a beautiful reddish brown with four white stockings, a white star on her forehead, with a star trail that runs down the front of her nose."

"Now you and your grandmother need to decide on a name for her. I brought you the paperwork that outlines her bloodlines. Her grandfather was Carl of Denmark and her grandmother was Glorious Girl."

"What do you think Grandma? Do you have a name for her?"

"Not yet. What do you think?"

"I've got it! We take the Carl from the grandfather, the Girl from the grandmother and we have Carly's Girl."

"That's very cute, Jason. And she was born on the night you and Carly got engaged. It seems perfect."

"I like it," said Roy.

"I can hear the racetrack announcer now – 'It's Carly's Girl coming up on the outside, she's going for the lead, giving it everything she's got, and it's Carly's Girl by a nose."

"You're a riot, grandma. Maybe you've been to too many races. Okay everyone, drink up! Here's to our new foal, Carly's Girl. You have to drink your own glass this time, Carly."

"I might be tipsy if I drink all that."

"No. We are going to give you some lunch to go with the champagne. Come on, everyone help yourselves!" said Grandma. "Let's put a little food with this champagne. When are you thinking about getting married? Have you talked about a date?"

"I don't think we've gotten that far, yet. But we could go down to the courthouse and get a marriage license today and find a Justice of the Peace to marry us. I know a few JP's. I don't think there is a waiting period once you get the marriage license. What do you think Carly?"

"I…I…I…"

"Jason, honey, that is not the kind of wedding every little girl dreams about. Carly needs some time to think about her wedding. You could have a nice ceremony here on the ranch. Nettie and I could help you plan it."

"Did you have dreams about your wedding when you were a little girl, Carly?"

"I don't think I ever thought about getting married. I used to dream about having a big brother who was going to come and save me and keep me safe. After I became friends with Sean, I pretended I was taken home from the hospital by the wrong family and the Benson's were my real family. I pretended they found me and took me in because I was their real daughter. Then they moved away and left me behind just like my other family."

Jason saw tears filling her eyes and running down her cheeks and put his arms around her.

"No one is ever going to leave you behind again, Carly. I will never let anyone hurt you again. We'll always be your real family and keep you safe. Everyone here loves you and wants you to be happy again."

"Amen," said everyone in unison.

"Carly, I would marry you tomorrow if you were ready, but I want you to plan a wonderful wedding. I want it to be your day. Little Lindsey will be the cutest flower girl ever!"

"Yes, I think she will love being a flower girl. I haven't told Christy yet. That might be hard."

"I'm sure your sister will be happy for you. I know she wants you to come back to Nashville, but she also wants you to be safe and happy. Let's go see your new filly!"

"I think she's your new filly, Jason."

"Nope. She's Carly's Girl. I named her for you so she's your girl now."

"Wow! I gained a fiancé and a filly in just 24 hours. I wonder which one will love me the most."

"I'll always love you the most, Babe!" Jason hugged her and swung her around off her feet just to hear her laugh and then they took off running toward the stables.

Once they were out of earshot, Roy looked over at Gwen and asked, "Did you hear what she said – that her family abandoned her? I thought her parents died when she was a little girl."

"They did die. Her father shot her mother and then killed himself – according to Jason. The neighbors took her in and cared for her, but they never told her the truth. They didn't tell her the parents were dead, so when she was little she always thought they had gone off and left her behind."

"That seems cruel. Why would they do something like that? What kind of people were they? They let her think she had been abandoned?"

"Evidently that's how they handled it. Jason said they told her not to ever talk about her parents or tell anyone they were gone. She had to pretend that Christy's parents were her own parents."

"I'm having a hard time wrapping my head around this scenario. If Jason's parents had died when he was little, you would have taken care of him, or Lucy and I would have taken him in and adopted him. But neither of us would have ever lied to him or let him think his parents had abandoned him. Did they ever tell her the truth?"

"Jason said her sister found out the truth and told Carly when they graduated from High School. She told Carly her mother was dead."

"She must have been about 18 by that time. There must be more to this story. It doesn't seem like anyone could be so cruel as to not tell a little girl that her mother was dead. So she was waiting for her mother to return for 12 years? That's incredibly sad."

"I think you're right, Roy. Seems like there is something wrong with this story.

"Well, it seems like you ladies have a wedding to plan. Let's make it a wonderful day for her."

Turn the page for an excerpt from
Nobody's Pretty Girl
A Carly Styles Novel 2

By K.J. Knudson

Available soon!

(Blank page)

Rehearsal and Rendezvous

Jason listened as the band rehearsed a few sets of songs. Carly's voice sounded better than ever, and he marveled at the resilience she had after such a long day. She had fallen asleep in the car, and he let her sleep until he saw the band members arriving. Mike came over to the car to greet them, and saw that Carly was asleep.

"Is she okay? We're so happy to see her again."

"Just a little catnap. It's been a rough couple of days, but she is anxious to rehearse with you and start singing again. She's been working on some new songs. I need to warn you that there will be a story breaking in the news about her again. They discovered bodies out in the woods where Jack found her, and some nosy reporters are trying to turn this into a major news event, painting her as the hero who escaped and brought down the serial killer brothers."

"Well, in a way that's true. I say thanks to whatever God is up there nearly every day that he let Jack find her and she has recovered."

"What are you talking about?" Carly asked, sleepily.

"We're talking about you, Carly. We're so happy to see you again. We can't wait to get you back on stage with us."

"Okay. Let's do it."

They rehearsed for about an hour and then the band members started packing up to leave. Carly was working out some chord progressions on the piano and Jason sat down beside her.

"Do you want me to stop? Are you ready to leave?"

"No. You don't need to stop playing. I love listening to you. I just came over to tell you I love you."

Carly smiled at him, and he felt mesmerized by her pretty green eyes. "Will you sing a song with me Jason. Everyone is gone. It's just the two of us here."

"No, Carly. You're the singer. I love hearing you sing."

"Please, Jason. Just one song. Please. I love you."

"Okay, Carly. One song. How about 'Colder Weather'. I know all the words to that song."

Carly started playing and then they were both singing. He wondered how she talked him into this so easily. *Must be her eyes, he thought.*

When the song ended, they heard footsteps and Mike came around the corner.

"Carly! You didn't tell me your man could sing! I started to walk out the door and I couldn't believe what I was hearing. You should sign him up for the band."

"No, no, no," said Jason. "I only sing when she begs me. I'm not a singer, I'm a lawyer."

"Could have fooled me, Jason. That was wonderful. Your voices are perfect together. Could we get you to sing that for an audience?"

"Oh, no. I'm not a musician like the rest of you. I never sang a note until I was in the Army. Then I did it mostly to win bets or alleviate boredom between missions."

"You never had voice lessons? That's hard to believe. You just started singing and you sound like that?"

"He's good, isn't he? He doesn't believe me when I tell him how good he sounds."

"He sounds so good I just hope he doesn't play the guitar, or I might have to find a new band."

"He plays the guitar, Mike, but we're not replacing you! Jason doesn't want to sing with our band. No worries!"

"Okay. I'll try to sleep tonight. Keep trying to talk Jason into singing that song with you on stage. It was terrific!"

Carly smiled. "I think it's a lost cause, but I can try. See you on Friday!"

Jason and Carly walked out and got in the car to go home. "I told you your voice was wonderful, Jason. You just didn't believe me."

"Okay, I'll believe you, but I'm not cut out to be a performer. That's your job, Carly."

She reached over and ran her hand over his leg and smiled up at him. "Thank you for singing with me. I really liked it."

"You're welcome. Do you want to go get some dinner? Are you hungry? Or we could head home. What's your choice?"

"I don't feel very hungry. Could we go somewhere to just be alone?"

"Alone? We could go home, is that what you mean?"

"No, that would take too long. I just want to be alone with you."

Jason was a bit puzzled and tried to figure out what she meant. "Do you want to stay somewhere in Nashville tonight?"

"That would be good. Can we do that?"

"We could stay at your house or at the Majestic Hotel if they have any rooms. What sounds good to you?"

"Not my house. Too many ghosts and bad memories there. How about the hotel? That sounds fun."

"What's going on here, Carly? You don't want to go back to the ranch tonight?"

"I just want to be alone with you, Jason." She reached over and kissed him and wrapped her arms around him.

Jason picked up his phone and searched for the Hotel. He found an available room and booked it. "Okay, I found us a room at the hotel. Do you want to go over to your house and pick up some clothes?"

"No, I don't need anything."

"You know you don't even have a toothbrush, don't you? I have a change of clothes I carry with me in the car, but you don't have anything."

"Maybe you'll let me share your toothbrush or we could get one at the hotel."

Jason laughed. "Okay, let's go."

They drove to the hotel and Jason grabbed his bag and checked in at the front desk. They got in the elevator and Carly gave him another kiss and one of her dazzling smiles. They got to the room and Jason sat on the edge of the bed and pulled her over to him.

"What are we doing here, Carly? What's going on?"

"I think you know, Jason."

She started unbuttoning his shirt and pushing it off his shoulders.

"If you don't start taking my clothes off this might take a long time, Jason."

Jason looked up at her and smiled. "Carly, is this what I think it is? Are you trying to tell me you're ready? Are you sure?"

"I'm sure Jason. I want you to make mad, passionate love to me. That's what you told me to say when I was ready."

"You told me you could never say that, Carly."

"Things change, Jason. It's time."

"I hope I'm not dreaming! Are you sure, Carly? Are you sure you're ready?"

"Yes. I love you and I trust you. Dr. Mac said that when someone loves you, you have to trust that they will never hurt you."

"I would never hurt you, Carly. I told you that the very first night you stayed with me at the ranch. I promised you I would never rush you or pressure you to be intimate with me. I told you that the decision would be entirely up to you when or if you wanted that kind of a relationship with me. I have wanted you since the first night we stayed together but I knew you weren't ready for a romantic relationship. We talked about doing little baby steps, remember?"

"Yes, but now I want to take a big leap of faith and you're still not taking my clothes off fast enough."

Jason started laughing. "Are we in a hurry, Carly?"

"We sort of are."

"We do have all night, you know. We don't check out until morning."

"If you don't stop talking, we might still be standing here in the morning."

"All right, Carly." Jason started laughing and slowly started peeling off her shorts and T shirt.

"You are so beautiful. This is like a dream come true."

Jason pushed the covers aside and pulled Carly down on top of him. "Are you sure you're ready, Carly? I want our first time to be amazing. I don't want you to be frightened."

"Yes. I want to be with someone who loves me. I need to know how that feels."

"Okay. I'm going to be very gentle with you. We'll take it nice and slow and easy. I want you to just relax and enjoy the feeling."

"Relax? Aren't you supposed to get me excited, Jason?" she teased.

"Don't worry, Babe. I'm going to get you very excited!"

"You sound pretty sure of yourself, Jason."

"I've been waiting for this night. I think I know what you will like."

"Again, pretty sure of yourself."

Jason loved this new side of her personality. Sometimes she would tease him or show him her sassy side. It proved that she was getting better and starting to let go of the horrors of her past. She was his fragile little bird, and everything tonight had to be perfect for her. He couldn't be just another disappointment in her life. She was giving him the chance to make up for all the hurt she had suffered at the hands of the kidnappers. She was giving him the chance to show her what it meant to be loved and cherished. He didn't want love to be just an empty word for her. It had to mean something. He took her hand and brought it up to his lips and kissed it. He stroked her cheek gently with the side of his hand. He felt a well of tenderness rising up inside of him. "You are so beautiful, so perfect."

She smiled up at him and he felt like he could just melt into her body. Their bodies intertwined in passion, and he listened for her soft murmurs of pleasure as they became one. She tried to stifle her murmurs as they climaxed, and he knew he had pleased her.

"I love you, Carly," he whispered. "You are the love of my life. Are you okay?"

"More than okay, Jason. I love you too. Can we do that again?"

Jason started laughing. "Yes, Babe. We can do it over and over for the rest of our lives. But you'll have to give me a few minutes, okay?"

"Okay, but don't take too long," she smiled."

"Are we in a hurry again?"

"We might be." Carly snuggled into his shoulder and tried to stifle a yawn.

"Are you tired, Babe?"

"Just a little."

Jason stroked her cheek again and smiled as he watched her falling asleep. He gently pulled her in closer to him. He loved the feeling of her soft skin against his body. She was always so soft and warm. He pulled the covers up over her and kissed her gently on the forehead. *Sweet Dreams, Babe*, he whispered. For now, he could just let her sleep. They had all the time in the world to be together, to make love to each other.

Acknowledgments

Nobody's Pretty Girl is my first full length novel. I've written many songs, but I never thought about writing a book until I had a dream one night about a beautiful singer/songwriter and heard the song her band was singing to her. Somehow, that morphed into this book. I had to go to the piano the next morning and play the song I heard in my dreams.

I want to thank all the family and friends who encouraged me to continue writing. I especially want to thank Ashley Mitchell, Events Specialist at Arapahoe Libraries, and all the up-and-coming writers from the Arapahoe Libraries Writer's Circle. Your comments and suggestions have been so helpful to me.

I also want to thank Suzanne Gelwick-Knight, Librarian at the Park Hill Branch Library and all the wonderful members of the Thursday Writing Circle who have shared their stories and poems with me and offered encouragement for my writing. You have inspired me to keep trying to be a better writer. Many thanks to Lauretta Dimmick who did the first reading and encouraged me to continue.

Many thanks to my son, Brett, who let me spend many long hours in his mountain home while he was away on work assignments. I think I did my best writing there in the peace and quiet, surrounded by the beauty of the Colorado mountains.

    Former public school music teacher turned entrepreneur, K.J. Knudson opened a temporary personnel service in Denver and managed it for 20 years. She currently lives life as a successful piano teacher. Most of her young students have no idea that she spends her after teaching hours toiling away at developing romantic suspense novels and performing her most recent song compositions at open mic venues.
    She is currently working on a new Children's picture book and will soon be publishing the second book in the Carly Styles series. She is the composer of countless piano solos for children, currently offering them for sale on a Teachers Pay Teachers website where her solos have reached the level of over 400 downloads. She lives in Denver, Colorado and enjoys frequent trips to the mountains to visit her son.

Made in the USA
Coppell, TX
18 February 2025

46123599R00105